MISS ALCOTT'S E-MAIL

Miss Alcott's E-mail

Yours for Reforms of All Kinds

a bio-memoir by

Kit Bakke

David R. Godine · Publisher

First Published in 2006 by
DAVID R. GODINE · *Publisher*
Post Office Box 450
Jaffrey, New Hampshire 03452
www.godine.com

LIBRARY OF CONGRESS CATALOGING-IN-PUBLICATION DATA
Bakke, Kit.
Miss Alcott's e-mail : yours for reforms of all kinds / by Kit Bakke.— 1st ed.
p.   cm.
Includes bibliographical references.
ISBN 1-56792-311-9
1. Alcott, Louisa May, 1832–1888–Correspondence—Fiction.   I. Title.
PS3602.A589M57   2006
813'.6—dc22
2006004895

First Edition
PRINTED IN THE UNITED STATES OF AMERICA

Publishers are very perverse
& won't let authors have their way
so my little women must grow up
& be married off in a very stupid style.
Louisa May Alcott in a letter to her Uncle Sam May,
January 22, 1869

Don't shut yourself up in a bandbox because you are a woman,
but understand what is going on, and educate yourself to take part
in the world's work, for it all affects you and yours.
Louisa May Alcott putting words in the mouth of Marmee,
Little Women, Volume II, 1869

꙳ ꙳ ꙳ ꙳ ꙳

All for Peter, Maya, and Tess
Dreams Come True

Contents

Why Louisa, Why now?

Life always was a puzzle to me,
& gets more mysterious as I go on.
Louisa May Alcott, 1874, age forty-two

Never have time to go slowly & do my best.
Louisa May Alcott, 1877

I was home alone, that rare treat for the working mother, when it occurred to me to write to her. To Louisa May Alcott. Why not?

Life, I think, requires more than simply showing up. Not that I expect a normal, ordinary person like me to move the tectonic plates of human history. But I can't help thinking that it's not quite enough just being in a family, making another family, earning one's keep and then exiting stage left.

Now in my mid-fifties, I have already lived longer than most humans in any century ever have. Being a healthy white American woman in 2006, the statistics say I'm likely to carry on for another twenty or thirty years. My personal genes agree: my grandmother lived to one-hundred-and-four-and-a-half. So I may be barely half done. What can I usefully do with all that future? I've already been in a family (mom, dad, two brothers); I've already made a family (mom, dad, two daughters); I've already earned a lot of keep (pediatric nurse, hospital manager, high-paid consultant). Now what? Where's the action? The freedom and fear, the fun and fight?

Sitting on our slightly dilapidated department-store sofa, Louisa May Alcott came rather suddenly to mind. I was reading, and had just looked up at our Chinese ink drawing of trees in a terrible winter windstorm. The bamboo is whipped horizontal by the wind, while the pine next to it is jaggedly, cruelly broken. My husband and I bought the picture from an earnest art student who explained that his picture celebrates the virtues and victories of flexible persistence over brute strength.

I looked back at the book on my lap, a biography of Jane Austen. I had been on an English literature jag for years, reading piles of eighteenth- and nineteenth-century Englishwomen's letters, journals, novels, autobiographies, and biographies. Early twentieth-century Edwardian was as modern as I wanted to venture (I did make an exception for the Bloomsbury set, though). I loved the elegant sentences of those days, the women's long, sweeping skirts, their tall French windows opening out onto terraces, and all those relaxed afternoon teas in the garden – such a welcome fantasy after a day of work, traffic, NPR news, and spaghetti dinners at the kitchen table.

But after September 11, 2001, I started thinking American more than European. Odd, because my husband and I were in Europe that September, treating his parents to a month in Siena, Sorrento, and Paris for their fiftieth anniversary. By the time we arrived in Paris in early October, my mind must have been secretly gearing up for the swivel from Miss Austen to Miss Alcott. I was unconsciously turning a mental corner as neatly as our Seine *bateau mouche* was spinning around the scale model of the Statue of Liberty at the end of our tourist dinner cruise. The French crew played "America the Beautiful" on the loudspeakers, and we all cried together.

Back home, I picked up a book of Louisa May Alcott's letters. Then her journal. Then a biography. I watched the George Cukor-Katharine Hepburn film of *Little Women*.* Then I visited the Alcott house in Concord, Massachusetts. Nathaniel Hawthorne lived right next door. Ralph Waldo Emerson lived across the road. Henry David Thoreau flitted in and out of the Alcotts' woods, tak-

---

* Which I didn't much like. The sisters were all too old and Katharine Hepburn was trying too hard.

ing Louisa and her sisters on nature walks. John Brown's grieving wife and family came for tea after his execution for masterminding and leading the Harpers Ferry raid. When the Civil War started, Louisa signed up to be a nurse in an army hospital. After the war, she chaired her local American Woman Suffrage Association chapter and was the first woman in Concord to register to vote.

Louisa's abolitionist zeal, her women's rights advocacy, her hospital work, her crazy commune days, her exceedingly eccentric father, her heartfelt desire to leave the world a better place, her industrious work habits, her humor, and her energy all materialized in full battle regalia in my living room. Louisa made her life, she didn't just live it. She wore her heart, as well as her brain, on her sleeve – always in the open, unprotected and brave.

"Being born on the birthday of Columbus* I seem to have something of my patron saint's spirit of adventure, and running away was one of the delights of my childhood," she once wrote about herself for a children's magazine. After visiting her sister Anna (Meg in *Little Women*) shortly after Anna's marriage to John Pratt, Louisa confided to her journal, "Very sweet & pretty, but I'd rather be a free spinster & paddle my own canoe."

Louisa was fifty-five when she died, about my age when I wrote the first letter. She suffered from chronic mercury (called calomel in her day) poisoning as a result of treatment she had received for typhoid twenty-five years earlier. She was not surprised that her life, unlike what I expect of mine, was winding down.

I had been through some of the same adventures as Louisa, but by my late thirties I had leveled out at an ordinary adulthood, indistinguishable from many other middle-aged, middle-class post-World War II babies. My revolutionary days in the passionate and violent Weather Underground were like the ruins of Pompeii, the sharp edges slowly silted over by the ash of graduate

---

* I cannot corroborate this. We do not today seem to know when Columbus's birthday was – probably between August 25 and October 31, 1451, a span which does not include Louisa's birthdate of November 29.

school, marriage, kids in college, professional career, husband with ditto, vacations, gardening, dinners in nice restaurants. Years of layered sediment had buried those volcanic days of the 1960s and '70s, when I lived in an unsubtle world of black and white values and overheated schemes for building the perfect society. Remember Eldridge Cleaver's simple and menacing, "You're either part of the problem or you're part of the solution"? Today, though, with the exception of financial donations and volunteer hours here and there, the personal and the private rule.

Louisa, on the other hand, never buried her scrapes, never laid aside her ideals, but mined them her whole life to create wealth ("I turn my adventures into bread & butter"), fame, and a string of good works. Plus she did it all husbandless in a time when the odds for female success were infinitesimal.

Her life, surely, would give me impetus and ideas for thinking about the rest of mine.

※ ⁊ ※ ⁊ ※

By the time my first letter reached her, she was the best-selling author of her century. "Fame is an expensive luxury," she wrote, "I can do without it. This is my worst scrape, I think. I asked for bread, & got a stone – in the shape of a pedestal." *Little Women* had earned her a celebrity with which she was uncomfortable, although she loved the money. She loved earning it, keeping track of it, and spending it – but mostly not on herself. She was the primary financial support for her parents, her sisters, and her sisters' children. She liked it that way.

She could also look back and know she had thrown her best energy into the two most important struggles of her American century – the abolition of slavery and the rights of women to be educated, to vote, to work, and to receive equal pay. Americans in the 1700s fought for independence; in Louisa's 1800s, the battle was for equal opportunity – and a more difficult and protracted struggle that has turned out to be.

Louisa May Alcott was not the first author to receive a letter from me. Once I made the mistake of mailing a short story I had written while I was in nursing school to a contemporary writer whom I much admired. Silly me. I liked this author's stories so much I thought for sure she'd love mine. She did write back, kindly but firmly, telling me that writers were very busy people and that I should never bother any of them ever again.

Presumably, though, dead authors would not be so busy. I couldn't resist Louisa's strong and opinionated personality, coming through so clearly in her letters, journals, and novels. The similarities between her life and mine – the nursing, the political activism – as well as the telling differences tempted me (a grown and otherwise rational woman) to send her an e-mail.

Given the mysteries of the universe, I caught her not dead, but in the last six months of her life, in the winter of 1887–88. Not so long ago, really. Just a hop, skip, and a jump from today – a time almost spanned by my own grandmother, a feisty redhead who was born on a southern Indiana farm, just eight years after Louisa's too-early death, and who lived to ring in the third millennium.

Over the course of several letters, Louisa and I gradually got our bearings. I explained, in words I hoped would make sense to a nineteenth-century mind, that I was a self-appointed spokes-woman for myself and some of my friends. We were all in our fifties, I explained, and were beginning to get our heads above water with the kids leaving home and the corporate climb cooling down. We were starting to think about the rest of our lives, and we were asking her for help.

Together, Louisa and I devised a mutually agreeable project. I would read everything I could find about or by her. I would then write short histories about all the interesting things she had done, the argumentative and creative people she had known, and how she had made her life work. I would send them to her for her correction and comment. In return for her editorial efforts, Louisa would have a chance to speak out one more time (an opportunity few can resist) *and* she could learn the twenty-first century fate of her own most heartfelt causes.

Through it all, I hoped to pick up some clues for my friends and myself about how better to live the thirty or so years that might remain to us. And besides, we would be giving Louisa a treat that could hardly be resisted – a peek into the future. I thought it would be a wonderful way to thank an author who had brought such pleasure to so many.

You may ask why she bothered to write that first letter back to me at all, but like many in her day, she was a compulsive correspondent. She wrote thousands of letters in her life. She routinely responded personally to fans, neophyte writers, and supplicants of various sorts. Once she received a request from a stranger who said she had no money to buy Christmas presents for her children. Could Miss Alcott help out? Louisa put together a box of useful goodies and mailed it on to the stranger, enjoying the role of secret Santa. Perhaps she saw this project as a similar gift.

❧⚶❧⚶❧

I wish I could explain more about the mechanics of our correspondence, but I can't, because, other than frying six surge protectors, I don't know how it worked. I sent my letters and chapter drafts to Louisa by e-mail from my Seattle living room, and she received them as handwritten ink on paper in her rooms in Dr. Lawrence's house in Roxbury, Massachusetts. She once told me my handwriting was neat and extremely legible, so there was definitely something odd going on. She wrote to me, using well-worn ink pens and paper, and they showed up in Times New Roman in my Outlook inbox. I was grateful for the technology transfer, as her own handwriting was also less than copperplate.

It's one of those Internet Effects, I guess. Or a Heisenberg thing, or Brownian motion gone amok. I didn't want to inquire too closely for fear the magic might vanish.

Her last letter to me was dated Leap Day, February 29, 1888, about a week before she died. Her last journal entry is from a few days later, on March 2, four days before her death:

Fine. Better in mind but food a little uneasy. Write letters. Pay Ropes [her coal supplier] $30, Notman [photographer] 4. Write a little. L to come. [Lulu was her dead sister May's almost nine-year-old daughter, named after her aunt Louisa, whom Louisa was raising.]

Louisa May Alcott died in Boston on March 6, 1888, a scant two days after the death of her difficult, omnipresent father, Bronson Alcott. Louisa and Bronson shared the same birthday, November 29; in her case, November 29, 1832.

⁂

I have included, along with the results of our project, most of our letters, deleting only a few repetitions and minor irrelevancies. The chapters are arranged roughly in the order of Louisa's life. Each chapter contains my introductory letter to her, the essay I sent to her, and her letter in response.

We begin with her first letter back to me.

Starting Out

Work is an excellent medicine for all kinds of mental maladies. . . .
You can be what you will to be.

Louisa May Alcott, 1859, age twenty-seven

November 15, 1887

Dear Ms. Bakke,

I must start by confessing my confusion over the title "Ms." I hesitate to guess, since I thought I understood quite well that one is either married or not married. For that we have the thoroughly descriptive & pleasant "Mrs." & "Miss." Perhaps you will respond that the same distinction is not made for men. True, but I hope you will agree with me that there are infinite ways in which it would be foolish for women to follow the same trails that men have built.

I fear that you have caught me feeling a bit low. I am tired, & the effects of my calomel poisoning are with me more than usual this week. Rest & quiet is my goal, & I must keep my correspondence to a minimum.

Even so, I admit that the singularity of this potential interchange is most intriguing. You say we are communicating across "time zones" in a way much imagined, but never reliably accomplished. I will have to take you on faith for that, as the concept of time zones is not familiar to me, although the railways are rumored to be trying to do something about time. Perhaps your letter is related? You say we are inhabiting different centuries? If so, this could be the most amusing correspondence I have had in years.

Back to your request. Perhaps if you can restate your interests in a more coherent manner, I will endeavor to respond in an economical & truthful way.

Yours sincerely,
Miss L.M. Alcott

November 16, 2005

Dear Miss Alcott,

I am astonished and delighted by your return letter. This is quite an amazing trick we have discovered. We seem to be in the same month, but you are in 1887 and I am in 2005. I think we must tiptoe forward and act as if this happens all the time. Let's just quietly get on with our business, as your friend Henry Thoreau did when he assumed that sparrows resting on people's hands was normal, and so they did.

I feel as if I know you, a little, already. The more I read about you (do you know we have books about you?), the more familiar you sound to me. You are exactly the sort of person I want to be talking with these days. When I told my friend Cindy about you, I said, "I know Louisa! And I need to know her better." Cindy is our same age and lives in Philadelphia, near where you were born. She and I became best friends in college (women go to college all the time now) when we discovered we both liked the Stones better than the Beatles (they were two English musical groups). The 1960s was an unbelievably terrific decade for music. You would have liked it yourself – very experimental, loud and dramatic, with lyrics by handsome young men all about relationships, nature, and politics.

Anyway, now my friends and I have lived through some of the same things you have: earning a living, coping with illness, trying to make sense of crazy families, trying to do good and be good – all that work you have done so well. We admire you particularly because you had to do it from a standing start. We, partly inspired by you and your wonderful Little Woman Jo March, had a running start.

I love the way you signed some of your letters to your women's suffrage correspondents "Yours for Reforms of All Kinds." *Of All Kinds* – I wish more of us thought like that today. So many of the noisiest people today care about only one issue and have only one reform in mind. They shout about their one position as if it's the only idea in the world. It's quite annoying, because any sensible woman knows progress doesn't work like that. I don't want to dishearten you, but many of the battles you fought are still, one hundred and twenty years on, not won. But be assured that none of the causes you care about have been abandoned.

One definite improvement in the years between us is people's general health, at least in the United States and Europe. Very few people die of tuberculosis any more, or scarlet fever, or in child-birth. We no longer poison people with mercury as a treatment for typhoid either. But don't think we are rolling in magic potions and pills. We still make plenty of mistakes – some well-meaning, like your mercury, and some not. I was a hospital nurse too – when I was in my thirties, like you – and did some painful and expensive things to patients that we now know did them no good. Medicine remains more art and less science than most patients want to believe. It's not so different today from your friend Ralph Waldo Emerson's story:

> On Wachusett, I sprained my foot. It was slow to heal, and I went to the doctors. Dr. Henry Bigelow said, "Splint and absolute rest." Dr. Russell said, "Rest, yes; but a splint, no." Dr. Bartlett said, "Neither splint nor rest, but go and walk." Dr. Russell said, "Pour water on the foot, but it must be warm." Dr. Jackson said, "Stand in a trout brook all day."

Patients today receive exactly the same conflicting advice for sprained ankles. Only the best doctors will acknowledge how little they know. Meanwhile, all sorts of new ailments have appeared, and as if the natural ones aren't enough, we twenty-first century humans are continually inventing new ways to harm ourselves and each other.

So there's much left to do, in medicine and everywhere else. Winning the vote for women, which finally made it into the Constitution in 1920, was, as you and your mother accurately predicted, only the opening act. Ending slavery in the South has turned out to be barely the first chapter of a very long and bloody story. We keep thinking we are finally reaching a happy ending when the plot stumbles, and there we are, back near the difficult beginning. Sometimes things inch along for the better; sometimes nothing much changes.

I know you said life was your college, but would that have been your preference, if you'd had a choice? Or were you just doing your usual trick of making the best of the hand you were dealt? Women today are as likely as men to go to college. Women today run their own companies, and become U.S. senators, Supreme Court justices, governors, and mayors (though not president yet). They are engineers, explorers, and scientists. Much of what your friend Margaret Fuller advocated so boldly in *Woman in the Nineteenth Century* has come to pass.

But all that higher education and honorable work doesn't stop us from occasionally devouring romantic novels about illicit love and tragic loss between wild, doomed, and always beautiful people. You like those tales too, don't you? Enough to write a few of your own, we have discovered. You should congratulate yourself, though, that your pseudonym A. M. Barnard kept your potboiler identity secret for decades until 1943.

Remember that section in your novel *Modern Mephistopheles*, where you had the evil Helwyze giving hashish to unsuspecting little Gladys? You gave her quite a night. From my own experience, I'd say you were writing from *your* personal experience:

By this time Gladys was no longer quite herself: an inward excitement possessed her, a wild desire to sing her very heart

4

out came over her, and a strange chill, which she thought a vague presentiment of coming ill, crept through her blood. Everything seemed vast and awful. Every sense grew painfully acute. She walked as in a dream, so vivid, yet so mysterious, that she did not try to explain it even to herself. Her identity was doubled: one Gladys moved and spoke as she was told – a pale, dim figure, of no interest to any one. The other was alive in every fiber, thrilled with intense desire for something, and bent on finding it, though deserts, oceans and boundless realms of air were passed to gain it.

And the *Atlantic Monthly* thought Nathaniel Hawthorne's son Julian had written it!

But, back to the reason for my letter. I am sitting in 2005 Seattle, looking back, looking ahead, and wondering if age is weakening my rudder and ripping my sails. I think it's time for a little course correction. You seem to have kept your rudder and sails in near perfect trim your whole life. That's why I think our correspondence might be worth pursuing.

What do you think? Might we try?

Yours truly,
Kit Bakke

November 25, 1887

Dear Mrs. (and I am taking a wild guess here) Bakke,

Although your enthusiasm is apparent, mine quails at the thought of so many battles still not won. I am not at all well these days, & expect death is waiting not so patiently around some nearby corner. Some days I am sure today is the day, & others I feel a bit better. Since Mother died, I often feel as if I am just marking time. I have been try-ing to work on a new story, however. I have a plan to smash through some of my old difficulties, at least on paper. That cheers me up.

You do ignite some new sparks, I must admit, with your offer of conversations about nursing and all the other old battles. I often think of my dear boys. We nursed both Union & Confederates, you know, & a wounded boy is a wounded boy, whatever the color of his uniform. Their clothes were mostly blown off them anyway, by the time they got to us.

You like my old blood-&-thunder stories? How did you learn that I am A. M. Barnard? Not that I didn't leave a trail a mile wide. Little Woman Jo, as you put it, wrote for the Weekly Volcano & the Blarneystone Banner, remember? Everyone knew I was Jo. Like her, I always loved my gothic stories. Still do! My tortured lovers were such a treat to invent. Sometimes I went beyond what even the lurid penny dreadfuls were willing to print. I don't know what was the biggest thrill – the unpredictable & violent heroine exacting painful revenge on the man who wronged her, or all the background mayhem of suicide, incest, mistaken identity, gambling, hatred, murder, love without marriage, marriage without love, hashish, opium & lonely castles in the cold, slanting moonlight. But I was always careful to put a trace of goodness in all my sinners. Just like life.

I can still quote whole passages from those stories, even to this day. "The rich hue of the garnet velvet chair relieved her figure admirably, as she leaned back, with a white cloak half concealing her brilliant dress. The powder had shaken from her hair, leaving its gold undimmed as it hung slightly disheveled about her shoulders. She had wiped the rouge from her face, leaving it paler, but none the less lovely." Ah, yes.

Even in 1869, as Little Women was sealing my fate, I wrote that little Perilous Play, where everyone takes hasheesh to while away a boring afternoon, & true love results. "Heaven bless hasheesh, if its dreams end like this!" says my hero Mark as he wins Rose's heart after they are nearly drowned in the storm. Did you notice how I kept hiding the moon behind threatening clouds? Fantasy is such fun.

I am pleased, as any author would be, to know that my touch is still appreciated. But I must push such delightful reveries aside for the moment, as I have an inkling that you have some work in mind for

*me. Never let it be said that Louisa May Alcott shies away from work.
It was my publisher Mr. Niles who suggested I try a girls' book, &
even though the idea didn't much interest me, I took it up. So, I ask
again, what are you proposing?*

Yours truly,
Miss L.M. Alcott

November 26, 2005

Dear Miss Alcott,

You are right. I do have a proposal. A Chinese revolutionary
whom I once admired wrote in his *Little Red Book* that a journey
of a thousand miles begins with but a single step. For all I know,
he stole it from Confucius, but anyway, here's my thought: our
journey would be to walk your life from front to back, top to bottom, Concord, Boston, and New York to London, Rome, and
Paris; Emerson and Thoreau to John Brown and Lucy Stone. We
would exchange letters about abolition, women's suffrage, and
nursing, about utopias and street demonstrations, about ideas,
earning a living and living with a purpose. We won't forget the
people you love or the books you wrote.

I'm hoping your journey will help me for the rest of mine.
There are points of correspondence between our two lives that
will make this back-and-forth fun for both of us. We were both
nurses taking care of dying people, we have both lived in communes and experimented with utopian ways; we both have taken
part in large and often violent movements to improve our country.
Finally, we both admit to have gotten ourselves into various
"scrapes" as you put it.

My proposal is that I send you short essays about your life,
from all that I have learned so far from reading your letters and
journal, and then you comment on and correct what I have written.

We'll do it over a few months, entirely at your convenience and pace. I hope this is not too much to tackle.

I especially want to know what it was like for you to grow up around people who were more interested in ideas than in money, and to live with people who thought they could change the world. We twenty-first century people need to be reminded of such a life.

I promise we won't dwell on *Little Women* because I know you are sick of it, but you should be pleased that it is still read by every new generation. Did you know its French title is *Les Quatre Filles du docteur March*? Interesting elevation of Mr. March's character, don't you think? The book is a great favorite among Italians too, where it's called *Piccole Donne*, a straight translation. In German it's titled *Betty und ihre Schwestern*. Everyone loves Jo as much as ever. Even so, we'll talk mostly about the grown-up books you cared about more: *Moods*, *Work*, and *Modern Mephistopheles*. And what about that story you say you are working on right now? Could we talk about that?

Besides abolition and women's rights, you have invested your time and money in so many other social and political problems. I want to give you credit for all you have done for education reform, prison reform, caring for orphans, public health, and the eradication of poverty. You have said that you need some solitude every day. Can you tell us how you find it?

You tell me that you don't expect to live much longer, but most of my generation will probably live another thirty years, maybe even more. We won't be perfectly healthy all that time, but we won't be bedridden, either. Some of our problems will be what we call chronic illnesses, which probably feel not very different from your calomel poisoning. How can we learn to live cheerfully and usefully even with our disabilities? None of us wants to become a boring old lady who can't stop talking about her health problems. We could use some of your strength. I just can't shake the idea that you are among the taproots that help keep the American tree true and upright.

But please forgive this rush of words, and take your time in responding. I hope you are staying warm and that Dr. Lawrence is giving you what you need. Also, happy upcoming birthday. I hope you plan to spend it in pleasant company.

Very appreciatively yours,
Kit Bakke

P S: Yes, your A. M. Barnard *doppelgänger* wasn't discovered until 1943, when Leona Rostenberg and Madeleine Stern found five letters to you from a Mr. Elliott, the editor of *The Flag of the Union*, imploring you to write more of the same and wishing you would allow publication under your own name. He said you'd make more money that way. That must have been hard to turn down. But you said you needed to keep your two identities separate. Why?

December 5, 1887

Dear Ms. Bakke, (Are you married or not?
I am getting impatient to know.)

You flatter me, & I don't respond to flattery any more. Never did much, come to think of it. Never got much, at least from the people who counted, so that probably explains it.

I have never understood why my life should be of interest to anyone. Where, might I ask, is my correspondence being kept that it is available for prying eyes in the twenty-first century? And I specifically ordered that my journal be burnt. I am getting a disturbing impression that my wishes were ignored. Wouldn't be the first time.

But I also have given up trying to predict the public's mood, as I have been wrong much of the time. Little Women's success, for instance, was a complete surprise. I didn't much enjoy writing it, & in many ways, didn't even enjoy living it. You are right that I hated the fuss that was made over it — & then feeling compelled to write in the same vein for the rest of my life! That has been an endless punishment. *I never got used to the autograph hunters & the people who thought they could just walk right up to my front porch & knock on my door, day or night. Are people still so rude? But I can't complain about the money: it continues to support Alcotts big & small in comfort & ease, several generations' worth.*

I do see some potential in this project. You already have done some studying, I see. Your request is interesting & sets my brain a-twirling. I will do my best to help. I do get lonely here in Roxbury, & I would like to learn a bit about what has happened to women in your century, & to so many of the causes & problems my family and I have cared about so much.

So, in return, I expect you to tell me about your century – or centuries, I guess, is more accurate. It appears the world staggered into its new millennium without apocalyptic disaster. Even so, I am very curious about people, as is any storyteller. You must be sure to tell me about yourself. I am at a significant & unfair disadvantage here, being without books & purloined papers from your times.

Finally, thank you so much for your concerns about my current health. I am reasonably well at the moment, thanks to my milk diet, but, perhaps like the chronic illnesses you mention, my health can change dramatically from day to day. Writing, sewing & knitting occupy all my energy between naps & headaches & cold. I am not able to play with my little Lulu nearly as much as I would like – although she certainly brightened my birthday. Friends sent me baskets of flowers & lovely wraps & some books with views of Europe. Sadly, pictures are the closest I'll ever get again to that delightful continent. Perhaps you read my little travel book about May and Alice Bartlett's and my Grand Tour?

Yours for reforms of all kinds – I had forgotten that I used that closing in letters; thank you for reminding me, it does bring back satisfying memories,

L. M. Alcott

December 6, 2005

Dear Miss Alcott,

I send you all my strengthening thoughts. I know how sad it is to be too ill to play with your own children. When I was in nursing school I had terrible migraine headaches, and could do nothing but lie rigidly in the dark and try to punch my brain down like rising bread so it wouldn't explode through my skull. My three-year-old daughter was puzzled to see me so horizontal and helpless.

Of course I will tell you as much as you want to know about myself. My story is not nearly as interesting or productive as yours, so I may forget to bring it up. Feel free to prod me, and I'll do my best to come clean.

So, yes, as a matter of fact, I am married. November 29, your and your father's birthday, happens to be my husband's birth date, too. We usually celebrate by having a quiet family dinner. Like you, he doesn't like a fuss. Like me, he is lucky enough to have had interesting and well-paying jobs. We both love visiting New York and Europe and have just enough to argue about to keep our conversations lively. Now, does my being married change your picture of me? If it does not, then that's why we use the term "Ms." If it does, in what way?

But enough. Let's sail on. How can we fail, with the resources of centuries to draw on? Time for you to look back, this time for the benefit of adults, not children. We'll twist the kaleidoscope a few degrees for each chapter and see what pictures fall into place. Here's your chance to say whatever you want to your new colleagues here in this century. I know you hate speaking in public. Here's a way to say whatever you want, right from your heart, without ever leaving your room. And no publisher, either, to put in an annoying oar.

Collaboratively yours,
Kit Bakke

11

December 13, 1887

Dear Mrs. Bakke,

Yes, of course knowing you are married changes how I think of you! Marriage is a complicated choice. Some women lose themselves in marriage & others find themselves. Tell me more about your husband. How many children do you have? I expect they are older than my little Lulu. It isn't often a forty-eight-year-old spinster is presented with an infant to raise! But what a dear she is, & how much life she has brought to my heart! I think, after I go, my sister Anna will become her new mother. Perhaps one day she will want to return to her father's family in Switzerland. But she'll never forget the warmth of being surrounded by Alcotts, & that will strengthen her all her life.*

Our project is acceptable, & I will do my best to accommodate it. I must admit to being spurred by the thought that my Little Women *has continued to so overshadow all else I have done. Perhaps we can correct that. The "blood of the Mays is up!" as I often said in the early sword-rattling, flag-flapping days of the Civil War. I look forward to learning about how the twentieth century treated our battles for the rights of women and how our struggles might fare in the twenty-first. I am equally curious about what has become of the descendants of the slaves, & what has resulted from our attempts to reform education, prisons & orphanages.*

And, dare I ask, are the poor still with us?

Not on your list, but since you brought it up, how is the publishing business run? Are authors well compensated for their works? Is international copyright law still such a muddle? Is the Atlantic Monthly *still in circulation? That charming Mr. Fields has been both a nemesis*

---

* Madelon Bedell, who wrote a book about the Alcotts, visited the ninety-five-year-old Lulu in Switzerland in 1975. She said Lulu looked just like pictures of Bronson Alcott, Louisa's father. The Alcotts were "*large*," Lulu told her. They threw their hearts into everything they did; caution was rarely part of any Alcott plan.

& a boon to me. I still chuckle over paying back his forty-dollar loan when he said I couldn't write & should stick to teaching. Like a bad penny, I'm just not that easy to get rid of, am I?

Cordially yours,
Louisa May Alcott

Getting Around Concord

It was a wild, windy day, very like me
in its fitful changes of sunshine and shade.
Louisa May Alcott, 1865, age thirty-three

December 14, 2005

Dear Miss Alcott,

I hope this first packet arrives to find you feeling energetic and ready to work. I have enclosed the first part of your history for your comment and correction. You will see that it's more about Mr. Emerson and Concord than it is about you or your parents. Your parents, as you well know, are so rich and complex that they deserve a chapter all their own. But we can't skip over Concord, can we? It's not just your hometown; Concord is a living being, a palpable, persistent presence in your life. I notice that no matter how vigorously you complain about its small-mindedness, you have never been able to leave it for long.

I hope the following does your neighborhood justice. You cannot imagine how lucky I think you are to have grown up around such intelligent and thoughtful people. My childhood neighbors certainly didn't chatter about ethics and the higher purposes of human life as yours did. What did that feel like?

Since you have very fairly asked about me, I will tell you that there were six or seven families on our road, and we kids played constantly together in the woods and the lake, while our parents helped each other out with projects on their houses or in their yards and had dinners together. Perhaps that part isn't very different from your Concord childhood. I grew up in a rural area, but most of the fathers went to work in Seattle, which was a small city in those days. There was a fair amount of scotch and gin drinking among the adults in the evenings, as I recall, and I guess that limited the depth of their conversation. Most of us kids were born at the end of a terrible war that had raged all over Europe, parts of Asia, and the Pacific Islands (much worse than the Franco-Prussian war you and May were caught in on your 1870 European trip), so our parents were just glad to be home safe. But what followed was not peace, exactly. It was a scary time called the Cold War, when the United States and other countries were stockpiling weapons against each other that were powerful enough – and this is not hyperbole – to destroy the entire planet. So that threat hung over everyone who was trying to get back to a normal life.

War must have been a common topic of grown-up conversation, because the most popular game we kids played in the woods was "Army Camp." We made little shelters in the underbrush from fir branches and rocks and then ran around attacking each other or barricading our camps against invasion. The boys let us girls play, but I remember spending more effort on defense than offense. Our woods were thick with Douglas fir, alder, salal, ferns, and blackberries – perfect for making secret camps. Sneaking around to find and occupy each other's camps was a lengthy part of the game. We all slept outside a lot too, using our fathers' old army sleeping bags.

You also invented lots of imaginative games, and put on swashbuckling plays for the whole neighborhood to enjoy. These days, though, in the twenty-first century, kids don't seem to have as much time for making things up. Their lives are far more structured, and guess who does the structuring? Grown-ups! It's too bad, because as you well know, grown-ups are not famous for knowing what's best for children.

My generation has been accusingly called the "Me Generation" because all we think about is me me me. I can see where that comes from, but unless I've completely whitewashed my own history, we weren't always so self-centered. We used to think about what would be good for other people.

When our elder daughter was growing up in the 1970s and early 1980s, she learned all about my generation's work to improve housing and job opportunities for black people and poor people, and about how hard we fought to end America's unconscionable invasion of Southeast Asia (yet another war – this time against Vietnam, with incursions into Laos and Cambodia). I'm afraid we gave her the impression that we were well on the way to fixing all the world's problems. She was angry with me when she grew old enough to realize that wasn't true at all.

Two steps forward, one step back. I am counting on your being able to help with this dance. I am looking forward to your comments on this first piece of your history. Here we go with our first small step.

Hopefully yours,
Kit Bakke

A MOST UNKISSABLE PERSON · GUILT
RALPH WALDO EMERSON · *MOODS*
HENRY DAVID THOREAU

Some people think that a person's dreams are closer to their true selves than what they do and say when they're awake. Louisa had weeks of dreams, wrought in the typhoid delirium she suffered while nursing in a dirty, freezing, makeshift Union army hospital during the Civil War. Her dreams of terror, endlessly failing work, and a boring, tedious heaven left memories so strong that she scribbled* them into her journal when her fever finally broke.

---

* Besides having dreadful handwriting, Louisa was a horrendously poor speller and had a hit-or-miss approach to grammar.

The most vivid & enduring [dream] was a conviction that I had married a stout, handsome Spaniard, dressed in black velvet with very soft hands & a voice that was continually saying, "Lie still, my dear." This was mother, I suspect, but with all the comfort I often found in her presence there was blended an awful fear of the Spanish spouse who was always coming after me, appearing out of closets, in at windows, or threatening me dreadfully all night long. I appealed to the Pope & really got up & made a touching plea in something meant for Latin they tell me. Once I went to heaven & found it was a twilight place with people darting thro the air in a queer way. All very busy & dismal & ordinary. Miss Dix, W. H. Channing & other people were there but I thought it dark & "slow" & wished I hadn't come. A mob at Baltimore breaking down the door to get me; being hung for a witch, burned, stoned & otherwise maltreated were some of my fancies. Also being tempted to join Dr. W. & two of the nurses in worshipping the Devil. Also tending millions of sick men who never died or got well.

Keeping a journal was standard operating behavior among the literate of Louisa's day. Sharing one's journal with friends was a common eighteenth- and nineteenth-century habit. Bronson Alcott shared his journal with Abba May, Louisa's mother (Marmee of *Little Women*) when the two were courting. Ralph Waldo Emerson and Bronson shared their diaries as part of getting to know each other. Emerson kept his for fifty-two years; he called it his "savings bank" and indexed it for use in constructing his lectures and essays. Bronson made time for journal writing over all other activities; he documented his life and thoughts in an almost endless scree of five million words. Louisa and her sisters shared their journals with their parents, who wrote encouraging (from Mother) or improving (from Father) notes in their margins.

Louisa grew up thinking she was an ugly duckling and no one ever told her anything that changed her mind.* She was tall for her age, reaching five foot six or seven, in a time when tall women were not routinely well regarded. She had a dark complexion, also not well regarded in an age of parasols, gloves, and wide-brimmed hats. Peering at the photographs of her that exist today, we can try to uncover the person behind the face. As with all photographs of that age, when an exposure required a minute or so of absolute stillness, there are no smiles. We see the dark, heavy hair. The dark eyes, staring straight at the lens, manage to look both critically penetrating and ultimately accepting. We see a strong, even heavy, jaw – much more like her mother than her father. The set of her eyes and the line of her chin convey quiet defiance and studied self-containment. There is nothing delicate about her. She looks like a working person. Here is a memory of Louisa, from a young male neighbor in the 1850s, when she was in her twenties:

> To me, as a child, she seemed a very unattractive and a most unkissable person, probably because she was quite a masculine type. Her sister May was very different . . . lots of beautiful blond hair.

A more perceptive neighbor described her at about the same age, saying that she had an "earnest face, large dark eyes, and expression of profound interest in other things than those which usually occupy the thoughts of young ladies."

Later, by the time Louisa hit her forties, she had put on a bit of weight and was forever conscious that it made her even less attractive. After she was famous, young readers of her books

---

* Carolyn Heilbrun suggested that not being beautiful in girlhood "enables women to develop the ego-strength to be creative and ultimately part of the instrumental rather than the expressive world in adulthood." Louisa herself noted in her journal, "Read memoirs of Madame de Rémusat. Not very interesting. Beauties seldom amount to much. Plain Margaret Fuller was worth a dozen of them."

would write to ask for a photograph, and she would refuse, knowing she looked so different from what they expected. When they came knocking on her door, she would hide or pretend to be a house servant, saying Miss Alcott was not at home.

Appearances always mattered. Even if no one was watching or judging you, God most certainly was. From an everyday, nineteenth-century religious perspective, everyone was a celebrity, and God was the most intrusive of paparazzi. Louisa might grow impatient and skittish with her earthly celebrity, always feeling that she would disappoint her adoring readers by being older or fatter or more tongue-tied than they expected, but she never avoided her watching God.

Louisa May Alcott was born in 1832, in Germantown, Pennsylvania, on her father's thirty-third birthday. Her generation played out their lives amid the chaos, pain, and high principles of the American nineteenth century: the Civil War, metastatic industrialization, women's rights, Darwinism, and all those social restrictions and expectations we today lump together as "Victorian." America was a growing country, thrashing around as dangerously and thoughtlessly as any strong, impatient adolescent.

The adults Louisa admired most, including her parents, took strong, risky, and public stands for the causes they felt were right for their community and their country. They repeatedly traded personal safety and comfort to shelter runaway slaves. Her parents frequently took in homeless and sick men, women, and children, sometimes rationing their own meals to two a day in order to spread their small stores among extra visitors. They worked publicly to improve education and employment opportunities for those with less than themselves. They did everything possible to make the freedoms their Revolutionary War grandparents and great-grandparents had fought so hard to win more equally available.

Humanity's place on Earth, our relationship with nature, the meaning of God, and the identity of the soul were topics of everyday dinner table conversation in Louisa's neighborhood. Her generation grew up in a ferment of social and personal improvement experiments; utopian communities like Brook Farm and New Harmony multiplied like mushrooms. These Americans truly believed they could get it right, and no one believed it more fervently than the Alcotts.

When Louisa May Alcott (Lu to her family) was fifteen years old, her parents were in one of their frequent financial panics. It was a cold and gray New England November in 1848. The warm colors of autumn were gone and the sparkle of winter was yet to come. The family made their usual plan, concluding that their only hope for survival was to move. This time, they chose to leave the country village of Concord, Massachusetts, and move to Boston, where Louisa's mother had an offer of work locating employment and housing for single and destitute women, and where her older sister Anna might find a teaching position. Bronson, Louisa's philosopher father, was never part of the family's financial support equation.

Remembering this particular move decades later, Louisa wrote:

> Always preferring action to discussion I took a brisk run over the hill and then settled down for "a good think" in my favorite retreat.
>
> It was an old cart-wheel, half hidden in grass under the locusts where I used to sit to wrestle with my sums, and usually forget them scribbling verses or fairy tales on my slate instead. Perched on the hub I surveyed the prospect and found it rather gloomy, with leafless trees, sere grass, leaden sky and frosty air, but the hopeful heart of fifteen beat warmly under the old red shawl, visions of success gave the gray clouds a silver lining, and I said defiantly, as I shook my fist at fate embodied in a crow cawing dismally on the fence near by, –
>
> "I will do something by-and-by. Don't care what, teach sew, act, write, anything to help the family; and I'll be rich and famous and happy before I die, see if I won't!"
>
> Startled by this audacious outburst the crow flew away,

but the old wheel creaked as if it began to turn at that moment, stirred by the intense desire of an ambitious girl to work for those she loved and find some reward when the duty was done.

This move was no more successful than any of the others. The family returned to Concord after failing to earn enough to pay the rent in Boston.

Concord provided the gravitational center of Louisa's life, and Ralph Waldo Emerson occupied the intellectual center of Concord. She left Concord dozens of times but always returned. She loved it and she hated it. In the middle 1800s it already had a couple of centuries of village history behind it and had been a Native American settlement for millennia before that. Concord played host to the first shots fired in the American Revolutionary War, on April 19, 1775 – right on the sturdy wooden bridge that still crosses the placid Concord River behind William Emerson's farmhouse.* William's great-great-great-grandfather Peter Bulkeley and some of his business associates bought the property from the indigenous peoples (who had been decimated by dysentery not long before) in 1635. The negotiations were so felicitous, from the buyers' perspective, that the village was named Concord.

Less felicitous, three decades later in 1692, were the witch trials running amok in Salem, just thirty miles to the east of Concord. Louisa and her neighbor Nathaniel Hawthorne were each direct descendants of two of the trial judges who presided over this fearful five-month outbreak of blinding prejudice and bullying superstition.† Besides trying, convicting, and hanging two dogs as witches, the judges devised several creative ways of

---

* It was Louisa's neighbor and William Emerson's grandson Ralph Waldo Emerson who coined the phrase "the shot heard 'round the world."

† Nathaniel Hawthorne felt so badly about his adamantly prosecutorial relative that he added the "w" to his family name (which for all previous generations had been spelled "Hathorne") and wrote several masterpieces about guilt-ridden people.

killing people, including a two-day event in which heavy stones were slowly added to a pile covering one victim who refused to recognize the validity of the court proceedings.

Louisa's mother Abba had a picture in her bedroom of her great-great-great-grandfather, the witch trial judge, Samuel Sewall. He was the only one of the frenzied Salem hierarchy to eventually return to reality and publicly apologize to the survivors. In 1696, in his official role, Judge Sam Sewall proclaimed a day of fasting and reparations for the official hysteria that killed twenty-four innocent citizens (and two dogs). For the rest of his life, he kept this annual day of remembrance. Judge Sewall is also remembered for his book, *The Selling of Joseph*, published in 1700 and believed to be the first antislavery tract ever published in the colonies. He argued the radical position that all men were created equal.

⁂

Ralph Waldo Emerson spent his childhood in Boston, but moved at age eleven to his grandfather William's farmhouse by the Concord River in 1814. Twenty-eight years later, in 1842, Nathaniel Hawthorne and his young bride Sophia Peabody Hawthorne rented the same farmhouse. By then Emerson had moved to a house of his own, along the Boston–Lexington Road, in the hills and fields on the southeast side of Concord. His property there included the shores of Walden Pond, which he let his friend Henry David Thoreau use for a couple of years of bean farming, writing, and transcendental meditation. Sophia Hawthorne once said of neighbor Thoreau that he had "alpine purity, diamond truth, stainless sincerity."

Emerson lived just across the road from Bronson Alcott's house, which Emerson and Abba's brother Sam May had helped Bronson buy after the family's second failed attempt to make a living in Boston. It was here in 1868 at age thirty-five that Louisa wrote *Little Women*, at a small, half-moon desk her father built into her second-floor bedroom wall, between two windows overlooking the Lexington Road. Thoreau, a man of many talents, had formally surveyed the property for them in September 1857, before winter snow buried all the land's features. Called Orchard House, it was already about 150 years old and sat surrounded by a small orchard of gnarled apple trees on a sloping twelve acres, long and narrow. The clapboard house and trim were, and still are, painted all the same chocolate brown; Bronson thought it more natural that way.

Previously, the Alcotts had lived next door to Orchard House, in a house they called Hillside – also partially bankrolled by Emerson – that was later occupied by the Hawthorne family (they renamed it Wayside), where Nathaniel entertained his friend Herman Melville.* Louisa was thirteen when they moved into Hillside. It was the first time she had a room of her own, which she loved chiefly because it had a door that opened directly onto the woods at the back of the house, so she could dash out for a run whenever she wanted, without seeing or talking to anyone.

Two doors down the road from Hillside/Wayside lived Ephraim Bull, who introduced his cultivated Concord grape to the world at the Boston Horticultural Society's 1853 exhibition. There is still a plaque in town honoring the site of the original Concord grapevine. Daniel Chester French, another neighbor, got artistic encouragement and his first sculpting tools from Louisa's youngest sister May (Amy in Little Women), an artist in her own right. French went on to sculpt the Minute Man statue by the Old North Bridge, as well as the grand, brooding Lincoln in Washington, D.C.'s Lincoln Monument.

Before and after his Walden Pond experiment, Henry David Thoreau lived on-again, off-again across the road at the Emersons' and at his parents' house in town. Later, in 1877, after Thoreau and his parents had died, Louisa bought the Thoreau house for her sister Anna and Anna's two sons. This is a reasonable starter picture of Louisa May Alcott's wonderfully active Concord neighborhood.

---

* Melville dedicated Moby Dick to Hawthorne. They shared each other's somewhat gloomy views of their fellow men.

When Ralph Waldo Emerson died in 1882, Concord's First Parish Church floor had to be reinforced to hold the weight of all the funeral attendees. Extra trains were put on the Boston–to–Concord track. Schools were closed for the day. By all accounts, Emerson was a genial character, always hospitable and happy to help out friends and neighbors.* The Alcotts and Thoreau were major recipients of his kindnesses, in the form of basics such as food and shelter, as well as the niceties of conversation and books. Louisa was acutely aware of Emerson's generosity and although she was embarrassed by her family's inability to feed and support itself, she was never too shy to accept his open invitation to visit his study, where she read Goethe, Shakespeare, and Milton. Children read those authors in those days.

Befitting Concord's continuing adulation of Emerson, the city maintains two complete versions of his study today. One is in his house, with some furniture similar to his, and the other is across the street in the Concord Museum, with Emerson's actual furniture. Both rooms are squarish and well lit with four large windows on the two outside walls and floor-to-ceiling bookshelves on the two inner walls. In the middle of each room is a round, dark wooden library table on a massive three-footed center pedestal. Emerson's chair, at the round table, is a small, unassuming rocker, with only a loose, thin cushion on the seat. Framed drawings and small etchings crowd much of the available wall space, among them a painting of goldenrod and asters against a black ground. This primitive charmer is hung over an uncomfortable-looking sofa, and was painted by Louisa's sister May as a gift to Emerson in 1874.

In the place of honor over a shiny black fireplace is an oil painting, *The Fates*, in a large, carved gilt frame. The subject of fate was a matter of much interest ("does control lie inside or out-

---

* One of Emerson's quotable quotes is "The ornament of a house is the friends who frequent it." Mark Twain, who wished he were as respected a writer as Emerson, punched that sentence into a decorative metal screen along the top of his drawing room fireplace in his elegant Hartford, Connecticut, home.

side man?") to the Alcotts and the Emersons, as well as to other Victorian thinkers and artists on both sides of the Atlantic. The three women in Emerson's picture, in classical robes of dark golds and umbers, hold a skein of thread that they have spun and woven into a tapestry. The thread represents the length of a person's life, and they are cutting it. It was painted by a friend of Emerson's, supposedly after an Italian Renaissance painting sometimes attributed to Michelangelo.

Louisa re-created her own friendly memories of Emerson's study in her novel *Moods*, which she began to write in her late twenties. *Moods* was Louisa's personal favorite of all her novels. She provided loving detail to the scene about the study. Her young heroine Sylvia visits the study of her older neighbor (and future husband) Geoffrey Moor and feels so at home that she borrows a book without permission. Her law-abiding sister Prue is scandalized.

> "Sylvia! Did you really take one without asking?" cried Prue, looking almost as much alarmed as if she had stolen the spoons.
> "Yes, why not? I can apologize prettily, and it will open the way for more. I intend to browse over that library for the next six months."

As a teenager, Louisa left bouquets of wild flowers at Emerson's doorstep. She wrote love letters to him, which she never sent. They were composed in the style of Bettina von Arnim, an accomplished German author, wife of a well-known (at the time) poet, friend of Beethoven, mother of seven, and – as a teenager – madly in love with Goethe. Bettina wrote impassioned letters both to Goethe and his mother, and eventually collected them into a book, *Goethe's Correspondence with a Child*, which became quite popular in America in the middle 1800s.

Louisa learned about the besotted Bettina from reading an article by Margaret Fuller in the *Dial*, a transcendental magazine founded by Bronson, Emerson, and their friends. Bronson suggested the name, as it was what he called his own journal. The men thought a quarterly magazine expressing the ideals of transcendentalism would be an excellent contribution to the American literary and philosophical landscape, but none wanted to take on the work of making it happen. Emerson turned to Margaret Fuller, the only woman he considered even marginally in their intellectual ballpark.* Margaret Fuller, educated to exacting standards by an impossible-to-please father, was reading and reciting Greek and Latin classics (in Greek and Latin) as a child. Her keen mind, poor social skills, and intense (people today might call her "high maintenance") personality frightened most men of her day.

Fuller wrote enthusiastically about *Goethe's Correspondence* and made Bettina sound like a woodland sprite, a little Thoreau-ish:

> Bettina, hovering from object to object, drawing new tides of vital energy from all, living freshly alike in man and tree, loving the breath of the damp earth as well as the flower which springs from it, bounding over the fences of society as well as over the fences of the field.

Bettina herself had less pastoral dreams in which she danced naked in front of Goethe, flying and gliding high in the air with an "airy tread," then sinking into his waiting embrace. "Passion is the only key to the world," Bettina boldly told Goethe's mother. Margaret Fuller and Louisa both loved Bettina's active outdoor imagery, and they loved the idea of falling for a godly man. Margaret Fuller, after a series of stiff, awkward, and unrequited infatuations in New England and New York, finally did exactly that a few years later in romantic, war-torn Rome.

Emerson enjoyed talking with children and had a knack for making them feel respected. His family was one of the few in Victorian America to include children at the adults' dinner table.

---

* A family name in Margaret Fuller's family is Buckminster, and indeed Buckminster Fuller is a cousinly descendant.

When preschool sons or daughters got restive with the finer points of transcendental conversations, he would give them an important task, like running outside to see what the clouds were doing so they could report on the state of the sky to the assembled diners. Emerson also invited his servants to eat at the table with the family, but they refused.

Emerson seemed to balance his life better than many of his friends. He practiced being a revolutionary without any apparent sacrifice of his own or his family's comfort. He was blessed with an entertaining and charismatic speaking style ("as good as a kaleidoscope," said one listener) and was much in demand as a lecturer. He didn't mind filling in, either. A contemporary wrote: "I was the curator [of a lecture series] for several years and had no difficulty in obtaining lecturers. And if any should fail to appear, we had the never-fail resource in Mr. Emerson, who had a supply of lectures which he always (with great courtesy) consented to deliver, and they were always acceptable. He required no previous invitation but was willing at the last moment [to] fill the vacancy." The income from lecturing and publications, plus having married two wives with some income of their own, allowed him to comfortably care for not only his own family, but for his friends as well.

Emerson's own childhood had been very different. His father died when his son Waldo was young, and his uncomplaining mother raised her six children with very few resources. He remembered hunger as a child and saw his mother go without food on her children's behalf. His mother made a deliberate choice to concentrate her small assets on her offspring's minds and souls, and hoped that their bodies would survive on their own. Emerson's aunt, who was born in the family farmhouse on the Concord River in August 1774, came to help her widowed sister-in-law with the children. Aunt Mary Moody Emerson had a strong, smoky character – eccentric,* witty, pious, and broody, a "woman

---

* Aunt Mary was often seen around town wearing a shroud. Her relatives recall her wearing out several in the course of her long life.

of acrid genius." She left a subversively freethinking but disciplined mark on her nephew. He sometimes copied her comments and letters to him into his lectures and essays on transcendentalism (generally without attribution). Criticism was mother's milk to Mary: more than once she said that tact was just another name for lying. She always liked people better when they argued back. In my own combative 1960s, we would have approved her view that one should act in the world, not merely react. "Scorn trifles, lift your aims; always do what you are afraid to do," she prescribed to her nephew Waldo, and he taught the same to his own children.

Mary Moody Emerson encouraged children to think beyond their daily routines. She was an inveterate pusher of the envelope, saying that it was a big mistake for a person to become "a nursling of surrounding circumstances." Her dislike of "surrounding circumstances" may be due in some part to the rather unpleasant fact that when her father died, she was the only sibling of five to be shipped off to a grandmother to be raised. Even when her mother remarried and had three more children, little Mary was left with her elderly relatives. She was brought back only as a teenager, when she could be of some help with the household chores.

Aunt Mary excelled at conversation. Conversation in the 1800s, much like today, could be gossip and shooting the breeze, or it could be harangue and hand-wringing about the day's headlines. On the other hand, conversation also could be a true discussion bristling with creative questions, and imaginative solutions, in which all participants were heard and no one claimed to know The Truth. This style of open exchange has perhaps become somewhat rarer today.

"Just spent a couple of hours . . . with Miss Mary Emerson," Thoreau wrote in his journal, "the wittiest and most vivacious woman. . . , certainly that woman among my acquaintance whom it is most profitable to meet, the least frivolous, who will most surely provoke to good conversation and expression of what is in you. . . ." He was thirty-six at the time and Miss Mary Moody Emerson was seventy-seven.

Thoreau worried that people weren't selective enough about what they put into their minds. "We should treat our minds, that is, ourselves, as innocent and ingenuous children, whose guardians we are, and be careful what objects and what subjects we thrust on their attention." (Louisa, if you only knew the trivia that bombards our minds today! Not only is there a continuous stream of it, but its methods of penetrating our brains have become perniciously clever. Figuring out how to fend off this incoming drivel is among the problems I hope our correspondence will address.)

❦ ❦ ❦

Emerson learned to read before he was three; his siblings did the same, and so did his own children. It was just expected. It was also expected that all the boys would go to the local college, Harvard. Which they all did. Emerson entered at age fourteen and finished at eighteen by paying his way as students do today – waiting tables, winning a few prizes, and, in his case, ghostwriting term papers for some of his fellow students.

He was not particularly satisfied with his life at eighteen. He recorded in his journal, "In twelve days I shall be nineteen years old; which I count a miserable thing. Has any other educated person lived so many years and lost so many days?"

Emerson went into the family business, the ministry, partly so he could marry a beautiful seventeen-year-old from Plymouth named Ellen Tucker. Sadly, but not unusually for the times, Ellen had tuberculosis and died less than two years later. His grief deepened to a yearlong depression, and he quit his ministerial post. He was so mopey that his friends pooled their money to send him to Europe. He spent some months sightseeing in Italy, attending Palm Sunday services in the Sistine Chapel and walking around on the roof of Milan's Duomo. He strolled the piazza in front of Santa Croce (where Machiavelli, Michelangelo, and Galileo are buried) in Florence, feeling that here was a church built for the human race. Florence was his favorite European city because it had cheap cafés and few beggars. He did not like

Venice, calling it a "city for beavers," and wrote that the canals kept people from knowing their neighbors.

He cheered up considerably in England, after talking to people like Carlyle, Coleridge, Wordsworth, and Harriet Martineau about revolution. Carlyle showed him his monograph, *Sartor Resartus*, which uses clothing and textile metaphors to discuss the contemporary social and political unrest in England and France and argues that revolutionaries need both a torch for burning and a hammer for building. Emerson liked it so much he arranged to have it published in the United States. Then he came home where he met and married a saint of a woman named Lydia Jackson, even though everyone could see that he was still in love with Ellen.

Some years after their marriage, the new Mrs. Emerson told her husband she had a dream in which she, Ellen, and Waldo were in heaven, and she gave her blessing to Ellen and Waldo as they walked off into the clouds without her. Emerson commended her (Lydia) for her large-mindedness and said nothing to contradict her interpretation. Ellen was still his true love.

Emerson didn't like the sound of "Lydia Emerson," so he renamed his wife Lidian, which is how her gravestone reads. She called him Mr. Emerson. They had four children, two girls and two boys. When their first daughter was born, Lidian suggested that the baby be named after his first wife, Ellen Tucker, and so she was. One of Louisa May Alcott's first publishing ventures, in 1854, was a book called *Flower Fables* – stories Louisa had told to little Ellen Tucker Emerson when she babysat the Emerson children.

Lidian was a bit like Louisa's mother Abba in her practical sensibilties and strong sympathy for the poor and downtrodden. They also shared the experience of being married to friendly but emotionally distant men. Both Abba and Lidian took in homeless people, sheltering, feeding, and clothing them with whatever they had available. Lidian had little patience for people who trod upon individual liberties. She once invaded a Shaker community that would not release a cousin who wanted to leave. Lecturing and debating them at length, she succeeded in her mission.

Lidian was active in the Society for the Prevention of Cruelty to Animals. Once, a rat was hiding in the Emerson chimney. After locking a family cat in the room with the rat for a whole day, the children came back to search the chimney to see if the cat had done its duty. They discovered a doughnut, placed on a ledge inside the chimney. Lidian had put it there, feeling sorry for the rat. When their house burned in 1872, Lidian was heard to express sorrow for the newly homeless rats hopping across the smoking clothing and papers scattered on the damp morning grass around the house.

We will leave the grown-up intricacies of Emerson's transcendentalism until later. For now, as Louisa did as a child, we can appreciate the cheerful, inclusive friendliness of the Emerson family, living right across the road from the Alcotts. Like his Aunt Mary, Emerson enjoyed conversing with the neighbor children and encouraged them to think independently. He was kind and appeared never to hold a grudge or publicly speak meanly of anyone. He liked talking to people, and he liked people. He would simply present his ideas in a friendly way and would never engage in personal arguments. His son Edward described his father's child-rearing methods: "Every day was to be fresh and new as a dewdrop from the hands of God. We may have failed yesterday, but we would never think of it again, and start right today."

Lidian, whose saintliness never overrode her sharp intelligence, found occasional moments to skewer her husband's transcendental excesses. Once, as she and Abba were comparing wifely notes, she put a slightly different spin on her husband's advice, paraphrasing it as "Never confess a fault. You should not have committed it & who cares whether you are sorry."

❧☙❧☙❧

Henry David Thoreau, fifteen years older than Louisa and fifteen years younger than Emerson, was Louisa's second love, after Emerson himself. Thoreau used to take the Alcott sisters on hikes, where he pointed out the best berry bushes and charmed the birds and squirrels so they sat in his hands. He told them that spiderwebs were handkerchiefs dropped by fairies. After his Harvard stretch, he took a job teaching in Concord's public school. He lasted only two weeks, resigning after realizing that he was expected to flog students who broke the rules.

Thoreau and Emerson admired and learned much from each other. Emerson noted in his journal in February 1838, after having a conversation with the twenty-year-old Thoreau, "My good friend Henry Thoreau made this else solitary afternoon sunny with his simplicity and clear perception. How comic is simplicity in this double-dealing, quacking world. Everything that boy says makes merry with society, though nothing can be graver than his meaning." Emerson often described Thoreau as brave, although in later years he called Thoreau an underachiever.

Thoreau moved in with the Emersons for two years in 1841, four years prior to his stint at Walden Pond.* Emerson told him, "Be yourself; no base imitator of another, but your best self. There is something which you can do better than another. Listen to the inward voice and bravely obey that. Do the things at which you are great, not what you were never made for." Thoreau made that message his own and might claim to have lived it as fully as any American ever has. Louisa honored both Emerson and Thoreau repeatedly in her fiction, casting them as lovers of her heroines, and sometimes as themselves, as in *Rose in Bloom* where her leading man Mac reads and is inspired by Emerson's *Self-Reliance* and takes long walks in the woods à la Thoreau.

So in this little Concord neighborhood of Alcotts, Emersons, and Thoreaus, the adults liked children. They were interested in children and how they discovered and played in the world. Natural

---

* There were rumors of hanky-panky between Thoreau and Lidian Emerson. Scholars generally interpret the evidence of continuing, high sexual tension between them as meaning they never consummated their relationship. Other scholars have proposed that Thoreau was gay. He never married, but did propose to Ellen Sewall, who rejected him.

history and human history, they believed, combined in a holy way to create beauty and ethics. They believed there was an exalted connection between people and the planet, and they thought that children understood this relationship better than adults. They heartily rejected any belief in original sin and subscribed instead to its opposite: children lived in an unstained state of grace. Paying attention to children, the Emerson and Alcott parents reasoned, could help all adults regain this connection to the goodness of life and nature.

These Americans were fans of Wordsworth and his friend Coleridge, who had romantically set up housekeeping in the damp and windswept Lake District of England at the dawn of the nineteenth century. Wordsworth's poem "Intimations of Immortality" was an anthem for them – speaking as it does of infants being born

> Not in entire forgetfulness,
> And not in utter nakedness,
> But trailing clouds of glory do we come
> From God, who is our home:
> Heaven lies about us in our infancy.

December 30, 1887

Dear Mrs. Bakke,

Yes, I count this as a fair beginning, & am pleased to remember those neighborly days. Your essay has distracted me from my headaches & dizziness, which never go away for long. I am glad to see the end of this 1887. Did get a few things accomplished though, including adopting Anna's son, my dear nephew John. Now he will clearly inherit all my copyrights. I don't want any legal hurdles to exist between my heirs & my money.

For someone who never met any of my neighbors (I assume!

*Although with your future poking its way into my parlor, perhaps I
am to be apprised of more surprises?), you have introduced them
reasonably well. We certainly left a trail of breadcrumbs & apple cores,
didn't we? Aunt Mary Emerson was quite a character. She was very
short & squat, you know, barely over four feet. In her shroud she looked
like a perambulating canvas-covered haystack.*

*Sometimes we did think what we were doing & thinking was
important enough to be remembered for hundreds of years, but at
other times we were grateful just to stumble from one day to the next.
My faithful & serene father, obviously, never doubted that his life was
worth being projected into the future. Five million words in his journal,
you say? That is truly prodigious. Bless his soul, would that he had
converted a tiny fraction of that effort into action – then the world
would surely be a better place!*

*But my rudder, as you call it, came straight from my parents, in a
sort of messy combination sometimes. I expect you will get to the fact
that the two of them weren't always steering into the same port. Dear
Father was such a trial at times, but so sweet about it, you know.*

*I was moonstruck by both Mr. Emerson & Henry Thoreau, as
everyone seems to have guessed. In a schoolgirl way, mind you. Mr.
Emerson was quite regal & good-looking, & so, so gentle & kind to me
– like a father, grandfather, uncle & godfather all wrapped into one.
And Henry, how I weep for him even now! I hope you will write more
about him. I still hear his flute from time to time. He was too good
for this world. (As is Mrs. Emerson, I must add!)*

*I will tell you some more gossip. Did you know that Mr. Emerson
opened his wife Ellen Tucker's coffin thirteen months after her death?
He loved her so much – he thought her so infinitely angelic that maybe
she would still be whole. He did the same later with his son Waldo's
coffin. The poor man was so devastated when Waldo died – just five
years old, scarlet fever, so quick. Fifteen years later, when Sleepy
Hollow was opened as our town cemetery, the Emersons moved him
there. During the move, Mr. Emerson peeked inside. It occurred to
me to make a gothic tale of such things, but I couldn't.*

Both Mr. Emerson & Henry helped so much to soften the never-

ending turmoil I had with my dear father. I do think the fact that we had the same birthday spooked us both, especially since we sprouted up into such different vegetables. Father never let me forget, in that quiet way of his, that I had inherited what he thought were Mother's least attractive traits.

I would prefer that you not go on about what I look like. Appearances, in real life, are not as germane as they are in fiction. It's how one lives that matters. I suppose, though, if my motley form gives heart to others as poorly endowed as I am, then it's all to the good.

Looking forward to seeing how you take a run at transcendentalism. I think you will find its wispy ways difficult to capture. My father, you know, said much the same thing as you quote Mr. Emerson saying to Henry. In my father's "Orphic Sayings," published (& much ridiculed, it pains me to add) in the Dial, he said, "Engage in nothing that cripples or degrades you." I suppose you will be talking more about the Dial when you talk about transcendentalism.

But first I think you need to tell your friends more about Mother & Father. They have never been far from my thoughts, even as I have become an old lady myself. Sometimes I wonder if all that filial closeness is good. You may notice in my books that I usually put parents off-stage. You are going to tell me, I trust, about your parents.

I am concerned about all the wars you keep referring to. I would have hoped that after the dreadful carnage of the Civil War that America would have learned its lesson. No sensible person could want a reprise of such suffering.

And yet . . . & yet, when I remember honestly, I was so eager to go to the front myself, & experience all the undeniable excitements of battle & the energy of fighting for just cause . . . perhaps that devilish yearning, in enough people, is enough to spark a war all on its own.

Lost in memory,
Louisa M. Alcott

Raising Louisa

People think I'm wild and queer;
but Mother understands and helps me.
Louisa May Alcott, 1846, age thirteen

There comes a time when children judge their parents
as men and women in spite of filial duty.
Louisa May Alcott, 1872, age forty

December 31, 2005

Dear Miss Alcott,

I am sorry about the looks part. People care about such things
now. They want to know what you look like; it makes you more
real to them. If it's any comfort to you, we are having an epidemic
of fat these days. Millions of women, and men too, are on diets
all the time trying to lose weight. We are being ambushed by far
more tempting, affordable food than our weak and shortsighted
wills can handle. People today don't get nearly as much exercise
as your generation either.

I agree with you that more needs to be said about parents,
and here it is. Yes, everyone who has read about you knows how
close you were to both your mother and father. Some think you
would have been better off if you hadn't been. People today tend
to believe that independence and freedom require some separation, physically and emotionally, from parents. I went too far in
that direction myself, during my radical politics days, when I dis-

appeared underground for about two years. For all my parents knew, I was dead on the side of the road somewhere. A mother myself now, I shiver at my heartlessness. But back then the bombs and firestorms our government was raining down on Vietnamese straw huts and mud-brick farmhouses weighed far heavier on the heartless scale. Not to mention our local police murdering black people for trying to register to vote. Just writing this to you reminds me of how much I still want to make my life count.

I'll tell you a little about my parents, although I don't claim to be objective or clear-sighted about them. My mother, like yours, is dead. My father, like yours, ages gently on after a somewhat tangential attachment to everyday life. He is a retired physician who has firmly believed all his life that there are physicians (the best people) and then there is everyone else (not so good). His single-minded passion for medicine turned everything he saw into a diagnostic problem. He has never ceased to marvel at the wonders of human biology. When I was a child, our dinner table conversation often involved diagrams of the alimentary canal on paper napkins. He described sexual intercourse to me and my brothers when we were not yet teenagers, lecturing to us (and drawing diagrams) as if we were medical students.

My mother would hover in the background, clucking "Now, Jack!", trying to bring him back to a semblance of family decorum. Her interests leaned toward local civic issues like voter education and clean water supplies. She was an active member of the League of Women Voters, an organization founded in the early twentieth century by women's suffrage veterans and dedicated to helping women have an intelligent and meaningful impact on the political process. She edited their local newsletter and wrote booklets about how our Washington State government worked. In 1954, when I was six years old, she surprised my brothers and me by ignoring us for a whole week. We had to be quiet all day and she wouldn't play with us; this was completely unprecedented behavior. She was listening to the radio (a kind of talking newspaper – an electric box that transmits people's voices from far away) to a governmental hearing. I learned later that these Army-McCarthy Hearings were about a senator even more dastardly than the pro-slavery Senator Brooks who beat your abolitionist Senator Sumner to bloody unconsciousness during legislative debates about slavery. By her actions, my mother was teaching us that it's important to know about the world outside our family living room, and that there are many wrongs out there, waiting to be redressed by informed and caring citizens.

You would have liked my mother. She made games out of learning, holding little math and spelling sessions at the end of summer to get all the neighborhood kids limbered up for school. Both parents raised me to feel extremely capable and smart. In fact, my brothers and I made the mistake of growing up thinking we were smarter than everyone we knew. All four of our grand-parents had graduated from college in the early 1900s, around the time another major war devastated Europe before the one I mentioned earlier. People called the first one the Great War, not imagining there was a worse one to come; then when it did, they had to rename it the First World War. But I digress. Academic success was the most prized accomplishment in my family, and it justified a huge range of other incompetencies. We were terrible at sports and awful at socializing and small talk. We also had a (possibly related) relaxed approach to laws and rules.

My parents did not take my brothers and me to church. They never taught us to believe in any Protestant, Catholic or Jewish God. This didn't seem strange to me, nor do I remember ever feeling discriminated against for not belonging to one particular church or another. I know it was different in your day, and that your family suffered snubs and economic hardship for your religious choices. Despite my own experience, I wish I could say that reli-gious intolerance was gone forever, but unfortunately it's still alive and well right here in America.

My dad was an anarchist in his early years. He acted as if the laws of the state were there for him to consider, but possibly to reject – a bit like Thoreau, now that I think about it. When I was a teenager, I once stole some clothing from a store. I was caught, and the store detective hauled me into her office. She called my house (we have these devices called telephones that allow people to talk to each other at any distance).

My dad replied patiently to the detective's accusation of my thievery, "I don't understand the problem. We have an account at your store – just put the clothes on our account, and send her home." The detective was appalled at his total absence of moral anger, social embarrassment, or anything resembling remorse.

I was just enormously relieved that my mom hadn't answered the phone. Her response would have been very different. I don't know if my dad ever told her about it. I hope not. My dad thought he was a genius. He said his friend Bill was the only person he knew who was smarter than he was. When they were in their thirties, Bill killed himself. After that, my dad started saying that being a genius was quite a burden, and maybe he himself wasn't one after all. For years though, I expected my dad to win the Nobel Prize in medicine. Mr. Nobel was a wealthy Swede, just your age. You may have heard of his invention called dynamite – he made millions from it. After he died, he said his money should go to funding an international annual prize for advances in the sciences, in literature, and in peace. Ironic, don't you think?

Moving right along,
Kit B.

PS: You are right that the transcendentalism part will be tricky. I asked a friend of mine who teaches philosophy at a college in Boston if transcendentalism is part of his curriculum. He gave me that look professors project when they have been asked a remarkably ignorant question. I guess transcendentalism is no longer considered a philosophy.

Still learning,
Kit

THE REFORMER IN LOVE

THE TEDIOUS ARCHANGEL · MRS. TROLLOPE'S VIEWS

BEHAVIOR MATTERS

Bronson Alcott, Louisa's father, was not as benign as Emerson.* Emerson confessed to a sort of morbid curiosity about Bronson's personality and what we would today call his "communication style." Bronson had an utter disregard for other people's feelings and a total absence of humor, both of which, Emerson privately vented, created a "monotonous" sort of neighbor, who "would be greater if he were good humored."

Both Emerson and Alcott had hardscrabble childhoods, but unlike Emerson's, Bronson's upbringing in a dirt-poor Connecticut farm family was not softened by a parent's interest in the life of the mind. Bronson's father was illiterate, his mother nearly so. There were more children† than books at home, and no college for anyone. Bronson, the oldest, tried farming but failed. He took to the road as an itinerant salesperson, hawking pots and pans, whistles and combs, needles and pins. After initial success, this also failed. In his twenties Bronson began to read and think on his own.

He became a schoolteacher, discovering he had interesting ideas about how children and adults could and should learn. The core of his approach was the Socratic conversation: just talk to children, draw out their ideas, and they will learn. The role of the teacher, he thought, was more to accompany children than to lead them. "Education, when rightly understood will be found to lie in the art of asking apt and fit questions, and in this leading the mind by its own light to the perception of truth." One of his

---

* Not everyone found Ralph Waldo Emerson so adorable. His wife Lidian complained that he was cold and solitary when she needed him the most. Margaret Fuller supporters fault Emerson from stem to stern for his general misogyny, making a case for his having led Fuller on and then coldly dumping her.

† Among the eight, there was a set of twin girls named Pamila and Pamela.

techniques was to have the children bend their bodies in the shape of the alphabet, similar to an approach used today to teach dyslexic children to read.* He also invented recess, believing that exercise and physical play were important parts of the school day.

In 1826 Bronson wrote out fifty-eight "General Maxims" for teachers, including ideas such as "To teach, distinctive from all sinister, sectarian and oppressive principles," "To teach, by keeping curiosity awake," "To teach by Comparison and Contrast," and "To teach, endeavoring to preserve the understanding from implicit belief, and to secure the habit of independence of thought and of feeling." There is early transcendentalist thought here, and this was long before he met Emerson.

This approach was remarkably revolutionary in an age when education was primarily rote memorization and recitation. It was also dangerous, because unchaperoned Socratic conversation can go down unpredictable paths, toward sex, for instance, ("let's think about where babies come from") or religion ("we are all children of God, just as much as Jesus was"). Which his schoolroom chats often did. Bronson's schools never lasted more than a few years before scandalized parents withdrew their children.

His best-known school was called the Temple School, in a Masonic Temple building on Tremont Street in Boston. It was here in the middle 1830s that both Margaret Fuller and Elizabeth Peabody worked as his assistants. Margaret Fuller went on to become America's most famous female transcendentalist (although she would not have used the title herself – thinking that transcendentalism was too narrow a descriptor for her views). She held conversations of her own in Elizabeth Peabody's Boston bookstore and library, edited the *Dial*, and wrote *The Great Lawsuit: Man versus Men – Woman versus Women* (later renamed *Woman in the Nineteenth Century*), an essay that combines stunningly erudite knowledge of both Western and Eastern

---

* Louisa remembered this fondly and had Jo March's husband Professor Bhaer teach his Plumfield students the same way.

civilizations with hard-hitting arguments for the social, political, legal, occupational, and economic equality of women.

Elizabeth Peabody was an active, busy woman who seemed to know everyone.* She was a fierce abolitionist and a fiery supporter of John Brown, famous for throwing herself so wholeheartedly into her thoughts and her causes that she would forget to dress herself properly before going out. Her friends would report seeing her walking blindly into trees or snow banks, her mind on higher matters. There is a story that once, deep in conversation, she unknowingly sat on several kittens, snuffing out their small lives before her companions could intervene.

Her bookstore, called the Foreign Library, was stocked with difficult-to-find European books on philosophy, economics, and politics – all of which were hot items her friends required to fuel their transcendental conversations. She was also an educational pioneer and is credited with promulgating kindergarten in America. It was her sister, Sophia Peabody, who married the guilt-ridden Nathaniel Hawthorne and lived next door to the Alcotts in Concord.

Bronson had a habit, which greatly irritated the financial and church powers in Boston, of teaching about Jesus as if he were a regular person. Jesus, Bronson would say in his calmly superior, otherworldly manner, was a person of considerable virtue, and one from whom we can all learn a great deal, but he was a person just like, well, just like Bronson. He talked with his young students about their own impressions of the stories in the Bible, as if they were stories like any other story.

He and his assistants wrote down what the children said about the Bible and published their words in 1837 in a volume called *Conversations with Children on the Gospels*. Elizabeth Peabody and

---

* Henry James probably used Elizabeth Peabody as his model for the kindly, dithering, and dedicated Miss Birdseye in *The Bostonians*, his condescending romp through Boston and New York's women's suffrage movement. He describes Miss Birdseye as "a confused, entangled, inconsequent, discursive old woman, whose charity began at home and ended nowhere. . . ."

Bronson had a falling out over this book, which she branded, correctly as it turned out, as too blasphemous for Boston readers.* One of Bronson's students, writing later of what it was like in his classroom, remembered, "His forte was 'moral influence' and 'sympathetic intellectual communion' by talking; and, oh heaven! what a talker he was! . . . The word *ideal* was ever in his mouth."

There were two other major counts against Bronson's Temple School. Not only did he talk about Jesus and God in a less reverent way than was expected, he also explained the physiology of childbirth to his young students, albeit in a cloudy Victorian way, and with full reference to God's role.† He alluded to the process of labor and delivery, which was unforgivably frank in adult mixed company and completely unacceptable when talking with children. Despite crediting God in the process, the published dialogue between children and teacher clearly indicates that a man and a woman shared the starring roles. Some "naughtiness" is involved, said a ten-year-old boy, and definite suffering and pain on the part of the mother. Charles, a practical student, said he thought the father ought to be the one to give birth as "he is so much stronger."

Boston was shocked to its puritanical core. Bronson was excoriated from every pulpit. There were calls for a grand jury. Although criticism of the book was rampant, actual readers were rare. Stacks of unsold *Conversations* were finally auctioned off to a luggage maker at five cents a pound to be used as lining material in suitcases.

---

* Louisa's third sister Elizabeth (Beth in *Little Women*) had been named after Elizabeth Peabody, but after this altercation, Bronson and Abba angrily changed their daughter's middle name from Peabody to Sewall, as there were plenty of Elizabeth Sewalls in Abba's family tree to be named after.

† He got slightly more graphic in his journal: "Sexual intercourse represents the synthesis of body and spirit. . . . Fluids form solids. Mettle is the Godhead proceeding into the matrix of Nature to organize Man. Behold the creative jet! And hear the morning stars sing for joy at the sacred generation of the Gods!" Later, when the English cofounder of Bronson's commune wanted to introduce sexual abstinence, Bronson vehemently vetoed the plan.

The final blow to the Temple School and to Bronson's teaching career came in 1839 when he acted on his belief that black children could learn as well as white ones, and that, in fact, there was no harm done to teach children of all colors in the same schoolroom. He admitted Susan Robinson, a black child, to the Temple School. Once again, the parents rebelled, and that was the end of that. Louisa was six at the time and Bronson was thirty-nine. It was the last time he ever held a full-time job.

Louisa's parents were an odd pair. Her mother, Abigail May Alcott (known as Abba), was as dark and active as Bronson was pale and inactive. She was a recognizable type: a hardworking woman who loved her children, supported them with praise all her life and publicly supported her eccentric husband – all the while keeping her own tart counsel in her journal,

> A woman may perform the most disinterested duties. She may "die daily" in the cause of truth and righteousness. She lives neglected, dies forgotten. But a man who never performed in his whole life one self denying act, but has accidental gifts of genius, is celebrated by his contemporaries, while his name and his works live on from age to age.

Abba was the practical glue that held the family together no matter what. As she aged, all that hard work eventually wore her down. In her fifties and sixties, the chip on her shoulder got flintier, and she became increasingly dependent on an uncomplaining Louisa. It was abundantly clear to the four daughters from their earliest years that Mother did all the work and got little in return. The girls reacted differently to this family truth, as children will, and it was all a real-life laboratory for Louisa's pen. Since Louisa was part of the experiment as well, her observations were colored by love and frustration. She once toyed with writing a story called "The Cost of an Idea" to detail how her father's transcendental philosophy adversely affected his wife and daughters, but she never wrote it.

Abba was a keen observer, and not much in the way of public relations pretense threw her off the scent of unfairness or persecution. Once, visiting a Shaker community in connection with her own family's commune at Fruitlands, she observed: "I gain but little from their domestic or internal arrangements. There is servitude somewhere, I have no doubt. There is a fat sleek comfortable look about the men, and among the women there is a stiff awkward reserve that belongs to neither sublime resignation nor divine hope." She was also perceptive enough to discover, by reflecting on her own frontline experiences as a social worker, the significant gap between a symptomatic versus a preventive approach to the problem of poverty. The symptomatic approach, favored by rich women wanting to feel good by charitable giving, was helpful first aid, she knew, but hardly sufficient.

Both Abba and, later, Louisa, spent considerable energy trying to convince rich, do-gooder wives that simple handouts would never amount to more than a tiny part of the solution to family poverty. If they were alive today, they would agree with the business advice against sitting downriver, shooting alligators as they appear. Abba and Louisa knew they had to slog their way upstream to wipe out those pesky alligator nests; when they arrived, they discovered that poverty's breeding ground was a well-defended and prickly thicket of laws denying women basic economic rights. Women in the nineteenth century were restricted to so few areas of work that they were forced to compete against their own overabundant supply, thereby driving all their wages below livable levels.*

As an eighteen-year-old, Louisa was paid four dollars for seven weeks' hard work as a house servant to a middle-class man and his sister in Dedham, Massachusetts. The job was described as being a companion to the sister, but after Louisa refused her employer's amorous advances, he assigned her to water hauling, wood carrying, snow clearing, and boot cleaning duty. To the cheers of her poverty-stricken but principled family, she quit and

---

* As women have continued over the past century to expand their employment options, more subtle mechanisms have served to keep women's wages lower than those of men's.

disgustedly returned the money. Abba wrote to her brother Sam that her life was "one of daily protest against the oppression and abuses of Society. I find selfishness, meanness, . . . among people who fill high places in church and State. The whole system of Servitude in New England is almost as false as slavery in the South."

Unlike Bronson, Abba May came from a family of excellent New England lineage, including Quincys and Sewalls, from the repenting Salem judge to a scattering of Revolutionary War heroes. The men in her immediate family were mostly ministers and lawyers, and their families were urban and solidly middle class. Her spirited and charming great-aunt Dorothy Quincy was John Hancock's wife. The Mays always had a powerful streak of wanting to do the right thing, and with their money and time, every generation had been involved in social and religious reforms of various kinds. Abba's father, Colonel Sam May, wrote this about the accumulation of money during one's lifetime, "Life was not given to be all used up in the pursuit of what we must leave behind us when we die."

Abba became smitten with Bronson, the itinerant salesman turned failed schoolteacher, when he visited her brother's house where she, in her mid-twenties, was staying to help with the birth of her sister-in-law's child. Her brother was the first Unitarian minister in Connecticut. He had read about Bronson's innovative teaching methods and was interested enough to invite him to his home to learn more.

It was love at first sight. The May family was surprised at Abba's sudden choice, but supportive of the marriage. Over time, however, their patience and support thinned; eventually, they tired of forking over money to the impoverished Alcotts. The May family men were irritated that Bronson seemed uninterested in providing for his growing brood, and began curtailing their financial support so that Abba could use it only for herself and her children, but not for any debts or support of Bronson.

Bronson was a shy lover and in the habit typical of the times, he let Abba know how he felt not by speaking, but by giving her his journal to read. They were married, more at her initiative than his, in the spring of 1830, she marrying "down" and he marrying "up." Louisa, at age eighteen, wrote of her mother, "I often think of what a hard life she has had since she married." Abba herself wrote, on hearing of a friend's becoming a mother once again, "How thoughtlessly this domestic martyrdom is enacted in married life. What a volume might be written on the heroines of private life – there is a courage of endurance, as high as that of action." Abba had five children and three miscarriages that we know of. There were the four daughters – Anna born in March 1831, Louisa in November 1832, Elizabeth in June 1835, and May in July 1840. Between Elizabeth and May, a son was born and quickly died, in April 1839.

≫⌐≫⌐≫

In 1832, the year Louisa was born, Mrs. Fanny Trollope published her wildly successful *Domestic Manners of the Americans*. Fanny, an imaginative self-starter of an Englishwoman, was fifty at the time, and it was her first book. Like Abba, Fanny had married a man who didn't mind letting his wife support him and their children. Also like Abba, she took a large view of her social responsibility as a human being. So in November 1827 she crossed the Atlantic, intent on helping another Fanny – the beautiful, headstrong Frances Wright* – found a utopian community for freed blacks in the United States.†

The utopia, in a Tennessee swamp, was a disaster, but Fanny Trollope stayed on in America, moving up the Ohio River to

---

* Fanny Wright, a Scottish heiress befriended by the aging General Lafayette, was extremely charismatic and gathered many admirers to her quirky projects. She was a bit flighty, however, and didn't stick to any one of them long enough to produce much success.

† The English were shortly (in 1833) to emancipate all the slaves in their colonies, long before all but a few Americans had owned up to the problem.

Cincinnati, taking copious notes all the while. Back in England, she shuffled them into a remarkably insightful and prescient manuscript describing firsthand the mostly uncivilized America into which Louisa was born.

> Had I, during my residence in the United States, observed any single feature in their national character that could justify their eternal boast of liberality and the love of freedom, I might have respected them, however much my taste might have been offended by what was peculiar in their manners and customs. But it is impossible for any mind of common honesty not to be revolted by the contradictions in their principles and practice. . . . You will see them with one hand hoisting the cap of liberty, and with the other flogging their slaves. You will see them one hour lecturing their mob on the indefensible rights of man, and the next driving from their homes the children of the soil [Native Americans], whom they have bound themselves to protect by the most solemn treaties.

Louisa's parents would have agreed with much of this, and they raised their daughters accordingly. But being Americans, they were participants, not observers, and could not, like Fanny Trollope, go back to Europe, dismissing the new Americans with a Seussian cadence: "I do not like them. I do not like their principles. I do not like their manners, I do not like their opinions." Like her countryman Charles Dickens, Fanny Trollope was another social reformer who was disappointed in the America she saw first hand and up close.*

Today, we don't much remember Fanny Trollope or the thirty-five novels she eventually churned out. English lit majors, though,

---

* Louisa herself was a great Dickens fan until she saw him in person at a lecture in London. She was disappointed and "found him an old dandy." This was two years before his death, when the stress of being the perfect Victorian gentleman in public and maintaining his life with actress-mistress Nelly Ternan on the sly was wearing him down.

will remember her son Anthony Trollope, the Barsetshire novelist and upstanding Victorian civil servant who also invented the public mailbox. Anthony, however, was mostly ignored by his mother, who was preoccupied by money woes, her useless husband, and nursing three of Anthony's siblings to their tubercular deaths. Anthony returned her inattention by critiquing her ability to have any opinions at all about Americans:

> No observer was certainly ever less qualified to judge of the prospects or even of the happiness of a young people. No one could have been worse adapted by nature for the task of learning whether a nation was in a way to thrive. Whatever she saw she judged, as most women do, from her own standpoint.

Bronson Alcott judged, as most men do, from his own standpoint as well. Emerson observed that Bronson was a "pure idealist, not at all a man of letters, nor of any practical talent, nor a writer of books; a man too cold and contemplative for the alliances of friendship, with a rare simplicity and grandeur of perception, who read Plato as an equal. . . ."

In 1842, when Louisa was ten, and the youngest Alcott daughter, May, was two, Bronson sailed (on Emerson's dime) to England at the invitation of several London-based transcendental reformers who appreciated Bronson's teaching methods enough to have started a school in his name. One was Charles Lane, of whom we shall read more later. Abba was not happy about being left with the four children for what she branded as an unnecessarily risky and expensive trip. She summed up for her brother Sam her dissatisfactions with her husband, "Our diversity of opinion has at times led us far and wide of a quiet and contented frame of mind – I have been looking for rest – he for principle and salvation – I have been striving for justice and peace – he for truth and righteousness."

Bronson was unusual in the nineteenth century, and he would be even more so in ours. He was a man who, once he grasped a wavering, idealistic dream of individual human perfectibility, never looked back. His calm detachment from the mundane appeared almost inhuman – enough to drive more reactive people over the edge of their uncertain control. He was by all accounts a man who never raised his voice, never became angry, and rarely deviated from a serene and optimistic outlook on life. Bronson was a lifelong vegetarian, bordering on the vegan. He considered fresh apples were the tastiest treat he could imagine.

Ignoring the ordinary was his forte. Odell Shepard, Bronson's biographer, pins him down perfectly, "His peculiarity was not that he was an idealist, for all true Americans are that. It was, rather, that he was nothing else." Indeed. It is amazing to twenty-first century eyes to see this man who clearly cared deeply for his wife and daughters, but felt not the least bit concerned that his chosen occupation, philosophy, kept his family in continual, un-remitting poverty. His neighbors appeared to notice his daughters' hunger more than he did – they would drop food baskets off at the Alcott doorstep, acts of charity which Louisa both appreci-ated and found humiliating.

To be fair, Bronson did demonstrate some marginally helpful skills as farmer and carpenter. He added several sagging addi-tions to both Hillside and Orchard House. For Hillside, he cut a nearby barn in two, moved the pieces to Hillside, and nailed the halves onto opposite ends of the existing house. The extensions still stand today. Louisa called Orchard House "Apple Slump" in honor of its small apple orchard and the primary architectural feature of her father's construction. He also maintained a vegetable garden and built bumpy furniture that fulfilled its function only because there was no alternative.

Bronson built a small one-room wooden schoolroom in back of Orchard House that he christened his School of Philosophy. He held summer classes there for several years, a precursor of today's university extension or adult education programs, draw-ing students and teachers from great distances. The building is there today and is still used for classes and conferences.

Although Emerson provided money to the Alcott family on a regular basis, his intellectual support of Bronson's ideas was decidedly mixed. Arguing with Bronson was exhausting and unsatisfying. His contemporaries would grasp tidbits of genius in his unstoppable flow of words, but then be overwhelmed with tedious overkill. Emerson finally gave up trying to engage him in intellectual dialogue, recording in his journal,

> Very sad, indeed, to see this half-god driven to the wall, reproaching men, and hesitating whether he should not reproach the Gods. The world was not, in trial, a possible element for him to live in. . . . Very tedious and prosing and egotistical and narrow he is, but a profound insight, a Power, a majestical man. . . . I think I shall never attempt to set him right anymore. It is not for me to answer him."

Emerson called him a "tedious archangel" and noted repeatedly in his journal that Bronson had no sense of humor, ever, at all. Bronson's reasoning was hard to follow, and he never admitted to error. He wore out his listeners with helter-skelter enthusiasms. Emerson wrote that Bronson was "quite ready at any moment to abandon his present residence and employment, his country, nay, his wife and children, on very short notice, to put any new dream into practice which has bubbled up in the effervescence of discourse."

At the same time as Emerson was providing money to the Alcott family, he was noting privately, "Unhappily, his [Bronson's] conversation never loses sight of his own personality. . . . His topic yesterday is Alcott on the 17th October; to-day, Alcott on the 18th October; to-morrow, on the 19th . . . this noble genius discredits genius to me." Emerson then summarized baldly, "I do not want any more such persons to exist."

Once, when the Emerson, Alcott, and Hawthorne families were all visiting together, Nathaniel contributed a poem, made up on the spot, about Bronson:

There dwelt a Sage at Apple-Slump
Whose dinner never made him plump;
Give him carrots, potatoes, squash, parsnips and peas,
Some boiled macaroni without any cheese,
And a plate of raw apples to hold on his knees,
And a glass of sweet cider, to wash down all these,
And he'd prate of the Spirit as long as you'd please,
This airy Sage of Apple-Slump.

Abba named the infant Louisa after her own sister, Louisa May Greele, who had died in childbirth. Bronson, feeling unappreciated, wrote to his father-in-law that the day was his birthday, too. He added that his new daughter's name was, to his wife, "full of every association connected with amiable benevolence and exalted worth. I hope its present possessor may rise in equal attainment, and deserve a place in the estimation of society." When Louisa was just two, Bronson's Pennsylvania school failed, and the parents took Anna and baby Louisa back to Massachusetts.

Bronson referred to his daughters as "living manifestations of my intellect." It must have been difficult to be his daughter. On the one hand, he treated everyone with full respect and dignity, down to the smallest child. On the other, he discounted the possibility that other people had emotions, fears, and hopes different from his own. He lived as if everyone were as fascinated by his own thought processes as he himself was.

His birthday letters to Louisa, for instance, are breathtakingly self-centered. They purport to be celebrating her birthday, but in fact are all about his own presence and expectations: "I would have you feel my presence and be the happier, and better that I am here. I want, most of all things, to be a kindly influence on you, helping you to guide and govern your heart. I live, dear daughter, to be good. . . ." Alternatively, they would be about how big sister Anna was better behaved than Louisa: "I wish we may all be as diffident and unpretending as this sister of yours. . . ." he wrote to Louisa on her sixteenth birthday.

His letter celebrating her seventh birthday went like this:

> You are Seven years old today . . . you have learned a great many things, since you have lived in a Body, about things going on around you and within you. . . . You feel your Conscience, and have no real pleasure unless you obey it. . . . It is G O D trying in your soul to keep you always G O O D.

Bronson thought of himself as a god, and he wanted to live among gods. This approach to parenting caused problems for the energetically human Louisa. The difficulty was exacerbated by the Victorian habit of equating the person with the behavior. Current fashion is to tell our children that while they may commit a bad act, they are not bad people. This was not the message in nineteenth-century New England. People *were* their behavior, and behavior mattered a great deal.

On Louisa's third birthday, she went down to the Temple School to celebrate with her father. They were one short on pieces of cake, and Louisa, the Birthday Girl, was pressured to be the one to go without. Much later she remembered, "As I was queen of the revel, I felt that I ought to have it, and held on to it tightly till my mother said, 'It is always better to give away than to keep the nice things; so I know my Louy will not let the little friend go without." No one seemed to think about cutting the pieces smaller, or maybe not giving any to the adults, because then the lesson of visible sacrifice would have been lost.

Particularly for nineteenth-century girls and women, the range of acceptable behavior was extremely narrow, and the punishment for stepping – or being pushed – outside those male-determined lines was severe. Louisa's semiautobiographical adult novel *Work* follows Rachel, a quiet, hardworking girl who is fired from her seamstress job for having been raped. Unable to find other work and ostracized by everyone, Rachel considers suicide, but is rescued

53

by a network of good-hearted women and a helpful minister. Later, she saves Christie, *Work*'s Louisa-heroine, from the same fate. *Work* is not the only one of Louisa's novels to portray desperate, trapped women who contemplate or attempt suicide.

Although Bronson rarely, if ever, expressed anger to his children, this is not to say he never disciplined them. He did, using "time out" techniques similar to those used by many parents today, as well as other, more highly manipulative methods. One can imagine twentieth-century cult leaders approving Bronson's emotionally charged punishments. In his school, for example, he would make a disobedient child hit him, the teacher, rather than the expected reverse. Instead of sending a naughty daughter (and it was usually Louisa – she was by far the most high-spirited and contrary of the four girls) to her room without dinner, he would go without food himself at the family table, for everyone to see and understand why.

Bronson puzzled over his difficult second daughter in his journal: "She does not, I think, fully comprehend the object of punishment: she is awed into obedience by the fear of results not love of yielding." Even when she was a baby, Bronson began to worry about Louisa's "unusual vivacity, and force of spirit . . . power, individuality, and force . . . great energy and decision of character," quite different from the easygoing, firstborn Anna.

Leafing through his daughters' journals, Bronson told Louisa that hers were about herself and her sister Anna's were about other people. This was no small criticism. In the Alcotts' day, duty and responsibility for others was routinely and publicly assumed without a blush or an apology. No "Me Generation" then. Providing concrete assistance and hard-earned goods to your friends and neighbors wasn't special or sacrificial; it was an everyday act. It was the only safety net around.*

---

* Survival was still fairly chancy in the middle 1800s. Thirty was the average age at death in Massachusetts in the 1870s. Babies and mothers still died at heartbreaking rates. Sniffles and chills were regularly fatal. Contagious diseases killed

Louisa, defensive and unhappy at her father's invidious comparison, responded in her journal: "Anna is so good she need not take care of herself, and can enjoy other people ... my quick tongue is always getting me into trouble, and my moodiness makes it hard to be cheerful when I think how poor we are, how much worry it is to live, and how many things I long to do I never can."

One of Louisa's few biographers, writing in the heyday of the feminist 1970s, is rabid in her dislike of both Abba and Bronson – Bronson for being so cold and inhuman, Abba for giving in to him too much. Bronson simply couldn't cope with Louisa's wild energy. Although an idealist, he was also a Victorian and had Victorian ideas of what women should be like. He was able to conveniently overlook this when it came to his wife's earning a living, but not so with his young daughters. Later, however, when Louisa began to support him, suddenly she became more acceptable. After 1868, when *Little Women* was a runaway success, Bronson's own philosophic lectures were advertised as being presented by "the Father of Little Women."

Louisa filled her girlhood journals with angst over her bad behavior – selfishness, meanness, jealousy. Early on, she accepted the worldview (her father's view) that she was a difficult child. Even her babyhood was marked by a demanding temperament, at least in comparison with Anna (whose middle name, by the way, was Bronson). Anna, who became a stay-at-home mom entirely supported by Louisa after her husband's early death, was always her father's favorite. Later on, when both Louisa and their youngest sister May had established careers but no children, Anna complained to her father that she had nothing to show for her life. Bronson responded that she was the mother of two sons,

---

a third of all infants and toddlers. Everyone had friends in their teens and twenties dying of tuberculosis. With no health, life, or fire insurance, people created their own protection by getting to know their neighbors. Letters and journals from those days are crowded with notes about taking a basket of apples across the road or being grateful for a jar of honey from a neighbor.

saying, "Here is what you have done. It is more than all the rest."

Bronson tended to blame Abba's side of the family for Louisa's misbehaviors, partly because the May family included such active people and partly because of the dark hair and olive complexion that Louisa inherited from the May family genes. Louisa's most meticulous biographer notes that Bronson thought Louisa's "fiery temperament . . . was bilious and demonic, unlike his own sanguine nature, . . . no doubt was left in his mind that his daughter was not a child of light." Bronson, despite his fierce support for the abolitionist cause, came to subscribe to the belief that Aryan types were closer to God than darker folk.

From this up-and-down childhood, of course, comes the solidly believable character of Jo March in *Little Women*: the archetypal story of the American "Tomboy Partially Tamed." Practically every episode of the story is true, but most accurate of all is the depiction of the unbreakable ties among the sisters and with their mother. Anna, before she married, tried to leave home several times and make friends separate from her sisters, but she always came back. "I think perhaps one reason why other girls are not more attractive," she wrote, "may be because I have been so much with Louisa who is so uncommonly interesting and funny that beside her, other girls seem commonplace."

January 6, 1888

Dear Mrs. Bakke,

All these memories are hitting me like Zeus's lightning bolts. Has it become so rare in your time for people to live according to their beliefs? Having parents with such strong characters was a mixed blessing like a hard rain in the desert, but I cannot believe it to be entirely unique. I did not realize that my father tried even the patience of Mr. Emerson! He never let on, wonderful man that he was.

It is quite difficult, as you say yourself, to form a clear picture of one's own parents. Our feelings confuse our thoughts about them.

They are as dear to us as our own skin, but then we discover that they have lives of their own & that their imperfections do not always serve the best interests of their children. It may well be a bigger problem if, as it apparently was for both of us, we have grown up seeing our fathers hovering like gods high atop alabaster pedestals.

Nor, however, do children always serve the best interests of their parents. I clearly disappointed my father in so many ways, & you perhaps did the same. I am piecing together a story about the future that is not particularly pleasant. Slavery in America was bad enough; now you appear to be describing an America that remains cruel to the negro, and is bringing pain & destruction to other countries as well. Even women still suffer basic occupational inequities? For shame! I take it you got your reforming & political energy from your mother? If so, that is something else we share. I must hear more.

I am also curious about the rest of your family. You mention brothers, not sisters. I would have loved a few brothers myself, but there were always boys around the village for me to race & climb fences with. I liked them better if I could beat them fair & square. Are your brothers alive today? Do you see them often? Tell me more. Do I have to coax everything out of you? I don't have the time to be patient, you know. And your husband – how helpful for you & your daughters that he is paid for his work!

A little more money would have made such a difference to us. But I daresay our difficulties made us all the stronger & wiser. I must admit, however, that buying presents for little Lulu is my most delightful activity. It is sad to think of my mother & other parents who rarely had such pleasures.

I have decided to reread my Transcendental Wild Oats, *to prepare for our discussion about communes & utopias. I got such a chuckle out of writing it, after I found that there was no other way I could treat it. It was either satire or be drowned in sobs.*

Curiously yours,
L. M. Alcott

Being Transcendental

A foolish consistency is the hobgoblin of little minds,
adored by little statesmen and philosophers and divines.
With consistency a great soul has simply nothing to do.
Ralph Waldo Emerson

Enthusiasm is the glory and hope of the world.
A. Bronson Alcott

January 14, 2006

Dear Miss Alcott,

Yes, I am looking forward to the utopian commune conversation
as well. Your migration to Fruitlands and some of your group-
living arrangements in Boston remind me of my 1960s and '70s
when I lived in several political collectives. We worked hard to
embody our new values and to reject the privileges that had
cushioned our childhoods. We believed that our riches were
directly related to the poverty suffered by much of the rest of the
world. It's impossible to ignore the enormous benefits the American economy reaps from systematically cheating the parts of the
world that provide most of our labor and raw materials. Our efforts
at communal living, like your father's Fruitlands, were attempts
to live outside that inequity and, hopefully, to eliminate it.

　　Before communes, however, we must cover some nineteenth-
century transcendental ground, since that was the engine that
drove so much of your life. As I said earlier, transcendentalism is

no longer a household concept, but since it saturated your air, I need to take a sniff myself. I am sure I will not get it perfectly right, but I have the impression that individual interpretation is part of its point.

Also, you ask about my brothers. Yes, it was fun growing up with brothers. I am the oldest, so in some ways that made up for the fact that I was just a girl. Being the only girl and the oldest child contributed, unjustifiably of course, to my feeling extra special. With fifty-odd years of repeated imperfection behind me, you would think I would have shed that cenceit about myself by now. Sometimes yes, sometimes no.

My brothers have both married and one has children. I liked them when we were young and I like them still today. They do not live close by, but we see each other several times a year and talk on the telephone, the device I mentioned earlier. I would say that they are quieter and more conventional than I have been – perhaps they have spent their lives trying to make up for my excesses and stumbles. They had to help my parents get through the worst of my revolutionary days.

My husband is the oldest of seven children, four boys and three girls, so I am also part of a much bigger family. All seven are married and four, including my husband, have children. Everyone lives west of the Rocky Mountains, a part of the country I wish you had been able to visit. One sister lives even farther west, in Hawaii. I enjoy it when we all get together; there is always much to talk about. You would appreciate their closeness and commitment to one another – a little like your extended family at Plumfield.

Our two daughters now live far from Seattle. One is in Hawaii, and the other is married and living in New York City. Both earn their own livings. It is not uncommon these days for daughters to leave their parents' home, even without being married. I think it is partly due to those improvements in health that I mentioned. We old people are still so healthy, I think we hardly deserve to be called old, and we certainly don't need to be taken care of. Besides, advancing age isn't respected nearly as much now as it was in your day.

Most parents today don't expect their children to plan their lives around them. We are glad that our kids have the chance to live their own lives without us parents being a burden. You, I guess, would never admit that taking care of one's parents is anything but a welcome and loving privilege. I'm not quite sure why we have come to think differently, nor am I sure it's a good thing.

But now we need to get back on track – at least as much as transcendentalism can be said to leave a track. The *Boston Times*, in its uncomplimentary review of the first issue of the *Dial* said: "One of the most Transcendentally (we like big words) ridiculous publications. . . . Duck tracks in the mud convey a more intelligent meaning."

Cheerio,
Kit

THE NEWNESS · AN ABSENCE OF HELL
POLL TAXES · NEVER WISH TO BE LOVED

If Ralph Waldo Emerson had lectured at my college campus in the mid-1960s, he would have spoken to cheering, packed audiences. We would have been highly receptive to his lilting, pied-piperish call to personal autonomy, whether or not we were high on marijuana. Louisa's neighborhood was the bull's-eye center of American transcendentalism, and even though the word was appropriated from the German philosopher Kant, the ideas were truly an American invention. No one knew at first how to label this slippery way of thinking about God, nature, man, life, the universe, and everything. Trying to describe transcendentalism was like trying to clean up a spill of liquid mercury. Some Bostonians gave up, calling it simply "the newness." One observer, clearly not happy with its scattershot flexibility, said it was "dreamy, mystical, crazy, and infideliterious to religion."

So what was transcendentalism about? Emerson answered in a lecture he gave in January 1842: transcendentalism is "idealism as it appears in 1842." Nice touch, that – implying that if the question were asked in 2042, the answer would be "idealism as it appears in 2042." Like most philosophers' answers, it leaves much to the listener – mainly more questions.

Transcendentalism particularly appealed to energetic people because it assigned active responsibility to human beings. Transcendentalists believed they could, indeed *should*, make meaningful choices in their lives. Transcendentalism appealed to serious-minded people who believed that their choices, and their lives, mattered.

More than most people, transcendentalists pondered hard on the meaning of life, and then tried to live that meaning in the real world. Kant originally used the word *transcendental* to suggest that each of us invents the world we live in; that is, the most important aspects of the world are known to us from personal reflection, not because scientific, political, or religious authority says so. This daring and empowering assertion caught the excited attention of the nineteenth-century New Englanders. As the ever-quotable Emerson put it, "the world of any moment is the merest appearance."

> The landscapes, the figures, Boston, London are facts as fugitive as any institution past, or any whiff of mist or smoke, and so is society, and so is the world. The soul looketh steadily forwards, creating a world before her, leaving worlds behind her.
>
> Values, truth, all possible futures, and divinity itself are entirely within each and every one of us.

Abba Alcott's good friend, the reformer and abolitionist Lydia Maria Child, sympathetically defined transcendentalism using the analogy of a woven tapestry. The back of a tapestry accurately denotes concrete reality – carefully counted stitches construct pictures of animals, mountains, flowers, or people. Most people live their lives on this back side of life. But the back only hints at the connected pattern and the flowing beauty of the front, which is where the actual value, the story, is made visible. That true picture can be seen only on the front of the tapestry, and that is the side of life that the transcendentalist is trying to live on.

This sort of individual power and creativity made perfect sense to people who were only a generation or so away from having successfully stolen half a continent from the greatest imperial power on the planet. Revolution was neither a dusty historical concept nor an impossible dream. Tackling all of reality didn't seem to be much more of a stretch. Bronson described Henry Thoreau, with whom he got along very well,* as a revolution in himself, a person who went beyond signing a declaration to actually living it. This translation of ideal to reality was the transcendentalists' approach to living. It's a tactic that is familiar to those of my generation who participated in the civil rights struggles of the early 1960s. The idea behind the lunch-counter sit-ins and the bus rides through the South was to act as if the Constitutionally-granted right to public services regardless of skin color was, in fact, the enforced law of the land – which if course it wasn't, not in the South, not at that time. The protesters faced a decade of murder, rampant property destruction and frightening intimidation before they could make the written law a reality for black citizens. Sadly, today we are still struggling with stubborn, trailing bits of white people's prejudices against people of different skin colors. But back to the nineteenth century.

Louisa's New England neighbors were an active bunch, forever founding magazines, giving lectures, starting schools, sheltering escaped slaves, sponsoring discussion groups, and establishing action committees. Emerson said that although "people wish to be settled" it is only so far "as they are unsettled that there is any

---

* Thoreau praised Bronson in *Walden*, calling him "the man of the most faith of any alive." One of the bonds between the two men was their common lack of interest in commercial or financial success.

hope for them." If transcendentalism did not change the way you lived, then you didn't get it. Julia Ward Howe, author of the "Battle Hymn of the Republic" and strong supporter of John Brown, said transcendentalism was like a century plant: "hard, dry and thorny . . . beautiful and inconvenient."

An 1837 review of Emerson's *Nature* commented, "The many will call this book dreamy, and perhaps it is so – It may indeed naturally seem, that the author's mind is somewhat one-sided, that he has not mingled enough with common humanity, to avoid running into eccentricity. . . ."

Eccentricity was an inextricable part of transcendentalism. Experimentation, personal and social, was the only way to make true progress. Transcendentalists placed themselves daily on the ragged edges of radical and unpopular thought on all fronts. They easily embraced Darwin's ideas of evolution, they were solidly abolitionist, they supported women's rights, and they did it all with personal panache and punchy turns of phrase. Once Emerson heard that Disraeli had asked, during a debate on Darwinism in the British Parliament, "Are we on the side of the apes or the angels?" On being told that Disraeli had come down on the side of the angels, Emerson said, "I would rather believe that man is advancing toward the angels than that he has fallen from them."

To be honest, the Concord transcendentalists were a bit equivocal in their support for the equality of women. Margaret Fuller easily saw the inconsistencies in their words and personally felt their lack of support. Emerson, for instance, had promised to write the introduction to her *Woman in the Nineteenth Century,* which would have greatly enhanced its sales, but he never followed through. At about this same time, he wrote to her about a mutual friend's new baby: "Though no son," he wrote, "a sacred event." Margaret wrote back, "I do believe, O Waldo, most unteachable of men, that you are at heart a sinner on this point."

Transcendentalists were often Universalists, a small sliver of Christianity as anarchic and opposed to church hierarchy as it was possible to be. A Universalist congregation in New York City was so sensitive to the dangers of authority that it refused to hold a regular Sunday service, being certain that even that small degree of scheduled formality would create intolerable risk to the congregation's liberty.* Universalists did, however, believe in heaven. With life so uncertain and death so common, even transcendentalists needed the optimistic expectation of a heavenly afterlife. On the other hand, they couldn't bring themselves to believe in Hell. They argued that no God would create such a dreadful place. People were good; life was good. But if not, the afterlife was certain to be good. An early observer of a Universalist service noted that the congregation "did not appear very religious; that is, they were not melancholy."

Universalists tell a nineteenth-century story of a Universalist and a Baptist riding through the woods one day. The skeptical Baptist says, "If I were a Universalist and feared not the fist of Hell, I could hit you over the head, steal your horse and saddle and ride away; could I still feel secure about going to Heaven?" The Universalist replies, "If you were a Universalist, the idea would never occur to you."

When Emerson once asked a servant in his household if she had been to church, she answered no, she "didn't trouble the church much." He responded without hesitation, "Then you have somewhere a little chapel of your own." For Emerson, "it was only a question for each person where the best church was – in the solitary wood, the chamber, the talk with the serious friend, or in hearing the preacher." Emerson said that to find work in your calling was halfway to the grace of prayer.

There was, unfortunately, a distinct anti-Catholic prejudice lurking under all this emphasis on personal freedom. The adults

---

* Universalism still exists today. The Unitarian Universalist Association's Web site, *www.uua.org*, describes it as "a religion that keeps an open mind to . . . religious questions. . . . We believe that personal experience, conscience and reason should be the final authorities in religion, and that in the end religious authority lies not in a book or person or institution, but in ourselves."

in Louisa's life, including Emerson, assumed that Catholics took orders from Rome and didn't think for themselves. From the transcendental perspective, not thinking for oneself represented the ultimate sin.

English Anglicans didn't escape transcendental criticism either, as Emerson satirically observed, "The gospel it [Anglicanism] preaches, is 'by taste are ye saved'. . . . It is not . . . a persecuting church; it is not inquisitorial, not even inquisitive. It is perfectly well-bred, and can shut its eyes on all proper occasions."

In 1838, Emerson was invited to give a speech to his alma mater's divinity school graduates. He delivered an incendiary transcendentalist lecture about the importance of thinking for oneself, saying, among other things, "Wherever a man comes, there comes revolution." He called on his audience to meet God directly, "without mediator or veil." It was better, he said, to learn from Jesus than to worship him. Shocked, the Harvard Divinity School authorities banned him from speaking on campus for the next thirty years. Similarly, Bronson Alcott's schools failed in part because he and his family were scorned for not attending any established church.

Transcendentalists, however, did not necessarily throw holiness and reflection out with the bathwater of organized religion. If anything, it was the reverse. They found holiness everywhere – in sunrises, on shimmering apple blossoms, and in the scent of warm gingerbread. Bronson wrote, "He who marvels at nothing, who feels nothing to be mysterious, but must needs bare all things to sense, lacks both wisdom and piety." Transcendentalism gave free will to all, but relied on people's understanding of their connection to nature and other people to prevent that free will from running amok.

※ ⁊ ※ ⁊ ※

If Waldo, Bronson, Abba, and their friends had been transported to a rock concert in Golden Gate Park in San Francisco in 1969 and had heard my long-haired friends in multicolored clothing singing, shouting and swaying, they would have enjoyed it and felt not far from home. It would not have been much different from one of their own conventions, called by the Friends of Universal Reform and described in the *Dial* by Emerson:

> A great variety of dialect and costume was noticed; a great deal of confusion, eccentricity and freak appeared, as well as of zeal and enthusiasm. If the assembly was disorderly, it was picturesque. Madmen, madwomen, men with beards, Dunkers, Muggletonians, Come-outers, Groaners, Agrarians, Seventy-day Baptists, Quakers, Abolitionists, Calvinists, Unitarians and Philosophers, – all came successively to the top, and seized their moment, if not their hour, wherein to chide, or pray, or preach, or protest.

Transcendentalists argued that people should not blindly follow the ways of the particular society into which they randomly happened to have been born. Merely because everyone around you says you should live your life in a certain way is never enough reason to do so. Trust yourself, Bronson would say with his quiet, convincing charisma, hypnotizing his young students into expressing thoughts they didn't know they had.

> Your first duty is self-culture, self-exultation: you may not violate this high trust. Your self is sacred, profane it not. Forge no chains wherewith to shackle your own members.

Emerson also left a treasure bag of epigraphs that stiffen one's soul* against the chattering advice of the elder generation: "Let him not quit his belief that a popgun is a popgun, though the ancient and honorable of the earth affirm it to be the crack of

---

* Nineteenth-century Christians, including the transcendentalists, were quite comfortable with the concept of a "soul." Transcendentalists even invented a communal soul that they called the oversoul.

doom" is perhaps a nineteenth-century version of "Don't sweat the small stuff." Listen to the wind in the trees, transcendentalists said, then listen to your heart. Louisa's closest connection with the divine always occurred during walks in the woods or runs in the fields.

Transcendentalists never imagined that the human heart could lead a person to become an ax murderer or a child pornographer. Their advice to the world was based on the firm belief that everyone was just like them, or was trying to become just like them.* Transcendentalists assumed that the people whom, in 1960s parlance, they urged to "do their own thing" were classically educated in European values, practiced in critical thinking, and attuned to human purposes beyond their immediate passions or self-gratifying whims. When confronted with clear and brutal evidence to the contrary, such as the existence of Southern slaveholders, their response was either national separation (who needs all those states, anyway?) or individual, fatalistic fanaticism of the John Brown sort. This black or white simplicity definitely attracted my Weathermen friends and me as we woke up to the enormity of our government's destruction of South East Asia and its utter unwillingness to enforce its own civil rights' laws here at home.

≽╼╤╾≽╼╤╾≽

Transcendentalists carried a double-barreled shotgun in their fight to improve the human condition. First, they aimed inward, believing that true and lasting social change could be achieved only through true and lasting personal change. Bronson and Henry Thoreau lived the most extreme, take-no-prisoners version of personal change, making them difficult companions indeed. Contemporaries noted that Thoreau, bristling with integrity, always preferred to say no rather than yes.

---

* Even today, Americans plague themselves – and the rest of the world – with this smugness.

Bronson's English admirer, Charles Lane, found Bronson's personal demands hard to bear. Lane wrote to a friend from Fruitlands, his and Bronson's utopian experiment:

> Mr. Alcott makes such high requirements of all persons that few are likely to stay, even of his own family, unless he can become more tolerant of defect. He is an artist in human character requiring every painter to be a Michael Angelo [sic].

Most transcendentalists carved out more gentle ways of living their ideals. "We live amid surfaces," Emerson said, "and the true art of life is to skate well on them." Think with the gods, he said, but live with the people. Emerson leaves the impression that he took daily life seriously, but not *too* seriously. If so, this goes a long way to explaining why Louisa was always so attracted to him. He was a welcome change from Bronson's unrelenting war on her imperfections.

Second after personal reformation, transcendentalists targeted for reform every social institution they could lay their sights on – schools, churches, the family, clothing, diet, health care, social services, the legal system, government. From this work came their utopian communities, the Universalist faith, their support for women's suffrage and the abolition of slavery, their advocacy for major reforms in prisons and education, and all sorts of ideas for more enlightened social structures. Bronson even took up architecture – building, in his own and Emerson's backyards, some Asian-influenced garden gazebos that he designed especially for contemplation, conversation, and inspiration. Lidian Emerson called theirs "The Ruin."

Transcendentalists encouraged active learning and active living. They urged everyone to be in an acutely observing and *present* state all of the time. If one took this approach, they believed, one could not help but improve the institutions of society and the well-being of all living things. Work and read, think and play.

Louisa May Alcott at about twenty: a neighbor boy described her as "most unkissable" but another said she often looked profoundly interested in things other than "those which usually occupy the thoughts of young ladies."

ABOVE: *Louisa's desk in her room at Orchard House looks out the front of the house, over the Boston–to–Lexington Road. This desk, built by Bronson, is where she wrote* Little Women. *The flower painting with the black background was painted by her youngest sister May Alcott.*

BELOW: *Bronson Alcott's drawing of Hillside, the Alcott's house where the action in* Little Women *took place. Louisa's room was in the back on the left. After the Alcotts left, they moved next door to Orchard House, and Nathaniel Hawthorne and his wife and three children moved in. Hawthorne renamed it Wayside.*

Bronson Alcott fishing for philosophical conversation in the Orchard
House front yard, facing the Boston–
to–Lexington Road. Note his bait:
three apples in a row.

Abba Alcott: Louisa inherited her
mother's chin and dark hair, as well
as her frustration and anger over
slavery and other economic, social
and political injustices.

Bronson Alcott and his youngest
daughter May posing in the gazebo
Bronson designed and built for their
backyard. He made an even more
elaborate structure for the Emersons.
Mrs. Emerson called it "The Ruin."

Ralph Waldo Emerson was a next-door neighbor and substitute father to Louisa. She loved him all her life. Emerson helped support the indigent Alcotts for years, until Louisa was able to take over with her Little Women *proceeds.*

Henry David Thoreau, an admirer of Bronson Alcott, took the Alcott sisters on hikes in the Concord woods. Louisa used him as a model for some of her most attractive heroes.

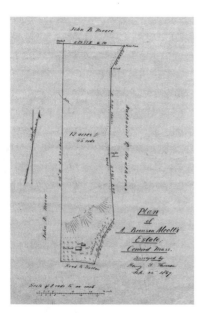

Henry Thoreau earned a little money as a local surveyor. This is his map of the Alcott's Orchard House property, made in September 1857. Note the Hawthorne property immediately next door. Rather than run the risk of meeting Bronson on the road, Nathaniel Hawthorne wore a path through the woods across its northern boundary.

John Brown hoped to end slavery without violence, but as he was taken to the scaffold he told his jailer that it seemed bloodshed would be necessary after all.

Margaret Fuller, looking quieter than most contemporary accounts of her would suggest. Louisa admired Margaret tremendously, and used her as a model for several strong women in her fiction.

Florence Nightingale with her pet owl Athena, who traveled in Florence's pocket. Florence was stronger than she looked in this drawing by her sister Parthenope. Parthenope would routinely collapse in Victorian hysterics whenever she was reminded of Florence's desire to work in hospitals.

ABOVE: *Bronson Alcott's innovative Temple School classroom in Boston, c. 1830. Note the students in a casual semi-circle as opposed to strict rows, and the adult observers at the back.*

BELOW: *Advertisement for a philosophical conversation by Brunson (sic) Alcott, described as "the Concord Sage and Gifted Sire of Louisa M. Alcott!" The "Dr." is illusory – Bronson was often ashamed that he had very little formal schooling, especially compared to his Concord friends Emerson and Thoreau, who both had Harvard degrees.*

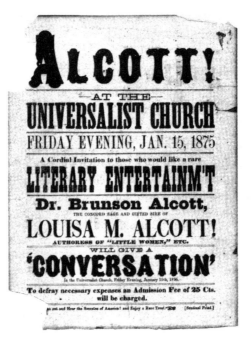

Life, they said, should be spent in activity that both exercises the body and stimulates the mind.

Thoreau, in a culinary metaphor, wrote in *Civil Disobedience** that a good man is like the particle of yeast that raises the entire loaf. The specific civil disobedience Thoreau had committed was to refuse to pay his poll tax in 1846.† He did not object to the existence of poll taxes. Radicalism, like idealism, has to be defined by its own times, and Americans did not abolish poll taxes until 1964, when it became clear that they were being used solely to prevent poor Southern blacks from voting. Thoreau didn't pay his poll tax because he objected to two specific activities that were being funded by poll tax revenue: slavery and the war against Mexico. Even then, he was not objecting to war in general, but to this specific war, which he viewed as a war not over principles or defense but over territory. Deciding that a single night in jail adequately made his point, he allowed himself to be bailed out by a relative and went home.

※ ❦ ※ ❦ ※

Transcendentalism, while encouraging action, also required hours of talking. This endless conversation irritated the women in Louisa's neighborhood because the men seemed to find it difficult to talk and work at the same time. Exasperated with all talk all the time, Abba Alcott once burst out "I do wish people who carry their heads in the clouds would occasionally take their bodies with them."

Lidian Emerson frequently found transcendentalists and their huge brains difficult to live with. She went so far as to write a pithy "Transcendental Bible," which she shared with her neigh-

---

* First published from Elizabeth Peabody's Foreign Library in 1849 in *Aesthetic Papers*, a one-hit wonder of a transcendentalist magazine – folding after this inaugural issue.

† Thoreau was not the first to see this propaganda value of going to jail at tax time; Bronson had done the same several years earlier in 1843.

bor Abba, poking fun at what she saw as transcendentalism's weak spots. It was truth-telling at its most subversive. Lidian precisely skewered her husband's writing style:

　　🦩 Never hint at a Providence, Particular, or Universal. It is narrow to believe that the Universal Being concerns itself with particular affairs, egotistical to think it regards your own.

　　🦩 Never speak of sin. It is of no consequence to "the Being" whether you are good or bad. It is egotistical to consider it yourself; who are you?

　　🦩 Never speak of Happiness as a consequence of Holiness. Do you need a bribe to well-doing?

　　🦩 Loathe and shun the sick. They are in bad taste, and may untune us for writing the poem floating through our mind.

　　🦩 Despise the unintellectual, and make them feel that you do by not noticing their remark and question lest they presume to intrude into your conversation.

　　🦩 It is mean and weak to seek for sympathy; it is mean and weak to give it. Great souls are self-sustained and stand ever erect, saying only to the prostrate sufferer "Get up, and stop your complaining."

　　🦩 Never wish to be loved. Who are you to expect that? Besides, the great never value being loved.

Louisa noted truthfully that "philosophy is a bore to outsiders," becoming frustrated when concrete action was overlooked. "Why discuss the unknowable till our poor are fed and the wicked saved?" But she agreed entirely with the basic idealism of transcendentalism and never stopped honoring Emerson, Thoreau, Fuller, and her father's philosophical and personal courage.

January 21, 1888

Dear Mrs. Russo,

So now I discover by the envelope that not only do you hide your marital status with the truncated "Ms." but you also do not use your husband's last name! What does Mr. Russo think about that? Is Mrs. Bakke your mother? Or did she not take her husband's last name either? Whose last name is it? Confusions abound in your century – not that I can claim mine to be an Olympiad of simplicity, as you are discovering yourself.

Since transcendentalism was mother's milk to me, it is hard to see it reduced to these cold words ᵴ few pages. As Father realized quite early, true transcendentalism exists in clouds of hope ᵴ private imaginings. It is best, although always imperfectly ᵴ only temporarily, instantiated in conversation ᵴ living . . . ᵴ never very well expressed in writing. Even Father's famous five million words fail to get us very far. I loved Henry Thoreau for many reasons, but one important one was his respect for Father. Henry once called Father the sanest ᵴ most good-natured man he'd ever met. He liked the way Father always assumed a better state of things than anyone else expected.

However, to avoid my becoming too transcendentally dewy-eyed, I must say you are right to point out its weaknesses in supporting ᵴ even understanding woman's place in the world. Perhaps that is the nub of my ambivalence.

So I am glad to be done with this part. Now we can move on to action, if I reckon rightly. Utopias! Abolition! It is time to roll up our sleeves ᵴ bring in the harvest we have labored so long to grow ᵴ protect. The proof, as women have always known, is in the pudding.

I am beginning to enjoy this project. I give myself away by indulging in silly metaphors.

Yours in partnership,
Louisa May Alcott

(over)

*P S: I am very pleased to hear that at least one of your daughters is
on our Eastern coast. Perhaps you & Mr. Russo should be here too?
Mr. Emerson went to California once, where he met a very interesting
Scotsman named John Muir, & my father went as far as Cincinnati.
Miss Fuller visited the Great Lakes. Not me. I have corresponded
& met people who have come to Boston from Chicago, & although
I have felt its allure, I have always been uncertain about the West.*

*Once a woman from a strange place called Oshkosh offered to
take me there. People would love me so much, she said, my feet would
never touch the ground. The mere thought horrifies me, & darkens the
West in my mind. I did send Jo's schoolboy Dan out West, but, as
you know from my latest Jo's Boys, he fell into a heap of trouble –
murder, jail time & finally he was killed. I couldn't think of what else
to do with him. He couldn't come back to Plumfield after all that.*

*My heart is firmly planted in New England, & if anything, I
glance further eastward, across the Atlantic, rather than westward,
for inspiration & comfort.*

*Henry, you know, refused several offers of western travel. He
always said that where you are is the best place to be. Ah me, I wish
your time could know a Henry Thoreau!*

L. M. A.

Experimenting with Utopia

This prospective Eden at present consisted of . . . ten ancient apple
trees . . . but, in the firm belief that plenteous orchards were soon
to be evoked from their inner consciousness, these sanguine
founders had christened their domain Fruitlands. . . .
About the time the grain was ready to house, some
call of the Oversoul wafted all the men away.
Louisa May Alcott, 1873, age forty-one

January 22, 2006

Dear Miss Alcott,

I must surrender on the naming issue. Years ago I told my husband
that I would swap Bakke for Russo after I had lived with him longer
than I had lived with my father. We have long since passed that
point, and now it's indefensible laziness that keeps me a Bakke.

I would have thought that with their love of nature in all its
untrammeled glory transcendentalists would have done more
traveling. I do not doubt the beauty of a clear bubbling spring
wandering through a Massachusetts apple orchard, or the view
of Wachusett draped in warm autumn color. But I think the true
wonder of nature lies in its endless variety. Natural beauty takes
on an extra dimension when you have seen a squat desert cactus
and a spidery rainforest orchid, or a towering blue iceberg *and* a
towering green sequoia.

Nature is on my mind because I recently returned from
Antarctica. I wanted to go to a place where people absolutely

cannot live without enormous artificial assistance, where we absolutely do not belong. I especially loved the icebergs. I know you saw icebergs on your trans-Atlantic crossings. Were you impressed at their majestic size and shimmering colors? The ice in Antarctica is thousands of feet deep and millions of years old. I went because I needed to be reminded that the human race is small and the universe very large indeed. The shiny, cold scenery helped to unsnarl me like a fly escaping from a spider's web.

I hope you will approve of the liberty I've taken in this essay. I found myself reminiscing about my own commune experiences and have included some of those memories along with yours. I am curious to know how you judge these twentieth-century efforts. This impulse to redecorate the human house from top to bottom must be both periodic and irrepressible. Every now and then, humans seem to produce a bumper crop of improving energy – like the urge to do spring-cleaning. Never mind that history is littered with constant failure.

Your mother would be interested to know that the Shakers still exist; except now that I think about it, their longevity proves her suspicion that they are not so utopian after all. Your father should feel vindicated at the way vegetarianism has continued to steam ahead into the twenty-first century. One of my brothers has been a vegetarian for decades. A vegetable diet doesn't always mean healthy eating though. He likes sweets, and sweets are all too available nowadays.

I know your family approved of Dr. Sylvester Graham's theories, including his use of unbolted flour, which today we call graham flour. His graham crackers are a staple in just about every kitchen cupboard in America today. They have been incorporated into desserts (Dr. Graham would probably be horrified) such as a bottom crust for sugary cheesecakes and a favorite camping treat of a graham cracker sandwich filled with melted chocolate and toasted marshmallows. They are called "s'more's" as in "I want some more." Here is a recipe for the graham cracker itself (not that anyone today makes them; we buy them in stores). Does it look like something you have made?

> Mix $1/2$ cup butter and $2/3$ cup brown sugar. Add in 2 cups graham flour, $1/2$ teaspoon salt, $1/2$ teaspoon baking powder and $1/4$ teaspoon cinnamon. Add in about $1/3$ cup water. Work well with hands, then let sit for about 30 minutes. Roll out on floured board to $1/8$-inch thickness. Cut into squares or rounds and bake on greased sheet pan in 350-degree oven for about 12 minutes.

Utopians have always been charged by the stodgy and unimaginative with living in a state of hallucinatory, irresponsible giddiness. Utopians have always responded that innovation and improvement require one to ignore the curbs that constrain exploration and change. In both your day and in mine, the river of communal energy overflowed its banks, fertilizing the fields and burying the roads. Our utopias and causes reflected the best and worst of our times. Apathy was not part of our vocabulary as well.

I think we're ready to swap some stories.

Your comrade-in-arms,
Kit Bakke Russo

GOD AS NATURE · THE WEATHER UNDERGROUND · BROOK FARM · WALDEN POND · FRUITLANDS

Enthusiasm and energy flooded the land during Louisa's girlhood. The late 1830s, '40s and '50s were a ferment of social experimentation, as the 1960s and '70s were for my generation. In both centuries, experimenters dared to challenge their social, political, and economic environments. For the Alcotts and their transcendental friends, it was the Industrial Revolution, which they saw as the Great Disaster. The individual spirit, so critical to staying on the right side of the tapestry, was being degraded and poisoned by repetitive factory work, and the factories themselves were destroying their beloved countryside.

Covering over nature with concrete, steel, and brick was bad. The transcendental life required a hands- (and feet-) on relationship with the visible natural world. The Concord neighbors believed our planet's matchless beauty and power went a long way toward reducing human envy, jealousy, and cruelty. Emerson, Thoreau, and others attributed their best thinking to walks in the woods or paddles down the river. In Emerson's first book, *Nature*, he wrote, "The noblest ministry of nature is to stand as the apparition of God." Wordsworth, whom both Emerson and Fuller visited at different times, wrote in his great poem "The Prelude" that living in the countryside of the English Lake District allowed him to be "removed from little enmities and low desires." Bettina von Arnim, Louisa's girlhood guide to forming crushes on older literary men, said, "Whenever we contemplate nature in calm meditation, it always lays hold of your heartstrings . . . what could have more easily freed me from the trivial things that oppress me?"

In her novel *Moods*, Louisa salutes Thoreau's account of his Concord and Merrimack river trip with his beloved brother John* in a chapter where her romantic triangle of lovers, Geoffrey, Adam, and Sylvia (along with Sylvia's brother Mark), paddle down a tranquil river. Floating along back eddies and resting on inviting grassy banks, they exchange questioning glances and converse on meaningful philosophical issues. When caught in a soaking rainstorm, the friends are taken in by an idyllic farm family gathered together to celebrate the grandparents' golden wedding anniversary. Louisa's description of this party, full of good food, country singing, plain talk, and warm hugs, absolutely oozes down-home wisdom, family stability and, especially, rootedness in nature.

Louisa loved the Concord countryside. Running along its gen-

---

* John died of lockjaw in 1842, leaving his brother Henry with a grief that heavily overlaid the rest of his life.

tle hills helped calm her excess energy. When she was twelve, she wrote in her journal,

> I had an early run in the woods before the dew was off the grass. The moss was like velvet, and as I ran under the arches of yellow and red leaves I sang for joy, my heart was so bright and the world so beautiful. I stopped at the end of the walk . . . a very strange and solemn feeling came over me as I stood there, with no sound but the rustle of the pines, no one near me, and the sun so glorious, as for me alone. It seemed as if I *felt* God as I never did before, and I prayed in my heart that I might keep that happy sense of nearness in my life.

In middle age, Louisa read through her journals, and added notes to some entries. To this one, she scribbled, "I have, for I most sincerely think that the little girl 'got religion' that day in the wood when dear mother Nature led her to God."

As in the 1960s, the nature-loving hippies of the 1840s launched their rural experiments to show their countrymen a better way of living gently on the Earth. In both centuries, the radicals realized that success required more than green fields and rustic skills. Creating the perfect society meant revising human relations as well. Visionaries in both centuries dared to reconstruct that most powerful and basic of units – the family. The ideal human group needed to be stronger than simple friendship, less neurotic than the average family, and more broadly inclusive than a two-person monogamous marriage. In the nineteenth century, attempts at these arrangements were called utopias (after the Greek for either "no place" or "good place").* In the mid-twentieth century, we didn't know Greek, so we used

---

* My father gave me Edward Bellamy's classic *Looking Backward: 2000–1887* (published in 1888), the story of a nineteenth-century Bostonian who wakes up in 2000 to find a highly structured utopia with no poverty, class strife, crime, or unhappiness. He appreciates the perfection but thinks it would be better to build it than live it. Louisa would have agreed.

three other words to label our experiments in better living: communes, ashrams, and collectives. Each attracted different types of searchers; communes tended to be more social, ashrams more religious, and collectives more political.*

I was in a sternly political collective. We all carried a red plastic-covered, pocket-sized copy of Mao Zedong's *Little Red Book* along with our carefully folded baggies of marijuana (no ziplocks in those days). We learned how to run small printing presses and how to pick locks. Some of us learned to make Molotov cocktails and fire handguns. Our pockets were also filled with toothbrushes, fake IDs, stolen long-distance phone codes, birth control pills, and spare change. We usually didn't know where we'd be spending the next night.

The most militant of the collectives called themselves the Weathermen, after Bob Dylan's song "You Don't Need a Weatherman to Know Which Way the Wind Blows." The idea was that revolution was inevitable: any fool could see that it was coming. I was a Weatherman. Later, we changed our name to the Weather Underground, thinking the name sexier, scarier, and even more militant. It also reflected a desperate change in our strategy, as we wanted to move from public street demonstrations to more violent, secretive and, we hoped, more effective actions. You cannot imagine, Louisa, how brutally Americans were behaving in Vietnam. Think of the most horribly wounded soldiers you saw in your Civil War hospital and imagine those wounds being suffered by children and grandparents. Imagine American corporations inventing weapons that were designed specifically to kill unarmed people in unsuspecting groups. One of those weapons was a gooey, flammable substance that was fired on people, stuck to their skins and burned them to death. Another was a small

---

* Sometimes people moved among the three. I had a friend who gave birth while tending toward the political side; she named her daughter Guevara after the dashing, but dead, exporter of the Cuban revolution. Later, she found that the easier life of a social hippie fit better. She renamed her child Guava.

bomb that shot thousands of tiny sharp knives into human bodies. These weapons were targeted daily on village marketplaces, schools and farmhouses.

Imagine this pain being perpetrated by your own government on a tiny agrarian country that had not the slightest capacity to deploy a single soldier on American soil. Finally, imagine the general population of the U.S. not only supporting the use of this horrific hardware, but actively punishing those (me!) who dared to object. Some of us thought often of John Brown in those days.

꒳꒷꒳꒷꒳

In July 1969 I went to Cuba on a Weather trip to meet a few military and political Vietnamese leaders. We flew from New York to Mexico City, looking like any other college kid tourists. But the Central Intelligence Agency (CIA) had gotten wind of us and greeted us on the Mexican tarmac. They photographed us, one by one, but didn't stop us as we filed onto the Air Cubana Ilyushin plane. We were bound for Havana, along with the Cuban soccer team, returning from a successful match in Mexico City. The cabin was draped with the Cuban red, white, and blue. Handsome team members in matching jerseys happily invited us to join in their singing, eating, and drinking as they celebrated their way home.

The Vietnamese had a far more eventful journey joining us in Havana. They modestly told us about hiking for two months westward through jungles, mudflats, and mountains to catch various means of transportation to Europe and then a plane to Cuba. They were tiny men and women, looking far younger than their ages, always immaculately and elegantly dressed, no matter how sticky the Caribbean heat. They had an unworldly, almost regal, air about them, as if they were tuned to one of Thoreau's different drummers. An incredibly disciplined, quiet, and kind group, they routinely retired early to their rooms, declining invitations to the nightly noisy, alcoholic, Cuban-hosted parties (partying was definitely a Cuban strength).

Before flying to Cuba, I was working in the Students for a

Democratic Society (SDS) national office in Chicago. We called ourselves the Action Faction before latching onto the Weatherman theme (our leadership, of course, couldn't resist calling itself the Weather Bureau). A group of us, mostly from Chicago and New York, had introduced the idea of the Weathermen as a successor to a splintering SDS at the June 1969 SDS Convention. Our organizing idea was that to be revolutionary, you actually had to foment revolution. Shortly after that meeting, we took off for Cuba to see what we could learn.

Besides getting the Chamber of Commerce tour of Cuba from our always friendly hosts, we immersed ourselves in a crash course in revolutionary life, both Caribbean and Southeast Asian style. We talked long and hard about how to use what we were learning as follow-up to our "You Don't Need a Weatherman" document published in the June issue of our newspaper *New Left Notes*. One of my jobs in Chicago was to print the paper. We had an old printing press, and I actually learned a few useful manual skills in the dirty, inky bowels of our office.

Like much nineteenth-century transcendental writing, our articles were turgid and long. Someone once said that Emerson's essays could just as well be read backward as forward, because his sentences didn't build on preceding sentences, and his paragraphs weren't conceptual building blocks. The same might be said for our Weather communiqués and agitprop (as we called our essays and articles). But the gist of our thinking was that we needed to go back to the United States, break up our four hundred or so Weatherpeople into collectives of eight or nine, send them to different cities around the country, and see what sort of revolution we could foment. College sweethearts abandoned without complaint: my boyfriend was sent one place and I to another. It was the least we could do to rid the world of militaristic, imperialistic, racist, exploitative, oppressive (and so on) America, in which we were shamefully among the most privileged citizens.

Despite our big ideas, I couldn't help feeling that these Vietnamese greatly overestimated the revolutionary potential of us clumsy white kids but, still, we came home (on a sugar freighter, through New Brunswick, Canada) determined to do our best to live up to their expectations.*

The ratio of play to work in a Weather collective varied with the part of the country it was in, the personalities of our comrades, and the demands of the upcoming action we were planning. We discovered early on that the Federal Bureau of Investigation (FBI) was remarkably unsuccessful at infiltrating meetings that included drugs and sex.

⁂

Louisa's parents' 1840s utopian crowd was not, like ours, made up of twenty-something college kids. Many were in their thirties and forties, married with children. They did not, as we did, have entire government departments out to destroy them.† My own FBI file, for instance, is more than four hundred pages of overwrought attempts by President Nixon and FBI Director Hoover to bring me to ground. Memos flew between FBI offices, as agents tried to find me in cities where I was and in cities where I was not. When the FBI classified me as a "Priority 1 Security Index Subject" (being more worrisome to them than the Agitator Index or the puny Reserve Index), they notified the 13th Military Intelligence Group, Evanston, Illinois and the Secret Service, Chicago, Illinois. This FBI memo comments that I am presently unemployed and have "no desire to seek employment at this time, indicating that full time on her part must be spent in attempting to correct the injustice raised by the imperialistic

---

* Being in Cuba that month, we missed the American walk on the moon, which received little notice in the Havana newspapers. Senator Edward Kennedy's drive off the bridge at Chappaquiddick and the death of his passenger Mary Jo Kopechne, however, received extensive coverage.

† Unlike us, they never lost sympathetic access to a significant portion of the respectable print media, except in response to their most confrontational abolitionist actions in the 1850s.

United States Government as a result of their present policies."
I feel a small victory smile coming on when I think of Government
secretaries transcribing the phrase "imperialistic United States
Government". Special agents filed wild-eyed descriptions of our
public demonstrations and actions. They harassed our frightened parents, intimidated old college roommates, and bullied
landlords and employers. Their intensity bears witness to the poisonous spume of official paranoia common in those days.

But there are heartfelt similarities between our two centuries
as well. We Weatherpeople shared with all utopians everywhere
the unquestioned faith that human history was on the verge of
dramatic progress and improvement. Optimism is characteristic
of Americans, but extra-strength optimism is required to estab-
lish whole new social structures. A certain crazed disregard for
one's own personal survival may also be necessary. In my experience, the utopians willing to risk their lives were optimistic about
the future of humankind in general, but not very cheerful or caring about their own futures. We had a strong sense of urgency,
an absolute absence of apathy, and an inflated view of our own
wisdom and abilities. We seriously believed we were changing
the course of human history. We were energetic, bossy, and
believed we had nothing to lose.

Our preference, like that of the Concord transcendentalists,
was to start small, with our own lives, and then move outward.
However, the immediate horrors of what the United States was
doing in Vietnam kept us from being so incremental. We were
never able to contemplate our navels for very long, because we
believed there was so much evil and stupidity to be swept off the
public stage.

My own all-consuming trajectory in those heady days was
jump-started during my sophomore year at an exclusive Ivy
League women's college. My friend Cindy and I discovered that
our live-in dorm housekeepers were excused from all nighttime
fire drills. To me, that meant the college didn't care if the hired
help lived or died. With my mother's let's-fix-it attitude coursing

through my body, I thought I knew the solution; they needed a union. They needed something to end the antebellum, plantation feel to their relationship with the campus. Did I mention that all the housekeepers were black?

I was editor of the school paper at the time, and I interviewed a few of them. They allowed me to take pictures of their small rooms on the top floors of our dorms, cramped under the eaves. I printed the interviews in the school paper, framing the pictures in heavy black lines. I also convinced some union organizers to visit the campus.

The unionization attempt never got off the ground, and I barely escaped expulsion from school. I also added insult to injury by selling antiwar buttons on campus. The faculty was my best customer. Calling me into her office, the dean was inarticulate with displeasure. "Would you do anything for money?" she sputtered, as if my crime was akin to prostitution and as if making money was the basest activity imaginable. "Well, no," I said lamely, thinking of various things I wouldn't do for money and not realizing it was a rhetorical question. Later I learned that the college dismissed law, medicine, and business as money-grubbing pursuits and expected all its best graduates to pursue academic careers.

I was interested neither in making money nor in academic tenure. I had my mother's beliefs about social justice and my father's sense of superiority and invincibility. In my senior year, I moved from campus issues to housing problems in our nearby godforsaken inner city. A group of us, ignorant but well meaning, led by a young Tom Hayden, thought we could help. I doubt our haphazard presence did, but it was another chance to meet hopeless people unfairly trapped in rotting housing and underserved neighborhoods by prejudice and capitalism.

Meanwhile, as the 1960s wore on, American atrocities in Vietnam were hitting the evening news with increasing frequency and specificity. We realized that the problems of poverty were complicated and unphotogenic compared to the stunning injustice of the war. We thought that both had the same root cause (our pseudo-Marxist thinking has us lumping racism, capitalism and imperialism into one untidy evil bundle) but believed we would have more success by first working to end the war, and then moving on to eliminate poverty. So we changed our focus.

In August 1968, in Chicago, the Democratic Party held its nominating convention for the upcoming presidential election. I was working in the SDS national office and knew about the various street demonstrations being planned to protest America's presence in Vietnam. Being a recent political science graduate, I was also curious about what exactly went on inside nominating conventions. So I applied to my weekly suburban Seattle newspaper for press credentials, saying I would write articles and take pictures for them. I lived a double life that week – demonstrating and being teargassed on the streets, then pulling out my press badge and going inside the convention hall as a legitimate reporter. My photographs published in the paper show lots of chain-link and barbed-wire fencing around the convention venues.*

Like the abolitionist-led Burns demonstrations in Boston in 1854, where Bronson took a brave stand against a phalanx of marshals, the Chicago Democratic convention was where the U.S. government took off its gloves and committed public violence on its own citizens.† More than five thousand National Guard troops joined the fray, in addition to the Chicago police with their military helmets and extra-long billy clubs. It was a hot summer week, and everyone's tempers were short. Official anger turned on the reporters when the violence itself became news. Delegates

---

* A year later, in Cuba, a soft-spoken Vietnamese woman pointed out our bus window at a stretch of barbed wire that was fencing in a cattle herd. She asked me, "What is that called? We have so much of it in our country." American forces deployed barbed wire all over the countryside, in an attempt to prevent Vietnamese villagers from harvesting their crops or visiting neighboring villages.

† Of course, the gloves had been off in the South for decades, but attacking white college kids and network newsmen was a new frontier.

inside the convention center watched demonstrators being beaten outside. Some were appalled at the violence; others were appalled that it was being made public. The former made speeches from the podium about the "Gestapo tactics of the Chicago police"; the latter tried to shout them down.

My final newspaper article quoted a conversation I had on the street outside the main convention hotel with a well-dressed man wearing a campaign button. He described himself to me as a "concerned citizen" who lived in Chicago. I wrote:

> I asked him what he thought of all these demonstrators milling around in the park and all the armed National Guardsmen in the street. He answered me with another question. "Why are there so many Jews over there [in the park]? I don't understand why so many Jews are traitors to their country."
>
> The prejudice and hatred evidenced by this man overwhelmed me as much as did the whiff of tear gas I got later that evening, as much as the hatred of the police towards the demonstrators and toward newsmen. Hatred, it seemed, was cheap in Chicago last week.

❧ᝰ❧ᝰ❧

Communities founded by people in an excited state of messianic and utopian fervor tend not to be very stable. Like subatomic particles, they glow only briefly and only under certain narrowly defined, artificially maintained environments. Two to five years is an average half-life for a utopian commune; those with strong religious underpinnings sometimes last longer.

Brook Farm, well known to the Alcotts, had a friendly six-year run in West Roxbury, then rolling farmland outside of Boston. It was founded in the spring of 1841 by George and Sophia Ripley, participants in Concord's transcendental club and sometime residents of the old Emerson house on the Concord River. Brook Farm's underlying principle was to encourage each of the one hundred or so residents to exercise equally both physical and mental muscle. Everyone participated in the farming and housework, and everyone had time to talk, walk through the woods, dream, and write. The hand and the mind of human endeavor were accorded equal value.

Besides making individual people more whole, Brook Farmers had hopes of binding together a society the Industrial Revolution was splitting asunder. Outside the farm's boundaries in both America and Europe, the rich were getting richer and the poor more miserable. Anyone who looked could see it. Karl Marx could certainly see it, as he walked the streets of Paris and London, busily formulating the notions he published five years later as the *Manifesto of the Communist Party*.

Visiting scholars like Emerson and Margaret Fuller arrived to lecture and contribute to the Brook Farm conversations. Bronson, when invited, refused to go on the grounds that the Brook Farmers ate meat and participated in the money economy by selling their excess butter and other goods for cash. John Pratt, who later married Louisa's sister Anna, had lived at Brook Farm as a child. Louisa immortalized him in *Little Women* as Meg's husband John Brooke.

Most of the letters and reminiscences we have from Brook Farmers are pleasant – the children especially seem to have enjoyed the life. Sixteen-year-old Arthur Sumner recalls living there with his family: "We Brook-Farmers were exceedingly happy people, and perfectly satisfied with our little isolated circle. . . . I don't believe anybody was ever hurt by being at Brook Farm. The life was pure, the company choice. There was a great deal of hard work, and plenty of fun – music, dancing, reading, skating, moonlight walks, and some flirting in pairs. After the dispersal, the people went back to the world, and most of them prospered. . . . It was a beautiful idyllic life which we led, with plenty of work and play and transcendentalism. . . ."

Nathaniel Hawthorne lived at Brook Farm from April to November 1841, looking after the pigsties. After he moved out, he continued on as trustee and chair of their finance committee. Ten years later, he looked back and wrote *The Blithedale Romance*. The story is a love/hate letter about the dark side of philanthropy set against the rural pleasures and utopian hopes that even Hawthorne could not deny. The book is remembered today mostly for its portrayal of a strong, beautiful, emotional, and doomed woman whom most have assumed is Hawthorne's take on Margaret Fuller. He didn't much like her. Henry James, in his 1879 biography of Hawthorne, wrote, "It is safe to assume that Hawthorne could not, on the whole, have had a high relish for the very positive personality of this accomplished and argumentative woman [Fuller], in whose intellect high noon seemed ever to reign, as twilight did in his own. . . . We may be sure that in women his taste was conservative."

The Brook Farm experiment died when the communal farmhouse, called The Hive, burned down and there was not enough money to rebuild. Emerson, ever the observer, thought that the Brook Farmers had overengineered their society with too many rules and systems. He concluded it would not have survived much longer, even without the fire. Emerson once said he didn't believe in communes, he believed in neighborhoods.

≈⊱⊰≈⊱⊰≈

Thoreau's homestead on the edge of Walden Pond could also be considered a utopian experiment. On July 4, 1845, when he was twenty-seven, Thoreau withdrew to a patch of land he borrowed from Emerson and spent two years, two months, and two days there, hoeing beans, watching the woods and the water, and writing. He invented raisin bread there,* but toward the end of his first year, he scalded his yeast, and spent the second year with

---

* Thoreau was an inventor outside the kitchen as well. He contributed several innovations to the family's pencil manufacturing processes, making Thoreau graphite pencils the best in the country. He was the first to add color (red and blue) to pencils. Outdoors, his acute and long-term observations of trees, bushes, and undergrowth resulted in the first written description of natural forest succession.

only unleavened breads. It is not quite accurate to say he withdrew to Walden. He kept up with his chores at his mother's house, walking to town daily to keep her supplied with water and firewood. He also hosted friends at his Walden cabin – the Emersons, Alcotts and others frequently came by to visit, either individually or *en famille*. He continued to help Lidian with her busy household, especially when Emerson was away on lecture tours.

Thoreau, like the Brook Farmers, was trying to integrate his life into a meaningful whole and to demonstrate a model of living in a world he felt was going horribly wrong. His angle was to separate the necessary from the unnecessary. He defined everything unnecessary as a luxury, and said that wanting and getting unnecessary things drove men directly into the hellish abyss of the money economy. Even worse, pursuing the unnecessary robbed us of the time needed to experience and appreciate the true adventures of life. "A man is rich in proportion to the number of things which he can afford to let alone," he said, thinking, no doubt, about videophones and plasma screens. Or, put another way, "When he has obtained those things which are necessary to life, there is another alternative than to obtain the superfluities: and that is to adventure on life now, his vacation from humbler toil having commenced." Thoreau, unlike most of us, knew that enough was as good as a feast.

When he finished his campout at Walden Pond, neighbors asked him why, if it was so wonderful, he decided to leave. He said, reasonably enough, that he had several lives to live, and this was only one. The world was big, life was short, and the landscape was in need of reforms of all kinds.

ᘛ᠊ᡧ᠊ᘚ᠊ᡧ᠊ᘛ

And then there was Fruitlands. In the spring (rural utopias always start in springtime) of 1842, when she was ten, Louisa and her family founded a commune called Fruitlands. It was Bronson's chance to try for perfection. The commune was to be populated by a "Consociate Family," his term to describe how blood relations and others would bond together to create the ideal human group.

Fruitlands spread across about fifty acres on the hills twenty miles west of Concord, near the village of Harvard. The land is on a ridge that today still has lovely territorial views of wooded hills and valleys. Bought in part with Emerson's money, it included a few drafty buildings for the utopians to occupy. Today the main building is preserved as a museum.

Louisa and her three sisters slept in the dark, splintery, unfinished attic crammed tightly under a steep roof. There are small, low windows at the pitched ends of the room, and the center is dominated by a large brick chimney. Headroom under the rough-hewn roof joists and exposed nail heads never exceeds about five feet. A bust of Socrates, saved from the Temple School, was the main decorative touch downstairs.

"The kingdom of peace is entered only through the gates of self-denial and abandonment" wrote Bronson, describing Fruitlands' founding principles for the *Dial* in 1843. English cofounder Charles Lane went on to sketch a typical day: "We rise with early dawn, begin the day with cold bathing, succeeded by a music lesson, and then a chaste repast [apples and unleavened bread]. Each one finds occupation until the meridian meal, when usually some interesting and deep-searching conversation gives rest to the body and development to the mind. Occupation, according to the season and the weather, engages us . . . until the evening meal, [then] we resort to sweet repose for the next day's activity." Members of Fruitlands would "perform the work for which experience, strength and taste best fit him. . . . Thus drudgery and disorder will be avoided and harmony prevail," wrote Mr. Lane, airily waving his magic wand as if latrines would build themselves.*

----

* Before they moved to Fruitlands, Mr. Lane lived for a while with the Alcotts in Concord. Emerson refused to have Mr. Lane to dinner, fearing that Lane's diatribes about the evils of meat, yeast, and wine would dampen the pleasures of the meal. Bronson, although a vegetarian, was often a guest, and once argued in favor of cannibalism, saying, as Emerson was carving the roast, "If we are to eat meat at all, why should we not eat the best?"

The Fruitlandian spin on perfection reduced the definition of necessary below even Thoreau's levels. In Bronson's commune, people were allowed to wear only linen, because cotton encouraged the slave trade, silk enslaved the moths, and wool belonged to the sheep. They ate a sparse, do-no-harm diet – no animal-derived products at all. Bronson and Lane estimated that if the whole world were vegetarian, humans would need to cultivate only one-fourth of the land then in use. The communards also ate no sugar or molasses (the slave trade); and no coffee, tea, or rice (trade and that damnable money economy). Water was their only beverage.

Occasionally, they formed their unleavened bread into the shape of animals or trees to make their sparse meals more enjoyable. They had few utensils and no plates (needless expense and fuss). They refused to use manure fertilizers (exploitation of animals) and seemed disinclined to weed their fields. They argued that the mealy worms that got into their apples and potatoes had just as much right to the nutrition as the humans did. Cold baths, they felt, made the bather more cheerful than hot ones. And they refused to stoop to using money, not that they had any, to solve any of their problems.

A contemporary account of Fruitlands describes Bronson as believing "that the evils of life were not so much social or political as personal, and that a personal reform only could eradicate them; that self-denial was the road to eternal life, and that property was an evil, and animal foods of all kinds an abomination." All this boiled down to more denial and privation than turned out to be acceptable to Louisa's mother Abba, or to any other sensible woman trying to keep her family's body and soul together.

Bronson believed that *being* was better than *doing*: "The greater part of man's duty consists in leaving much alone that he now does." Although this echoes Thoreau, Fruitlands' founders stretched "leaving much alone" to unsustainable limits. Thoreau may have spent days watching the birds flit along the shore and leaves falling from trees, but he also was not averse to growing crops and cooking dinner. Bronson had no time for such mundane matters. Human labor, he and Lane argued, was the root of all evil, whether you were the buyer or the seller. Their argument, as it has come down to us in contemporary magazine articles and letters, gets a bit confusing, as sometimes they supported boycotting the exchange of labor for money and sometimes they opposed performing the labor itself.

Bronson enlarged on this energy-saving theme: "Being in preference to doing, is the great aim, and this comes to us rather by a resigned willingness than a willful activity, which is, indeed, a check on all divine growth. Outward abstinence is a sign of inward fullness; and the only source of true progress is inward."

Mr. Lane appeared to have a peculiar fixation on cattle. With spirited antipathy, he concluded a cow-free world would be a better world. He was quite certain that the care of cows distracted people from seeking the Spirits of Devotion and Wisdom. Cows also took up far too much acreage, although what else he would use it for was not clear. He cleverly tried to buttress his argument for eliminating cows by taking the bovine perspective: "the driving of cattle beyond their natural and pleasurable exertion," for instance, to plow a field, was wrong.

"So long as cattle are used in agriculture," he stated unequivocally, "it is very evident that man will remain a slave. . . . Debauchery of both the earthly soil and the human body is the result of this cattle keeping." Not to mention that humans had to "wait upon them as cook and chambermaid three parts of the year." Lane was a man whose eccentricity rivaled Bronson's.

Fruitlands' population in 1842 included the four Alcott sisters, their parents, one woman who came as a teacher for the girls, three men, and Lane's ten-year-old son. In the end, Miss Anne Page, the teacher whom Louisa described as a "stout lady . . . with vague yearnings and graspings after the unknown," was discovered eating forbidden cheese and fish and was exiled from Bronson's Eden. One of the men, a Mr. Joseph Palmer, well known in the neighborhood for having been incarcerated for an entire year in the Worcester jail for refusing to shave his beard (at that time, beards were a custom of Jews, not Christians), milked a cow. He too was kicked out.

Mr. Palmer's harrowing story of that year in jail is a stirring story of random prejudice and stupidity. Forty years later, in 1884, the *Boston Daily Globe* interviewed Palmer's son, a dentist, about his father's life. "He was looked upon as a monstrosity," Dr. Palmer said. "When asked once why he wore it [the beard], he said he would tell if anyone could tell him why some men would, from fifty-two to three hundred sixty-five times a year, scrape their face from their nose to their neck." Mr. Palmer turned out to be the most practical of the Fruitlanders, being the only one who understood that fields can't effectively be plowed without a plow. In the end, Mr. Palmer, who owned the adjacent farm, bought Fruitlands from Emerson and renamed it Freelands, opening it as a home to homeless men willing to work for their food.

The Deadheads and misfits of 1843 visited Fruitlands, thinking it would be cool to live without rules for a while. None, however, stayed any longer than it took for them to realize there was no milk or honey in this utopia. Emerson, a summer visitor, wrote in his journal, "The fault of Alcott's community is that it has only room for one. . . . Alcott and Lane are always feeling of their shoulders to find if their wings are sprouting. . . . They look well in July. We will see them in December." He went on to say that what his friends needed most were feet in cowhide boots planted firmly on the ground.

Emerson never joined any of these utopian communities. He did not believe in social theories that threatened to break up families, nor did he "wish to remove from my present prison to a prison a little larger." Rather, he wrote, "I wish to break all prisons." Charles Lane was no fan of Emerson's, describing him to a friend in England: "Mr. Emerson is I think quite stationary; he is off the Railroad of Progress, and merely an elegant, kindly observer of all who pass onwards." Margaret Fuller, increasingly frustrated with Emerson's unwillingness or inability to acknowledge that even transcendentalists treated women as inferior to men, would have agreed.

Despite the ethereal disposition of its male founders, Fruitlands worked well enough over the summer, when it was warm and the apples and berries were abundant. The men happily comported themselves as "unworldly persons" carefully avoiding "the cares and injuries of a life of gain," and the children played in the unplowed fields, collecting berries and making doll families from twigs, leaves, flowers, and rags.

But as summer receded over the yellowing horizon, Abba realized this would not last. Louisa remembered her mother once staring Charles Lane down with her keen, skeptical eyes and asking, "What part of the work do you incline to yourself?" She probably had already guessed his answer: "I shall wait till it is made clear to me. Being in preference to doing is the great aim. . . ." and so on, as the weak and ill-fed kitchen stove threatened to go cold behind him.

❧☙❧☙❧

Bronson and Charles Lane's belief that practically everything was corrupt reverberates familiarly to those of us who were 1960s hippies and revolutionaries. I can vividly recall our siren call to "tune in, turn on, and drop out." We suburban white baby boomers exploded from our childhoods chock full of vitamins, fluoride, polio vaccines, backyard barbecues, Disneyland, college, and all the pocket money our parents, warding off memories of war and depression, could afford. We swaggered with superb health, wealth, and good fortune. But I and others of my generation could not ignore the fact that our well-fed, well-educated, triumphant existence rested entirely on America's imperial aggression and our undeniably white skin. Guilty as charged, we planned to live the rest of our lives spending our ill-gotten wealth to build a far better world, which, amazingly enough, we were convinced we knew how to do.

I lived those Weather-commune dreams in the industrial flats of Cleveland; in Chicago's rundown westside tenements; on the scrubby, orange uplands of New Mexico; and in the pockmarked, stucco flatlands of Oakland, California. We moved a lot. My group was never more than ten or eleven people, about the same as Fruitlands. No children though (we didn't give up our middle-class access to birth control). The leader in my New Mexico cell was a guy who had done a tour in Vietnam flying helicopters. He came back embittered and dangerous, jumpy in mind and body, and it was his unpredictability that finally spun us apart. But for a while we were tapped into that same hotline as the founders of Fruit-lands, believing we had found all the right answers that, some-how, everyone else had missed.

We churned about just as they did, clumsily, making mistakes. But we were not without individual courage, as we awkwardly worked with the same conundrums as the nineteenth-century utopians, trying to find that elusive, perfect balance of freedom and discipline. We rejected our parents' rules (and practically everything else they had worked so hard to give us), but we were quick to invent just as many restrictions of our own. Everything was serious and nothing was off-limits. We held frequent Maoist criticism sessions, confessing our failures to each other, worry-ing about our weaknesses, and concocting naïve improvement strategies. We had long talks too – about what to do when some-one didn't do his or her chores, who should own the means of production, and when might be the right time to throw a Molotov cocktail at an army recruiting office.

One of our funniest ventures* was the night we went out to spray paint "Free Fire Zone" on the walls of the Berkeley FBI office building. Whole villages in Vietnam at that time had been declared "free-fire zones" where anything that moved – man,

---

* To us, that is; I think the western branch of the Weather Underground indulged in a more humorous perspective on life than did our east coast com-rades – maybe because the weather was better.

woman, child, dog – was a legitimate target for U.S. napalm, cluster bombs, and bullets. We thought painting "Free Fire Zone" on an FBI building would provide an appropriately balancing message. The Berkeley police, thinking differently, rudely interrupted us in the act. We sprayed only the letters "Free Fir" onto the wall before we were scattered. Speculation was rife in the press for weeks about the identity of this mysterious, incarcerated Fir and when the next attempt to free him might occur.

It never occurred to us to consider any of our graffiti or window breaking as simple criminal vandalism. We were engaged in a righteous political war using the typical tactics of the practically powerless underdog. We did another paint job one evening when we were casting about for something new to do: we sprayed black paint on the little windows of all the parking meters along a busy commercial street, thereby freeing Berkeley villagers from paying parking fees for a couple of weeks.

One of our hardest decisions came after one of our pet dogs was hurt and needed $50 worth of veterinary care. We could barely scrape the money together, and decided, sadly but in the spirit of great revolutionary sacrifice, that we could have no more pets. In New Mexico, we had a terrible time slaughtering an old sheep for food. None of us city kids found it easy to wield the knife. I can't remember now who finally did it, but it wasn't me.

Guns were more impersonal than knives. One day we went to a gun show – in the Midwest somewhere – for educational and procurement purposes. It was held in a school gym; sellers had put up card tables along the edges of the basketball court. American flags were draped over the folded-back bleachers. The neighborly gun traders were delighted to see us, pleased as punch to supply us with as much firepower as we wanted, providing us with handy tips along the way. Anyone who liked guns was a friend of theirs. Our obvious political differences were not seen as deal breakers, which I found quite surreal.

They were heady and exciting times – how could we not be on a full-time high when we knew we were reshaping the destiny of

America? We saw a lot of America (which of course we spelled "Amerika" or even "Amerikka"). We were always madly hitch-hiking across country – sometimes to make a court appearance somewhere, sometimes for the next demonstration, every now and then just for fun. We were picked up by nice families, by travel-ing salesmen, by off-duty highway patrolmen, and once by an Oklahoma farmer who offered me $5 for sexual favors. There we were, thinking globally, acting locally, just like the Fruitlanders, who thought that by not eating animal flesh or dressing in cotton, they were combating human misery around the world.

⇟⇞⇟⇞⇟

Louisa was the only Fruitlander with the guts to write about how the experiment actually went, but not until thirty years after it closed its six-month run – in the winter, just as Emerson had foreseen. Using her childhood journals and lecture material from her father and Charles Lane, Louisa shaped their adventures into a short, lightly fictionalized memoir called *Transcendental Wild Oats*. With its evocative title, it reads a bit like a schoolgirl lark. She and her sisters were swept along, children who had no choice but to make the best of the grown-ups' fantasies. They endured the cold baths and lack of food, taking each day pretty much as it came, as children at the mercy of adults almost always do. Louisa also drew on her Fruitlands memories, rewritten to include hot food and an equitable sharing of the chores, to create Plumfield, Jo's home and school in *Little Men* and *Jo's Boys*. By turning Fruitlands into Plumfield, she was making life better, at least on paper, for the people she loved.

Louisa's contemporaneous journal* from Fruitlands is differ-ent from the two fictional accounts – the pain comes through.

---

* It is interesting to compare the Alcott girls' journals with those of that other famous American family of four girls. Laura Ingalls Wilder and her sisters were contemporaries of Anna's two sons and lived a thousand miles to the west. The Ingalls daughters wrote in their journals about friends' visits, babies, games, and

She records long and deep conversations about personal improvement, after which she would cry her ten-year-old self to sleep for her inability to curb her bad temper and cross ways. Both Louisa and Anna record doing a fair amount of ironing too, which strikes me as oddly nonutopian. The Fruitlanders would meet in the afternoons and evenings to discuss such subjects as "What is man?" Louisa recorded: "These were our answers: A human being; an animal with a mind; a creature; a body; and soul and a mind. After a long talk we went to bed very tired."

Communes and utopias always and everywhere face one unavoidable and inevitable challenge: what to do with the human drive to create families and have a private life? Bronson and Charles Lane repeatedly discussed this question: "Can a man act continually for the universal end while he cohabits with his wife?" Family implies a narrowing of loyalties, a selfishness, and a preference for one group of persons over all the rest. Emerson said that one of the best reasons for having a house is so one can choose whom to let in and whom to keep out. Equality and fairness to everyone is ultimately impossible as long as people form into families.

Preference for kin is the rock upon which many utopian ships are smashed. So it was for my commune – all the group sex in the world couldn't keep couples from forming. So it was for Fruitlands, but not the group sex part. For them it was the opposite: Mr. Lane argued for celibacy; Bronson tried, but failed.

There are, of course, secondary shoals, icebergs, and other barely submerged hazards to the survival of utopias. Lack of adequate food and shelter and diminished resources of all sorts are their common contributing factors to their failure. People are flighty; they drift away; their attention spans are caught by other enthusiasms. Factions and cults, loveless variants on family, are commonly seen during utopian death throes. Direction, vision,

---

fun. Absent were soul-searching pages of introspection and agony about bad behavior. Perhaps life on the South Dakota frontier was difficult enough, and the internal challenges that plagued the Alcott girls did not need to be invented.

and commitment subside as optimism dims. It is in this phase when people get hurt.

Fruitlands started up in the cheerful, flowering springtime and broke apart in the cold, unforgiving winter. Abba's desperation over her increasing inability to provide food and warmth to her daughters drove her to franker conversations with her husband than perhaps he had ever heard her initiate before. She wrote in her journal,

> I hope the experiment will not bereave me of my mind. The enduring powers of the body have been well tried. . . . I hope the solution of the problem will not be revealed to them too late for my recovery of their atonement of this invasion of my rights as a woman and a mother. Give me one day of practical philosophy. It is worth a century of speculation.

Bronson, finally noticing Abba's state, turned in a cowardly way to his daughters. Louisa records in her journal, "Father asked us if we saw any reason for us to separate. Mother wanted to, she is so tired. I like it, but not the school part or Mr. L[ane]."

Finally, an exhausted, cold, and frustrated Abba forced Bronson to choose between his real family and his consociate family. Twenty-four years later, as Bronson basked in the glory of having a famously family-oriented author for a daughter, he changed his tune: "Sown in the family, the seeds of holiness are here to be cherished and ripened for immortality."

In the end, for Fruitlands in 1843 and for me in Berkeley in 1973, plain old-fashioned person-to-person loyalty and love won out. I took my baby daughter and went off to nursing school. Mrs. Alcott finally convinced Mr. Alcott that his path lay with his little women. Fruitlands broke up.

January 23, 1888

Dear Kit,

Now I feel as if I know you well enough to call you by your first name. Perhaps I know even a bit more than I want to. You didn't at first appear to me as a violence-prone person, but now I am not so sure. Do I understand correctly that women as well as men have been involved in these warlike activities you describe? Breaking windows? What are Molotov cocktails? No women were in John Brown's brave raid on Harpers Ferry, but now that I think about it, there was that wonderfully courageous & gun-carrying Harriet Tubman. I still get thrills today thinking of how we women saved Frank Sanborn from being captured by government agents. You will tell that story, won't you?

I am fascinated that people are still striving for perfection. That is good & bad, in my opinion. I have found it much easier to create a happier world on paper than in reality, that's for certain. But to try is often necessary & always honorable. There is a tendency for wrongs to multiply themselves if no one stands up to object. I must admit that Father & I do not agree on the being vs. doing debate – I believe wholeheartedly in doing. The way to get something done is to do it!

Some people need more, I think, than just to hear other people object to the inequities of the world; they need to see real examples of what the better life would look like. I tried to describe a latter-day feminine utopia several times, as you must have seen, especially at the end of Work. *I am going to try again with* Diana & Persis *although I may make the husbands so wonderful that I will keep them in too.*

I am glad to see that there was some fun in your utopias as well (although I must admit that perhaps the humor of your scrapes doesn't translate so well into my nineteenth-century mind). But, if I were in a position to give advice, which I guess I am, thanks to you, I would applaud your fun & strongly urge people of all centuries to take more time for games & pleasure. That means taking the time to find the things you truly enjoy (not simply copying what someone else says is fun) & then making the time to do them. There's a real utopia for you!

Although I also had some experiences with ingesting various substances, & though indeed they provided some amusement at certain times, I do not think they can be relied upon. The world is far richer in other opportunities, & despite my Perilous Play story, one doesn't usually escape scot-free. Not everything I wrote had a moral lesson, you know.

Another thought about utopias. . . . It is better, I think, to live in & work for the betterment of our large & imperfect world than to start completely over in one tiny corner. Even Father realized that in the end. There is never enough support going into these tiny experiments & not nearly enough momentum coming out.

It is time, is it not, to talk about the abolition movement? It was the crucible of my life, much like this war in Vietnam must have been for you. (I must confess, I do not know anything about this Vietnam. Did they succeed in repelling the American invaders?) Having seen the effects of war up close myself, I know it is a sorry affair on every side.

Father is much on my mind these days. He is not at all well, & my own lack of health prevents me from visiting him at my Louisburg Square house as much as I would like. Neither of our problems, by the way, do I attribute to our vegetable diets. Father has held strictly to his; I must admit that at special events, when he is not present, all his little women, including me, have let a few animal products pass our lips.

It will do me good to move on to our abolitionist days, as Father was one of the bravest soldiers on that difficult front. I do hope you tell the whole story of the Burns incident and Father's most courageous role on those infamous courthouse steps.

Yrs truly,
Louisa

Ending Slavery

But the counsels of the Abolitionists were spurned, their sentiments and purposes were shamelessly misrepresented, their characters traduced, their property destroyed, their persons maltreated. And lo! our country, favored of Heaven above all others, was given up to fratricidal, parricidal, and for a while we feared it would be suicidal war.
Sam May, Louisa's uncle

You must be sure to say that no house nowadays is perfect without having a nook where a fugitive slave can be safely hidden away.
Ralph Waldo Emerson, helping his son design
a house for a class project

January 30, 2006

Dear Miss Alcott,

Since I admire you so much, I am not yet comfortable with any less formal greeting, although I use your friendly first name in our essays, because I want people to "connect" with you, as we say these days. Maybe I'm being contradictory, but that's nothing new. In any case, you are absolutely welcome to call me Kit. What with all the feminist freight weighting down last names these days, Kit seems easier anyway. To answer your question about the war: the American military did finally give up and withdraw from Vietnam. Nowadays American tourists go there to swim on the beautiful beaches and enjoy the delicate Vietnamese cuisine.

So, yes, on to abolition. We were lucky, both of us, to have had such defining battles going on while we were young enough, and old enough, to be part of them. As you say, being able to fight the honorable fight is a pleasure and a privilege. You had the good fortune to have parents who were as subversive and abolitionist as you. My parents were calm and private liberal Democrats, not given to attending street marches or demonstrations of any form. A political fanatic was the last thing they expected their daughter to become.

My mother was kindness itself and firmly opposed to rude displays of any sort. Wrongs should be righted, yes, but with the vote, not a bludgeon. "Two wrongs do not make a right" and "If you can't say anything nice, don't say anything at all" were her two favorite pieces of advice. She never gave up believing that rational understanding among people was possible, and she was convinced that rational understanding always led to fairness and that fairness inevitably created peace.

But back to the streets – I recognize those wild feelings you describe from those big antislavery parades and demonstrations, because I've felt them myself. It was the same for us, demonstrating and marching to end the U.S. government's invasion of Vietnam. Many in my generation were raised to believe that the U.S. was the most humanitarian and progressive democracy in the world. Our parents thought they were being kind to protect us from troubling inconsistencies; despite Senator McCarthy, they did not raise us to be cynics. So when we grew old enough to notice the official and systematic persecution of black people and the outrageous and deadly destruction in Vietnam, we were initially at a loss about how to respond. We couldn't believe that our parents would allow such evil into the American paradise. Those of us who were accused of the most excessive response may have been those who most believed our parents' rosy picture of an enlightened, benign, and democratic America.

My parents were like many Americans who finally saw the perfidy of what was going on, but since they didn't catch on as quickly as most of us younger folk, for a time they couldn't see why we were making such a noisy, illegal, and impolite fuss. When I was jailed for some particularly aggressive street fighting, my father refused to bail me out. I spent three days in Chicago's Cook County Jail. He was very angry and afraid that I was throwing away my life. Many years later, I found letters he'd written to his parents, describing his own disgust with the government, and telling his parents he morally and theoretically supported my position.

I am sure my jail conditions in Cook County were better than those you saw in your visit to New York's Tombs that winter in 1875, but Chicago had a justifiable reputation for being fairly unpleasant – physically, mentally, and aesthetically. When the police arrested us on the street, they pulled off the helmets we were wearing to protect ourselves from their billy clubs, threw the helmets on the ground, and proceeded to smash them to bits in front of our eyes. They said our heads were next. It was frightening. I felt safer in the courtroom, where I ignored court procedure and acted as if I were in one of my many high school debate tournaments. I talked directly to the judge, trying to convince him that the war in Vietnam was wrong. I got the impression he was listening; I was sentenced to time served (three days, longer than Thoreau's incarceration).

My conservative Norwegian grandfather,* who loved to argue with my liberal Scottish grandmother, was adamantly opposed to John Kennedy's candidacy for president in 1960. I debated with my grandfather too. He opposed Kennedy in part because Kennedy was Catholic; I thought religion was irrelevant to being president. The Kennedys were a very wealthy Massachusetts family. I hope you think it good news that some Irish Catholic immigrants in your neighborhood did quite well for themselves in the twentieth century.

---

* My grandfather gave me five shares of Kaiser Aluminum as a college gradua-tion present. When he found out that I sold them to help pay legal expenses for some friends who were arrested in Ohio for antiwar demonstrating, he didn't speak to me for two years.

When the votes were counted, Kennedy won, though not by much. That was forty-five years ago. We still have in front of us the opportunity to elect the first Jew, the first black, the first woman, the first Muslim, the first atheist, and we could go on and on through all the different national immigrant groups that have so enriched this richest of nations. I wonder in what order all those presidential firsts will occur?

But all of that will be a mere footnote to your much more monumental fight to end America's habit of buying, enslaving, and selling people.

Historically yours,
Kit

P S: Exciting as these time were, let's not forget the question I am laying at your feet: now that we're older, how do we remain helpful and useful to the cause of liberty, justice and peace?

UNCLE TOM'S CABIN · BLOOD ON THE SENATE FLOOR · HARRIET TUBMAN'S TACTICS ST. JOHN & THE SECRET SIX · TYRANNY RULES THE PEACEABLE MAN

Louisa was a child of actively abolitionist parents. Abolitionists between 1830 and 1860 formed societies, supported each other's families when times were hard, attended demonstrations, gave lectures, wrote letters and articles, and socialized primarily with each other. The Alcotts shopped (when they had any money) at stores where the goods were certified to have been produced by non-slave labor. They donated clothing and other items to various fund-raising events for freed slaves. Other problems needing reform were on their list, but none was approached or attended to with as much focus and fire as ending slavery in America.

It was a long battle, demanding attention and investment for almost forty years. Bronson helped organize the Massachusetts Anti-Slavery Society in 1829, along with William Lloyd Garrison and Abba's brother Samuel May. Abba was a charter member of the Massachusetts Female Anti-Slavery Society.

In 1830, two years before Louisa was born, William Lloyd Garrison, a twenty-five-year old newspaperman from Newburyport, Massachusetts, was jailed for being unable to pay a $50 fine for calling a slave ship owner an "enemy of his own species." Garrison, a physically slight man given to skin ailments, moved to Boston, where, a year later, he launched his antislavery newspaper the *Liberator*. "I am aware," he wrote in the first issue, "that many object to the severity of my language; but is there not cause for severity? I *will* be as harsh as truth and as uncompromising as justice. On this subject [slavery], I do not wish to think, or speak, or write, with moderation." Garrison published the *Liberator* weekly for thirty-five years, closing down without ever missing an issue when the Civil War ended in 1865.

Garrison helped set the tone of the abolition movement for the next thirty years, or rather, one of its tones. Like all movements and causes, it was liable to splinters, disagreements, and internal power struggles. Garrison initially supported the American Colonization Society, which wanted to move American free blacks to Haiti or Africa. Although this sounded reasonable to some at first glance, it soon became clear that deporting free blacks was all the society wanted to do. They had no interest in ending slavery or increasing the number of free blacks in the United States. When Garrison thought this through, he rejected the Society's goals and realized that his own aim was immediate and universal emancipation.

In 1835, Garrison was rescued by police from a crowd of angry proslavers who were dragging him, tied to a rope, around the streets of Boston. The police put Garrison in jail, using the old trick of saying it was for his own safety, although no one believed it. Bronson was his first visitor. When proslavery forces held a meeting in Boston's Faneuil Hall, Abba was scandalized, writing to Mary Peabody that they had turned the Cradle of Liberty into the "Coffin of Freedom." In the years 1835 and 1836, abolitionists counted more than three hundred riots for their cause, and this was almost thirty years before the Emancipation Proclamation.*

Garrison also supported women's rights and disagreed irreconcilably with Frederick Douglass, the most famous black man of his time, on this point. Garrison tended toward nonviolence and passive resistance and did not believe in participating in the political process. Abba and her brother Sam were Garrison's friends and fervent supporters. Sam quit his pulpit in Connecticut to work full time in the movement. When Abba died in 1877, Garrison attended her funeral and, according to the *Concord Freeman*'s contemporary account, "indulg[ed] in a few reminiscences" of the old abolitionist days with a grieving Bronson and Sam.

The first active abolitionist elected to Congress was Joshua Giddings of Ohio (where John Brown lived for a time) in 1838. Fiercely heckled and censured on the floor of the House for an antislavery speech, he resigned his seat. But his constituency reelected him and he returned, finishing his speech from the exact phrase where he had been forced to leave off.

Margaret Fuller argued in the early 1840s that women had a special responsibility to fight slavery because "the films of interest are not so close around [women] as around the men." Being an underdog always makes it easier to support other underdogs. Fuller went on to say that women didn't have to put themselves in personal danger to fight slavery; there were many small ways any respectable woman could make her point, such as telling her husband that she had no need for the "glittering baubles, spacious dwellings, and plentiful service" that slavery provides.

---

* Lincoln's document fell far shorter than most of us remember from high school history. It freed only the slaves living in the Confederacy, who were not, at that time, under Lincoln's Union control anyway. It did not free the slaves living in the four slaveholding states (Missouri, Kentucky, Maryland, and Delaware) that were fighting on the Union side. Politics is tricky business, and Lincoln was a master.

Displaying great economic and political naïveté, general feeling among abolitionists, all the way up to the April 1861 Confederate attack on Fort Sumter, was that slavery could be ended without an all-out war. Even John Brown, for all his firebrand reputation, summed up his Harpers Ferry attack plans by saying, "We shall by this means conquer without bloodshed, awaken the slaves in the possibility of escape, and frighten the slaveholders into a desire to get rid of slavery."

Brown came to believe violence was the only way late in his life and quite reluctantly. On his way out of his jail cell to be hanged, he handed this note to his jailer: "Charles Town, Va., December 2, 1859. I, John Brown, am now quite certain that the crimes of this guilty land will never be purged away but with blood. I had, as I now think, vainly, flattered myself that without very much bloodshed it might be done." In our smaller scale, we anti-war activists were also guilty of thinking we could stop the war by modest means. We tried letter-writing campaigns, we wore buttons that said "Stop the War," we organized peaceful marches and educational events. Once, while I was still a college student, a group of friends and I decided we would stop eating. We hoped that a public fast objecting to the war would encourage the government to rethink its aggressive militarism.

About a dozen of us vowed to eat nothing and drink only orange juice for two weeks as a protest against the war. I was very hungry for the first three days, but then felt fine. Our action brought some media coverage, including an article in the *New York Times*, but the war didn't end. I think I lost about ten pounds.

※ ※ ※ ※ ※

Nineteen-year-old Louisa avidly read Harriet Beecher Stowe's *Uncle Tom's Cabin* when it came out in 1852. It was the country's first best-seller; half a million copies were sold by 1857. Like movie tie-ins today, her book spawned a rash of commemorative plates, spoons, and china figurines as well as songs, plays, musicals, and poetry. Mrs. Stowe was fêted and vilified on both sides of the Atlantic. The Richmond, Virginia papers sputtered in true *ad hominem* style that she was a "coarse, ugly, ill natured, ill mannered old woman." A Kentucky man wrote to his newspaper that Mrs. Stowe should be given all the rope she wanted, as she was bringing on the breakup of the Union all that much quicker, which was just what the South wanted.*

Mrs. Stowe† said she wrote *Uncle Tom's Cabin* as an outraged response to the passage of the 1850 Fugitive Slave Law. Requiring Northerners to return escaped slaves to slavery was simply the last straw. "These men and Christians cannot know what slavery is; if they did, such a question could never be open for discussion," she wrote, adding, "The object of these sketches is to awaken sympathy and feeling for the African race; as they exist among us; to show their wrongs and sorrows, under a system so necessarily cruel and unjust as to defeat and do away the good effects of all that can be attempted for them, by their best friends, under it." In other words, it was time to stop working within the system; there was no such thing as a kinder, gentler slavery.

Mrs. Stowe was not the only person galvanized into concerted action by the Fugitive Slave Law. Concord, including the Alcott's house, was a major stop on the eastern branch of the Underground Railroad, which operated most actively during the 1850s.**

---

* George Orwell called *Uncle Tom's Cabin* the quintessential "good bad book": "It is an unintentionally ludicrous book, full of preposterous melodramatic incidents; it is also deeply moving and essentially true; it is hard to say which quality outweighs the other."

† Mrs. Stowe and her family lived next door to Mark Twain in Hartford, Connecticut. She was a short woman of much energy: she had seven children, she painted flowers (much like May Alcott), and she invented a number of labor-saving kitchen designs such as shallow shelving, countertop work surfaces, and "stations." Her hydrangea and lilac bushes bloom in her yard today.

** Neighbor Nathaniel Hawthorne, however, was not a fan of the abolitionists. His opinions provoked a family feud between his wife Sophia, trying to be loyal to her husband, and her fiercely activist sisters.

Daniel Webster disgusted many of the New England abolitionists by helping develop the Fugitive Slave Law's wording and intent. Emerson was incensed, titling a long journal entry "Bad Times" and railing against Webster, saying, "All I have and all I can do shall be given and done in opposition to the execution of the law . . . The word *liberty* in the mouth of Webster sounds like the word *love* in the mouth of a courtezan." Louisa, too, was scandalized, peppering her journal and letters with references to Webster's traitorous turn. Lidian Emerson expressed her opinion by draping her front gate in black bunting on July 4.

In addition to maintaining safe houses and passages to Canada for escaping slaves, in the 1850s the abolitionists needed to expand their protection to blacks who, before the law, had been safely working and living in Northern cities. Abolitionists set up vigilance committees to physically prevent blacks from being taken into custody by bounty hunters and slave traders. Occasionally, abolitionists would storm local jails to release captured blacks. Bronson, whose unworldliness gave him an enviable lack of fear, actively participated in these fights.* Louisa tracked each one, cheering or grieving with each success or failure. The most dramatic event of this sort in Boston was the capture and return of Anthony Burns in June 1854.

Anthony Burns was working in Boston, having escaped from slavery in Virginia just a few months previously. Grabbed off the sidewalk while he was he walking home from work, he was thrown in jail. An abolitionist crowd, including Bronson, attacked the courthouse, trying to free him. In the course of the fight, thirteen demonstrators were arrested, several were badly beaten, and one U.S. marshal was killed.

There was confusion and some bungled execution of the plan after the marshal was killed. In the ensuing tense standoff, the abolitionists noisily occupied the street at the bottom of the court-

---

* There is some record that Bronson considered going to Virginia to try to rescue John Brown from his prison cell.

house stairs, and the government forces massed behind the great courthouse doors. Both sides brandished their weapons. Bronson broke away from the crowd on the street, and slowly, alone, climbed up the no-man's-land steps to the courthouse doors. The crowd hushed. Reaching the top step, Bronson turned to the crowd below him and, pointing his cane at the doors, said quietly, "Why are we not within?"

Government reinforcements had arrived, however, preventing further assaults on the building. Burns remained behind bars. During his trial, Burns's lawyer tried to convince the judge to rule the Fugitive Slave Law unconstitutional. This failed, and Burns was remanded back to Virginia and slavery. Tension was high on Boston's streets as Burns was moved from the jail to the ship waiting to take him south. Abolitionist forces lined the route with black flags, American flags were hung upside down from windows, and a huge coffin marked "Liberty" was suspended across State Street. Louisa excitedly participated from the pavement of Court Square. Richard Henry Dana, one of Burns's lawyers, described the scene in his journal:

> Every window was filled, & beyond the lines drawn up by the police, was an immense crowd. . . . Gen. Edmonds gave orders to each commander of a post to fire on the people whenever they passed the line marked by the police in a manner he should consider turbulent & disorderly. So . . . the city was really under Martial law. The entire proceeding was illegal . . . as the procession (of Burns and his guards) moved down it was met with a perfect howl of Shame! Shame! & hisses.

In response to this setback, the abolitionists busily set up new committees to kidnap and harass the bounty hunters and government officials who spearheaded and supported these wretched searches and seizures. Petitions were circulated to remove Burns's trial judge from office, which succeeded in 1858. Money was raised to purchase Burns's freedom and send him to school, both of which were accomplished. The abolitionists raised the political stakes to an unacceptably feverish level; Burns was the last runaway slave to be captured in Massachusetts.

On May 22, 1856, when Louisa was twenty-three, Massachusetts Senator Charles Sumner was giving a speech on the Senate floor opposing the proslavery forces in Kansas. Enraged, Preston Brooks, a representative from South Carolina, invaded the Senate chamber and attacked Sumner, beating him on the head with his silver-tipped cane. Brooks thrashed Sumner into bloody unconsciousness, inflicting head injuries that lasted for years. The southerner eventually resigned from Congress, but only after it became clear that momentum was building to expel him for this display of ungentlemanly partisanship. However, he was soon re-elected by his supportive constituency and returned to Washington. Emerson noted in his journal,

> South Carolina is in earnest. I see the courtesy of the Carolinians, but I know meanwhile that the only reason why they do not plant a cannon before Faneuil Hall, and blow Bunker Hill Monument to fragments, as a nuisance, is because they have not the power. They are fast acquiring the power, and if they get it, they will do it.

Senator Sumner was an abolitionist hero, even before being caned. He argued as early as the 1840s that public schools should be desegregated (after all, he said, if society is desegregated, schools should be too), and he spoke in favor of universal enfranchisement of freed slaves. When asked if he'd ever looked at the other side of the slavery issue, he responded, "There is no other side."

After the caning incident, Sumner returned to Boston to a large welcoming demonstration. Louisa was there. "After dinner," she wrote to her sister Anna,

I went out to see the Sumner demonstration. . . . Eight hundred gentlemen on horseback escorted him & formed a line up Beacon St. through which he rode smiling & bowing, he looked pale but otherwise as usual. . . . The only time Sumner rose along the route was when he passed the Orphan Asylum & saw all the little blue aproned girls waving their hands to him. I thought it was very sweet in him to do that honor to the fatherless & motherless children. . . . The streets were lined with wreaths, flags, & loving people to welcome the good man back. . . . I waved my cotton handkerchief like a meek banner to my hero with honorable wounds on his head & love of little children in his heart. Hurra!!

I could not hear the speeches at the State House so I tore down Hancock St. & got a place opposite his house. I saw him go in, & soon after the cheers of the horsemen & crowd brought him smiling to the window, he only bowed, but when the leader of the cavalcade cried out "Three cheers for the mother of Charles Sumner!" he stepped back & soon appeared leading an old lady who nodded, waved her hand. . . .

I was so excited I pitched about like a mad woman, shouted, waved, hung onto fences, rushed thro crowds, & swarmed about in a state of rapturous insanity till it was all over & then I went home hoarse & worn out.

There is something so invigorating about being committed to something bigger than one's self. Horace Mann, who married Mary, the third Peabody sister, said in 1859 to Antioch College's graduating class, "be ashamed to die until you have won some victory for humanity." This sense of larger purpose, shared by the abolitionists and by the 1960s anti-war and civil rights activists, fuels the revolutionary fires and turns setbacks into rallying points on which to build the next effort.

Louisa loved being part of a group of like-minded people

doing undeniable good and enjoying themselves at the same time. "Went to Readville & saw the 54th colored Regiments both there & the next day in town as they left for the South. Enjoyed it very much, also the Antislavery Meetings." She fought the battle on several fronts and leaned, as was her style, toward the dramatic. In February 1860, she submitted a story called 'M.L.' about the love and happy marriage of a freed slave and a rich white woman to the *Atlantic Monthly*. When it was rejected, her comment was that the *Atlantic*'s editor (who was James Russell Lowell at the time) "won't have 'M.L.' as it is antislavery, and the dear South must not be offended." If there was anything white men were more afraid of than free blacks competing for their jobs, it was free blacks competing for their white women.

Some abolitionists put together their version of the American flag in the late 1850s. It had only nine stripes and twenty stars (the real flag, of course, had thirteen stripes and, at that time, thirty-three stars). Abolitionists may have disagreed with each other about some things, but they definitely did not agree with Lincoln that saving the Union was the most important issue. They were more than ready to jettison the slaveholding states. Both abolitionists and Southern rebels believed that only by splitting America into smaller and smaller sections could one finally form a society of people like-minded enough to build a perfect society. Fruitlands and Brook Farm were experiments in secession no less than Mississippi or South Carolina.

Lincoln rejected the splinter approach to a better America. The abolitionists' vision did not extend, as Lincoln's did, to a future where the country could stand whole and united without slavery. Unlike Lincoln, abolitionists took the Southerners at their word when they said they could not and would not live without slaves. By designing houses with hidey-holes for escaping slaves, Emerson was assuming a future in which people would continue to need to help other people escape slavery.

If I were to characterize the Weather Underground's path to a better America, it would be that things had to get a lot worse before they got better. In every way. Death, chaos, and mayhem would awaken the complacent (white) population to the depredations America was wreaking around the planet. As I contemplated this strategy on one of many hitchhiking trips across the country, I was struck by a small thought: one possible implication of this push to make things worse was that it would be politically correct to throw litter out of car windows. Since I found myself strangely unwilling to add candy wrappers to the nation's forests and streams, I began to expand my thinking; perhaps the initial premise was flawed. The accidental explosion in New York in March 1970, which killed three of my Weather friends, helped considerably to clarify my thinking. As great as my anger was, amateur-level suicidal terrorism was not an escalation I could wholeheartedly embrace. I didn't know if this meant I wasn't properly committed or if it demonstrated actual rational thought.

❧ ❧ ❧ ❧ ❧

Louisa met Harriet Tubman when she visited Concord, raising money and telling eye-opening stories of her nineteen trips south to help more than three hundred slaves safely escape to the North. Tubman, who always carried a gun, was a hunted criminal, with a reward of $12,000 offered for her capture. Louisa and her family's abolitionist crowd, whom Louisa called the "regular Anti-Slavery set," were always part of the movement's most active leadership.

Tubman's successes were due in part to her stern tactics and lack of sentimentality. She followed homegrown utilitarian strategies, maximizing the greatest good for the greatest number. Her escapes were timed for weekend nights when a slaveholder's guard might be down. Babies were doped with opium to keep them quiet, and she had helpers who stayed back a few days to pull down signs that slaveholders might post about the escapees.

> The expedition was governed by the strictest rules. If any man gave out, he must be shot. "Would you really do

that?" she [Tubman] was asked. "Yes," she replied, "if he was weak enough to give out, he'd be weak enough to betray us all, and all who had helped us; and do you think I'd let so many die just for one coward man?" "Did you ever have to shoot any one?" she was asked. "One time," she said, a man gave out the second night; his feet were sore and swollen, he couldn't go any further; he'd rather go back and die, if he must." They tried all arguments in vain, bathed his feet, tried to strengthen him, but it was no use. . . . "I told my boys to get their guns ready, and shoot him. They'd have done it in a minute; but when he heard that, he jumped right up and went on as well as any body."

In early 1861, Louisa started writing *Work*, which she first bravely called *Success*. Her chapter about being a domestic servant included a Harriet Tubman character, transformed as a brave and benevolent cook named Hepsey, who was saving money to go south to rescue her old mother.

※ ※ ※ ※ ※

Franklin Benjamin Sanborn and Bronson were among the most active abolitionists in Concord. Sanborn, a neighbor about Louisa's age, ran a school at which Louisa's youngest sister May was the art teacher. The students included the Hawthorne and Emerson children, Henry James's two younger brothers, and John Brown's daughters Anne and Sarah. In his long life (he died in 1917), Sanborn went on to be involved in many social service activities and was a founding member and president of the American Social Science Association.

He was a good friend to the Alcotts, helping Louisa get her poem about John Brown published in Garrison's *Liberator* and serializing her *Hospital Sketches* in his magazine, the *Commonwealth*. He also helped Bronson earn some money as a not very successful, one-term superintendent of schools in Concord in 1860. He may have hired May to work in his school, more as a way to funnel money to the Alcotts than because he thought her especially well qualified. On the down side, he has a reputation among historians for having taken advantage of his friends by writing self-serving histories of Concord's transcendental elite.

Sanborn was one of the so-called Secret Six who helped plan and finance John Brown's raid on Harpers Ferry. Louisa called Brown "St. John the Just." Ending slavery was the only reason Brown got out of bed every morning for most of the fifty-nine years of his life. He said he viewed the Golden Rule and the Declaration of Independence as one and the same. Except for fighting to free slaves, he did not believe in violence.* In the month before he was executed, Southern ministers and preachers came to his jail cell in Charles Town, trying to convince him that slavery was a Christian institution. He refused to pray with them, saying they knew nothing about Christianity and that though he might respect them as gentlemen, it was only as "heathen gentlemen."

John Brown came to Concord in 1857 and again in 1859 at Sanborn's invitation, publicly raising money to prevent slavery from being legalized in the western territories, but secretly planning more direct action. He had plenty of support among the transcendental abolitionists of Concord and Boston. Abba's brother Sam said Brown's raid "was the beginning of the end of our conflict with slavery." Despite being called the South's worst nightmare, John Brown went to Harpers Ferry not so much to light the fire of armed black insurrection as to capture the mountainous territory around the town. Harpers Ferry was in the middle of the best route out of the parts of the South where the majority of slaves lived. At the time of his raid,† he was still hoping to free the slaves by helping them escape their captors, not by

---

* John Brown also had a sense of humor. When President Buchanan put a bounty of $250 on Brown's head, Brown offered $2.50 for Buchanan's.

† The first man killed during the raid, shot by one of Brown's troops, was Heyward Shepherd, a free black man, who was the baggage master on the train they stopped.

killing their captors. Ironically, as the war drew to a close a few years later, the battered and disoriented Confederacy itself armed the slaves, desperately trying to shore up their exhausted and shrinking military.

When Louisa found out about Brown's raid and capture, she wrote to a friend, "We are boiling over with excitement here for many of our people (Anti Slavery I mean) are concerned in it. We have a daily stampede for papers, and a nightly indignation meeting over the wickedness of our country, & the cowardice of the human race. I'm afraid Mother will die of spontaneous combustion if things are not set right soon."

After John Brown's capture by U.S. Marines led by a young and upcoming Col. Robert E. Lee, Louisa wrote to her friend Alfred Whitman, an alumnus of Sanborn's school, who had moved to Kansas,

> What are your ideas on the Harpers Ferry matter? If you are my Dolphus [Louisa's pet name for him], you are full of admiration for old Brown's courage & pity for his probable end. . . .

When I was just beginning my anti-war activity in Philadelphia in the mid-1960s, the United States had a draft, not volunteer, army. My male friends were legally required to carry their draft cards, so one of the obvious methods of protest was to publicly burn your draft card. A man's likelihood of being called up to fight in Vietnam was determined by a series of (shrinking) exemptions and an annual lottery system. While still in college, I helped organize one of these draft-card burnings and was impressed at the bravery of some of my friends as they lit their cards. We chanted antiwar slogans as we watched the cardboard squares burn down to their fingers and the ashes drop to the street. I had only a foggy notion of the dangers the cardholders were bringing down on themselves, but I assumed that, beyond singed fingers, they certainly would be arrested, face jail time, be sent to Vietnam, or be forced to escape to Canada.

I was disappointed to discover, a week or so later, that at least one of my supposedly firebrand friends had simply reported to his draft board that he'd lost his card and needed a replacement. It was another one of those lessons, still so new to me, that things were not always as they seemed. Louisa was not so naïve, but she still became highly frustrated with the same wishy-washy commitment she saw from some of Concord's female citizens as she tried to whip up support for women's suffrage – but that's for later.

※ ※ ※ ※ ※

In April 1860, five months after Brown had been executed,* federal agents stormed Sanborn's house in the middle of the night, intending to arrest him. In a letter to a friend, Louisa called it a kidnapping and described the heroism of her friend, Ann Whiting, who helped foil it.

> Annie Whiting immortalized her self by getting into the kidnapper's carriage so that they could not put the long legged martyr in. One of the rascals grabbed her & said "Get out." "I wont" said Annie. "I'll tear your clothes." "Well tear away." "I'll whip up the horses & make them run away if you don't get out." "Let them run to the devil but I shant stir." & the smart little woman didn't till the riot was over. Young Warren charged at the foe with a rake & Sanborn's boys rushed about like heroes.

Sanborn then wrote a long article, "Mr. Sanborn's Account of His Own Arrest," that appeared in Horace Greeley's *New York Tribune*. He gave full credit to his sister and Annie Whiting for effecting his rescue, and commented at length on the lack of due process and the fact that he had to stand around for hours outdoors

---

* After he was convicted, kindergarten inventor Elizabeth Peabody was so outraged at the death sentence that she journeyed all the way to Virginia to plead, unsuccessfully, with Governor Letcher for clemency.

in the cold night in handcuffs and stocking feet. The town formed another vigilance committee to protect Sanborn, and Louisa was one of its members. Her journal is strewn with comments like "Glad I have lived in the time of this great movement, & known its heroes so well. War times suit me, as I am a fighting May." Ellen Emerson echoes Louisa with "I am so glad that such a thing has happened in my day," but adds, since she inherited a thread of her father's observational distance, "The town is in a high state of self-complacency, it flatters itself that this is the spirit of '76."

When Thoreau heard about the Harpers Ferry raid, he waxed more emotional than people had ever seen him. He poured his anger into his journal – ten thousand words of praise for Brown and literate vitriol for the government, the press, and the judicial system that executed him. Thoreau then converted his thoughts to a fiery lecture, which he took on tour. At Concord, the fearful city fathers refused to ring the bell to announce his talk, so he rang it himself.

Thoreau's response to Brown's execution was cynical and desperate. He described the government as a "semi-human tiger or ox, stalking over the earth, with its heart taken out and the top of its brain shot away . . . a government that pretends to be Christian and crucifies a million Christs every day! . . . It is more manifest than ever that tyranny rules. . . . I do not wish to kill or be killed, but I foresee circumstances in which both these things would be by me unavoidable. . . . The same indignation that is said to have cleared the temple once will clear it again." Of the press that uniformly condemned Brown (including pacifist Garrison in the *Liberator*), Thoreau said, "I do not chance to know an editor in the country who will deliberately print any thing which he knows will ultimately and permanently reduce the number of his subscribers." The *Springfield Republican* returned the favor, albeit ungrammatically, "This Thoreau seems to be a thorough fanatic – why don't he imitate Brown and do good by rushing to the gallows."

Brown's raid on Harpers Ferry, with his twenty-one-man army (which included three of his sons, two sons-in-law and six blacks)* was a case study in mishandled revolution. In the end, ten were killed during the fight, including two sons; seven were captured and hanged and six escaped. Three Harpers Ferry residents, one marine, and one slave owner were also killed.

Those of us who fancied ourselves revolutionaries in the twentieth century would, I think, recognize ourselves in Brown's dedication, vision, tactical errors, and optimistic delusions (I wonder if we would have had Thoreau's impassioned and consistent support?). The way Brown rented a local farmhouse to case out the Harpers Ferry area, the way he trained his men, the way he collected money from liberal businessmen back in the big cities, the way both he and the government wildly misjudged each other's strengths, the way the press inflated the attack – all remind me, with both fondness and frustration, of my own Weather days. As does W. E. B. Du Bois's description of Brown's Harpers Ferry raiders, most of them in their twenties, as

> idealists, dreamers, soldiers and avengers, varying from the silent and thoughtful to the quick and impulsive; from the cold and bitter to the ignorant and faithful. They believed in God, in spirits, in fate, in liberty. To them the world was a wild, young unregulated thing, and they were born to set it right.

The *Atlantic Monthly* published a six-part article about John Brown by Sanborn in 1875, when it was safe for both editor and author to do so. Sanborn stated his purpose: to write a clear, factual history so that the "vaporization of genuine history may be deferred as long as possible." The article runs to more than a hundred pages of close text with no pictures, drawings, or headings and is avail-

---

* The widow of one of the blacks, Lewis Sheridan Leary from Oberlin, Ohio, remarried and in time had a grandson named Langston Hughes, the prize-winning poet and storyteller who died in 1967. Hughes wrote of the "sweet fly-paper of life" in New York's Harlem, a phrase that I think Louisa would have much appreciated.

able on the Internet. In it, Sanborn includes a number of letters from Brown never before published, as well as a short autobiography Brown wrote in 1857 to the son of one of his supporters, who was then a student at Sanborn's school. Brown urges the young man to have a specific plan to excel in whatever he takes an interest in doing:

> This kind of feeling I would recommend to all young persons both male & female: as it will certainly tend to secure admission to the company of the more intelligent; & better portion of every community. By all means endeavor to excel in some laudable pursuit. . . . I wish you to have some definite plan. Many seem to have none; & others never stick to any that they do form.

Hard to find fault with that.

※ォ ※ォ ※

The abolitionists grew increasingly impatient in the run-up to the Civil War. After all, for almost forty years they had been making their point that it was wrong for human beings to own other human beings in a country with a publicly articulated belief in human rights. A schizoid America standing tall for liberty and democracy against the corrupt monarchies of Europe, but corrupting itself by actively selling and owning other human beings was driving thinking people crazy on both sides of the Atlantic.

This was especially true of the many English people, like Mrs. Trollope, who very much wanted to admire America, but who were decades ahead of Americans in their condemnation of slavery. Eighty years earlier, Thomas Day, a pioneering Yorkshire industrialist, the Darwin family, and Josiah Wedgwood of porcelain fame, all openly sympathized with the American rebels. The irony of slavery, however, did not escape them, "If there be an object truly ridiculous in nature, it is an American patriot signing resolutions of independence on one hand, and with the other brandishing a whip over his affrighted slaves," wrote Day in 1775.

But the abolitionists had to wait until the Civil War was halfway over before Lincoln officially incorporated emancipation into the Northern cause. Lincoln was hesitant about embracing emancipation because he knew that his Union army was sharply divided over whether freeing the slaves was worth the fight. He didn't want to introduce a deal-breaker into his sometimes uneasy political/military alliance. Despite the abolitionists' work, there was much more agreement in the North that the war was about proving that a republican, federalist government could exist without tearing itself apart at the least sign of disagreement than it was about ending slavery. "The central idea of secession is the essence of anarchy," Lincoln told his countrymen. Anarchy was the key problem, not slavery. Enough Northerners agreed and were willing to risk death to keep the country together. In 1863, an Ohio blacksmith, a private in the Union army, wrote home

> Admit the right of the seceding states to break up the Union at pleasure . . . and how long will it be before the new confederacies created by the first disruptions shall be resolved into still smaller fragments and the continent become a vast theater of civil war, military license, anarchy and despotism? Better settle it at whatever cost and settle it forever.

When Fort Sumter was attacked, everyone, including Louisa, was ready to fight the war, however Lincoln defined it. In truth, she loved the martial atmosphere – the flapping flags, the town meetings, the newspaper dispatches, and the recruits and volunteers marching and camping around town. "September 1859:" she wrote in her journal, "Great State Encampment here. Town full of soldiers, with military fuss and feathers. I like a camp, and long for a war, to see how it all seems." It tasted like a bigger world and thrilled Louisa in a very unladylike way. Ellen Emerson wrote her brother that some situations were preferable to peace, and she signed the letter "your warlike sister."

When war was declared in April 1861, Louisa wrote,

War declared with the South, and our Concord company went to Washington. A busy time getting them all ready, and a sad day seeing them off, for in a little town like this we all seem like one family in times like these. At the station the scene was very dramatic, as the brave boys went away perhaps never to come back again.

I've often longed to see a war, and now I have my wish. I long to be a man, but as I can't fight, I will content myself with working for those who can.

The rush and high of seeing the world in white and black, wrong and right, with no gray spaces in between is bracing and seductive. I both fueled and fed off that feeling for as long as I could in the 1960s and early '70s. In the end, as in wars everywhere, people die, and where life continues, it may appear ugly or muddled, making invalids and cynics of many survivors. One truth, though, is not lost and, I think, should never be lost: no matter how high the cost of liberty, in the end the cost of repression is always higher.

⁂

The *Atlantic* published a contemporary account of the Civil War in July 1862. Titled "Chiefly about War-Matters, by a Peaceable Man," it was written by Louisa's reclusive next-door neighbor Nathaniel Hawthorne, then fifty-eight years old. In it, he describes his journey south from Concord to Virginia in March and April 1862. He records that he wanted to see the war for himself, being tired of dispatches from newspapers and the telegraph.

Whenever Louisa mentioned Hawthorne in her journal or in letters, she always painted him as odd, albeit in a different way from the rest of her unusual friends and relations. "Mr. H. is as queer as ever and we catch glimpses of a dark mysterious looking man in a big hat and red slippers darting over the hills or skimming by as if he expected the house of Alcott were to rush out and clutch him." The *Atlantic* apparently thought him strange as well, as they published his article only after excising bits* that they didn't think were properly respectful of Lincoln and editing his comments with frequent footnotes such as "We do not thoroughly comprehend the author's drift in the foregoing paragraph, but are inclined to think its tone reprehensible, and its tendency impolitic in the present stage of our national difficulties."

In his article, Hawthorne described his trip south to visit Harpers Ferry and noted its tactically impossible position at the bottom of a valley. He wrote, "I shall not pretend to be an admirer of old John Brown . . . nobody was ever more justly hanged." He went on, "Any common-sensible man, looking at the matter unsentimentally, must have felt a certain intellectual satisfaction in seeing him hanged, if it were only in requital of his preposterous miscalculation of possibilities." The *Atlantic*'s abolitionist editors, scandalized, footnoted that sentence with "Can it be a son of old Massachusetts who utters this abominable sentiment? For shame!"

Refusing to be caught up in the feelings of the time, Hawthorne's Peaceable Man noted his prescient thoughts about the freed slaves he saw on the road: "I think . . . that, whoever may be benefited by the results of this war, it will not be the present generation of negroes, the childhood of whose race is now gone for ever, and who must henceforth fight a hard battle with the world, on very unequal terms." He concluded by imagining that secession might still be a reasonable option. The *Atlantic* scolded in its final footnote, "We regret the innuendo in the concluding sentence. The war can never be allowed to terminate, except in the complete triumph of Northern principles." The footnote went on to question the Peaceable Man's loyalty to America for some sympathetic comments he made after meeting some sad, imprisoned white Southerners.

---

* The *Atlantic* had also meddled with an article by Thoreau a few years earlier. Thoreau had written about the majesty of a pine tree, saying it was as immortal as he himself was and may well end up in heaven, towering over him still. The *Atlantic*'s editor, Lowell, felt this crossed the line into unacceptable pantheism and deleted the sentence.

Louisa's entry about Brown's death in her journal caps her fervent attraction to the high emotions of the abolition movement:

> Glad I have lived to see the Antislavery movement and this last heroic act in it. Wish I could do my part. . . . The execution of Saint John the Just took place on the second. A meeting at the hall, and all Concord was there. Emerson, Thoreau, Father and Sanborn spoke, and all were full of reverence and admiration for the martyr. I made some verses on it, and sent them to the *Liberator*.

The poem was published in the January 20, 1860, edition. Its last stanza reads

> No monument of quarried stone,
> No eloquence of speech,
> Can grave the lessons on the land
> His martyrdom will teach. . . .

Louisa served tea to several of Brown's family in the spring of 1860, a few months after his execution, when the grieving family came to receive comfort from their Concord friends. In a letter to her sister Anna, Louisa described John Brown's widow Mary Ann, who came along with Isabel, her daughter-in-law, the widow of her son Watson, and Isabel's now fatherless infant son. Watson Brown was twenty-four when he died at Harpers Ferry, shot as he carried a white truce flag out of the building where he, his father, and a few others were hiding. He had written to his wife Isabel a few weeks before he died, shortly after his son's birth.

> Oh, Bell, I do want to see you and the little fellow very much, but I must wait. There was a slave near here whose wife was sold off South the other day, and he was found in Thomas Kennedy's orchard, dead, the next morning. Cannot come home so long as such things are done here. . . . There was another murder committed near our place the other day, making five murders and one suicide within

five miles of our place since we have lived there; they were
all slaves. . . .

Louisa's description of the Browns' visit is clearly written to
entertain as well as to inform. She had a knack of being serious
and having fun at the same time. She gives Anna a picture of a
chaotic afternoon. As the word gets out that the Browns are visiting the Alcott house, more and more uninvited people showed
up, expecting tea and cookies along with a sighting of the abolitionist celebrities. Louisa wanted to make sure that her favorite
people were fed first – besides the Browns, this meant Emerson
and her Uncle Sam May. "I filled a big plate with all I could lay
hands on, and with two cups of tea, strong enough for a dozen,
charged upon Mr. E and Uncle S, telling them to eat, drink and
be merry, for a famine was at hand. They cuddled into a corner;
and then, feeling that my mission was accomplished, I let the
hungry wait and the thirsty moan for tea, while I picked out and
helped the regular Antislavery set."

Louisa gossiped to her sister about the Browns:

Mrs. Brown, Sen., is a tall, stout woman, plain, but with a
strong, good face and a natural dignity that showed she
was something better than a "lady," though she *did* drink
out of her saucer and used the plainest speech. . . . The
younger woman had such a patient, heart-broken face, it
was a whole Harpers Ferry tragedy in a look. . . . The
bright-eyed, handsome baby received the homage of the
multitude like a little king, bearing the kisses and praises
with the utmost dignity. He is named Frederick Watson
Brown, after his murdered uncle and father, and is a fair,
heroic-looking baby, with a fine head, and serious eyes
that look about him as if saying "I am a Brown! Are these
friends or enemies?". . . C. and I went and worshipped in
our own way at the shrine of John Brown's grandson, kiss-
ing him as if he were a little saint, and feeling highly hon-

ored when he sucked our fingers, or walked on us with his honest little red shoes, much the worse for wear.

After the Emancipation Proclamation, Lincoln appointed Samuel Gridley Howe, another one of the Secret Six and the husband of Julia Ward Howe* to head a government commission to figure out what to do with the freed slaves. Howe started by asking the basic question: Would blacks persist as a separate group in America or would intermarriage eventually absorb them into a larger mixed race population? Despite obvious evidence to the contrary, some contemporary scientists argued that absorption was genetically impossible. In the end, Howe plumped for a separate but equal approach, something Louisa didn't agree with, at least in her fiction. Her adult stories of happy cross-color marriages were far ahead of her times.

The abolition movement in the 1850s spiced the most lively and emotional years of Louisa's life. With the exception of her trips to Europe and a trip as a famous author to New York City, the 1850s are the only years when her journals and letters consistently lean more toward joy and energy than duty and doggedness. While she championed women's suffrage and many other reform activities after 1865, her heart and mind always dwelled close to those heady decades from the late 1840s until the war was over. It was the right cause at the right time in her life, imprinting her as so many of my generation were imprinted by our opposition to the war in Vietnam and our support for civil rights in the 1960s and early '70s.

Eight months after the attack on Fort Sumter, Sophia Hawthorne was helping Louisa pack her bags for her departure to the

---

* She was also an acquaintance of Louisa's. They met in 1856 in Boston, where Louisa described her as "a straw colored supercilious lady with pale eyes & a green gown in which she looked like a faded lettuce." Mrs. Howe wrote the "Battle Hymn of the Republic." The lyrics "as He died to make men holy, Let us die to make men free" refer to John Brown, whom she had met and liked in the spring of 1859.

Union Hotel Hospital in Washington, D.C. Louisa's petition to work as a nurse had been finally accepted. Her sister May and Nathaniel and Sophia's son Julian walked Louisa to the railroad station, with Abba weeping and waving a tear-stained handkerchief from the doorstep. Louisa doesn't mention Bronson's whereabouts, although Sophia later told her daughter that Bronson referred to Louisa's departure as being akin to having "sent his only son off to war."

<hr>

January 31, 1888

Dear Kit,

Ah me, abolition was indeed my favorite cause. It was meaty; it was righteous; it was exciting; it brought good people together. Did you know that John Brown was a direct descendant of one of the brave Pilgrims aboard the Mayflower? Peter Brown was his name. Did you say your husband's name was also Peter? It's a good name, although I can't say I used it much in my stories.

Be that as it may, I am saddened to think about your comment that there is still much redressing left to do. You are confirming one of my Uncle Sam May's worries as he saw that negroes in the south were being systematically denied the land & education they needed to become useful citizens, even into the 1870s.

It is true, I believe, that only the big jobs are worth investing one's life in. Aiming too low never bags the big ones.

Do you agree with me that the forces conserving the status quo always have the easier task? It's an irritating & quite unfair fact of life. I have always been more interested in the future than the past. That's what I find so irksome about Concord. Its esteemed citizenry seems perfectly happy to rest on its eighteenth-century laurels forever. As if the Old North Bridge will answer for every injustice into eternity.

It's nothing more than a historical excuse for sitting on your hands. Pah!

Now, what was I saying? Oh yes, there is considerable inertia, I think, attached to the present, since there is only a single present to protect. On the other hand, there are thousands of possible futures. But because only one can become the new present (assuming your concept of time zones has not changed that), the advocates of the multiple contending futures need to fight it out among each other, as well as fight against the current state of affairs. It gives the status quo an unfairly heavy thumb on the scale.

That's why we learned to fight with words & demonstrations, as well as with bullets. The former is the only way we underdogs can live long enough to win. Forces us to be smarter, too – the Boston Tea Party, for example. America's own history tells us over & over that these less deadly weapons are good ones for certain times in the battle, & that our struggles, if we ply them with enough energy & cleverness, can be won. You ask me not to forget your question about continuing the fight once the health & energy of youth has faded. I sigh over that one every day. Just not forgetting the question is a clear step in the right direction. I find life gets increasingly cluttered with age; it's harder & harder for me to keep my eye on the right ball. I try to wake up believing that every day is a new chance to do better. If that doesn't quite get me bouncing out of bed, I forgive myself in advance for always coming up short. It's when I don't even try that I can't forgive myself.

So what is next for our correspondence? Nursing, I hope. My goodness, the work it took me to convince all those ponderous bureaucracies to let me do it! First I was too young, then I was unmarried. Do they still hamper nurses so stupidly in your day?

When I think back, I believe my campaign to become a nurse was the only time – the only time! – in my life that I seriously invested effort in something that didn't, even marginally, benefit my parents or sisters. Then to have it snatched away from me so quickly. . . . Alcott luck has never been very good.

I do so wish I had lasted longer. Getting typhoid & having to leave the hospital was a crushing disappointment. I'll never forget any of my boys, & I so loved wandering around Washington, D.C. The swamps & construction & war made it all the more interesting to me. Most of all, I loved New Year's night 1863. I startled the whole hospital by throwing open my window & happily adding to the racket of the people celebrating on the streets, cheering my lungs out for the Emancipation Proclamation. Despite your quibbles, it was a great document.

Happier than I've been in a while,
Louisa

P S: Please do call me by my first name. This project is doing me good – almost as much fun as playing with Lulu.

Earning a Living & Having Fun

Do not be too timid and squeamish about your actions.
All life is an experiment. The more experiments you make
the better. . . . What if you do fail, and get fairly rolled in the dirt
once or twice? Up again, you shall never be so afraid of a tumble.
Ralph Waldo Emerson

Working for a living shuts a good many doors in one's face,
even in democratic America.
Louisa May Alcott, 1870, age thirty-seven

February 4, 2006

Dear Louisa,

All right, I will try to call you Louisa. But by any name, and no
matter how much respect I have for you, I must tell you that we
are not quite ready for the nursing conversation. We need to
spend a few pages remembering that you did more than anti-
slavery work in your twenties.

Being in one's twenties is such a terrific time of life, don't you
agree? Even if history is not exploding, all sorts of personal experiments are. We don't want to miss any of yours. All that energy!
All those assumptions about living forever! All that conviction and
planning to become famous and rich! Remember? You moved
away from your family for the first time; you tried all sorts of ways
to earn a living; you had fun; and you started submitting your
writing for publication. You did what twenty-somethings do in

137

whatever century they inhabit. I think those events are worth at least a nod. If you get impatient, you can tell me to hurry along.

Trying to be organized,
Kit

PS: I also want to remind you of all the fun you had in Europe. You've always been a hard worker, but I want to point out to you (and to my workaholic friends – they know who they are) that you knew how to indulge yourself from time to time. Remember how you enjoyed the Brittany countryside? And literary London? And that opera in Lugano? And Paris with Laddie, what more can I say? What better place for your sister May to find true love and artistic success. Margaret Fuller, too, was more at home in Italy than New England. She wrote from Rome, "Here is a great past and a living present. Here men work for something besides money and systems. . . . 'Tis a sphere much more natural to me than that the old Puritans and bankers have made." I think finding such observations justifies all my poking around in other people's mail. :)

It's so easy to understand why you are using Europe as your setting for your optimistic tale *Diana and Persis*.

Ciao, K

THE AMERICAN BOOTSTRAP · LOVE AND NOT OBEY
THE CRASS BROWN BABY · THE ROMANTIC POLE

Earning a living was one thing Bronson Alcott *never* did. It never seemed to have occurred to anyone other than Abba's family that Mr. Alcott should contribute to the family coffers.* There is a photograph of him sitting on a wooden bench he made and

---

* Like the romantically starving (male) artists in Parisian garrets and the romantically starving (male) English Lake District poets, Bronson was never pressed (except by Abba's family) to give up his philosophizing in favor of earning his

attached to a very large elm tree in the Alcott front yard, on the edge of the Lexington Road. The arms of the bench are bent-wood, and the elm tree, easily six feet in diameter, serves as the back of the bench. Bronson is uncompromisingly upright, lean-ing slightly forward, dressed formally in dark suit, vest, black tie, and white shirt, with his white hair stringing down to his shoul-ders. His is wearing a tall, rounded, light-colored hat and holds his silver-headed cane across his knees. At his side, on the bench, is a careful row of three ripe apples.

Bronson is fishing, and the apples are his bait. He is waiting for people to swim along the Lexington Road, on their way into or out of Concord. He will offer them an apple and, in return, engage them in philosophical conversation. He will sit there for hours, sunning and watching – a patient toad waiting to pounce. Hawthorne, next door, so much dreaded the possibility of talking to Bronson that he wore a path across the steep hill behind the back of both houses to avoid passing the elm tree. Louisa, unfor-tunately, could not use this tactic. Her frequent stays in Boston, begun as soon as she was old enough to leave home, were the best escapes she could manage.

Making a living by laboring for wages, as opposed to marrying someone who would make the wages for the both of you, was an unusual concept for a white, nonimmigrant woman in Louisa's day. Hundreds of novels, plays, and songs for hundreds of years track the only plot available to respectable women before the twentieth century – the search for a suitable husband. Most of those stories end with the wedding, as nothing of interest was expected to follow. Think classic Jane Austen: all six of her novels end in weddings, sometimes double ones.†

---

keep. These men all did whatever they wanted, after first finding a patron to man-age the mundane matters of feeding and clothing; or, failing that, a wife or a sister, (or in Bronson's case, a daughter) to figure it out for them.

† In Austen's defense, I would say she wrote in this vein because it sold better, not because she thought marriage was the better choice for women. Certainly she didn't follow her own script, turning down at least one proposal herself.

This, however, was not Louisa May Alcott's view of either life or fiction. When she did marry off a heroine, she took pains to inform her readers that matrimony did not end that character's useful, public life, nor did life necessarily become a bowl of cherries after the "I do." In her novels, marriages are only one of a continuing series of events in a woman's life, never the last word. Almost. The exception is *Taming a Tartar* in 1867, where she did give the marriage vows the last word, but with a twist. This gothic romance concludes with the Russian prince reminiscing with his new bride Sybil about their wedding. The story is told from Sybil's point of view, and she interrupts her husband's tale with a telling clarification. Her husband begins:

> "I might boast that I also had tamed a fiery spirit, but I am humble, and content myself with the knowledge that the proudest woman ever born has promised to love, honor and –"
>
> "*Not* obey you," I broke in with a kiss.

Before striking it rich with *Little Women* at age thirty-seven, Louisa had tried most of the genteel and a few of the not-so-genteel occupations available to Boston women: teaching, sewing, acting, nursing, and being a kitchen maid and servant. Perhaps the only job she never tried was factory work. In Louisa's day, factory work was on the lowest social rung; it was left, by the 1850s, to Irish immigrants. Once, at her most desperate, Louisa accepted a factory job, but the next day a teaching position turned up, and much as she disliked teaching, she was grateful for being rescued. As for prostitution, several of her heroines seriously considered it, and perhaps she did too, but we have no evidence that she ever tried it out. And it is doubtful that she would have been successful.

From her seventeenth year onward she regularly noted her earnings at the end of each year in her journal. Work was one thing she never avoided; she said it was her salvation. "Work is such a beautiful & helpful thing & independence so delightful

ABOVE: *Louisa's year-end journal summaries for 1861 and 1862. Note her careful accounting of her earnings. See her note "began Moods."* Hospital Sketches *was her first big success.*

BELOW: *Louisa's autograph. The lines above it read, "Of all sad words the saddest are these / to an author's ear, 'An autograph, please.'"*

By the Author of "LITTLE WOMEN."

WORK

A STORY OF EXPERIENCE!

BY LOUISA M. ALCOTT,

With 30 CHARACTER ILLUSRATIONS, by SOL EYTINGE.

Price, $1.75.

ROBERTS BROTERS. Publishers.

Louisa initially titled this book Success *although it was published as* Work. *It is a thinly veiled account of her failure to make a living at all the occupations open to women in the 1850s and 1860s. The story weaves together poverty, rape, suicide, mental illness, despair and happiness in various guises.*

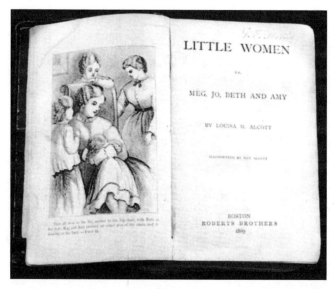

The first edition of Little Women. *Sister May's drawings received negative reviews and were scrapped in subsequent editions. Louisa's honest publisher advised her not to sell the copyright outright (a common convevntion at the time), but to receive royalty payments instead. The book's instant and continued success supported generations of Alcotts.*

ABOVE: *This drawing was included on a "Louisa May Alcott Calendar" in the late 1880s. The artist, Lisbeth B. Comins likely knew Louisa, which makes the error in spelling her name all the more odd. Louisa was widely known as "The Children's Friend" for her ability to capture and describe the struggles of children trying to be good.*

BELOW: *Louisa reluctantly posing as an author. She used her status to leverage her work in support of women's suffrage.*

ABOVE: *Orchard House as it appears today.*

BELOW: *Louisa's gravestone in Sleepy Hollow Cemetery. Note the spare change. The Emersons, Thoreaus and Hawthornes are nearby, along with the rest of the Alcotts. Their graves are more conventionally strewn with flowers.*

that I wonder there are any lazy people in the world." She loved the feeling of strength and freedom that came with earning a living. Money brought her heart to the surface; money allowed her to obey her generous desires to support her family, have fun, and help the world.

It was to the big city that twenty-two-year-old Louisa May Alcott went in 1855 to seek her fortune and her identity. Her journal is short that year. "I don't waste ink in poetry and pages of rubbish now," she wrote in April 1855 from her Boston garret, "for I've begun to live and have no time for sentimental musings." She knew the city from the time her parents had moved the family there in two earlier failed attempts to earn a living, and now she was eager to make it her own. She was young and strong, as most of us were at one time, and, not surprisingly, saw the urban scene as the place to be. Closer to the abolitionist action, Boston also offered the concerts, plays, and lectures she loved. Boston, she said, "is nicer and noisier than ever . . . my beloved old town whose very dirt is interesting to my eyes." She wrote to her sister Anna that she would take it as a good omen that the skies cleared as she moved closer to Boston. "I feel hopeful in my mind and more determined than ever to try my experiment and be independent of everyone but my own two hands and busy head."

She had faith in the American bootstrap, even daring to believe it applied to women. "I want more fives, and mean to have them too," the twenty-four-year-old wrote home. Later, to Anna, "You ask about funds, &c. I have eight cents in the bank at present, $10 owing me, and a fortune in prospect." Here is the voice of a brash young person speaking in any century.

But brashness doesn't necessarily produce revenue, and unemployment eventually becomes exhausting and debilitating. She wanted to prove that Alcotts, despite their track record, weren't destined to be objects of eternal charity. In her journal, some of her public bravado is replaced with a private desperation. Money is a constant topic. Once, when there was no work and no money, she cryptically tells her journal:

My fit of despair was soon over, for it seemed so cowardly to run away before the battle was over. I couldn't do it. So I said firmly, "There is work for me, and I'll have it," and went home resolved to take Fate by the throat and shake a living out of her.

What the "it" was that she couldn't do, she doesn't describe. However, as several of her young heroines contemplate suicide on a Boston bridge well known to Louisa, it is not hard to imagine the same thoughts occurring to their creator as well.

A woman in her twenties looking for work in the 1850s had advantages and disadvantages compared to the 1970s when I was doing the same. There were far fewer jobs available in 1850, but they required skills that most women already had – sewing, washing, teaching, child care, cooking and indoor service, and, of course, sex. Louisa gravitated to private teaching in a home environment. The work was little more than babysitting elementary-school-aged girls in their homes, reading stories with them, and going for walks. She didn't enjoy doing it. Either the children were unresponsive or the mothers were bossy. She also took her turn as a house servant, which, as we saw, was even less successful.

Sewing worked better for Louisa because it could be done at home and on her own schedule. She would go around soliciting orders – that was the hard part – and then whip up men's shirts and handkerchiefs while thinking up stories in her head. She was by this time writing and submitting stories and poems to various magazines around town. Her first published work came out in 1851 when she was a teenager, under the name Flora Fairfield – an undistinguished five-stanza poem titled "Sunlight" about the joys of sunshine, flowers, dew, birds, and heaven.

Louisa loved acting. She and Anna had excelled in neighborhood productions back in Concord. For a while Louisa thought she might make a living at it. "I had hopes of trying a new life. . . . I felt as if I must find interest in something absorbing. . . . Perhaps it is acting, not writing, I'm meant for. Nature must have a vent, somehow." But her parents were adamantly opposed. Like factory work, it was outside the bounds of someone with May family credentials. Later, Louisa saluted this dream in chapter 3 of *Work*, letting heroine Christie take up acting for a while. Louisa herself performed periodically all her life for charity fund-raisers, perfecting several over-the-top Dickensian characters.

乡未乡未乡

When my first daughter was born, various species-preserving genes began to replicate, telling me that I needed to live a longer and more stable life than I previously had mapped out for myself in my Weather days. The search for steady money loomed as large in my life in 1973 as the search for a believable explanation to an eighteen-and-a-half-minute erasure in a White House audiotape was looming in President Nixon's.

Deciding on nursing as being the most likely to do no harm in an increasingly harmful world, I found I was a few science credits short of a successful application. Infant daughter in tow, I walked to the local community college (tuition: $2 per semester) to take the qualifying exam for an organic chemistry class I needed to be accepted to nursing school. Several other refugees from the revolution and I were herded into the lab to take the test standing at gummy black counters amid sinks and Bunsen burners. The professor, looking harassed, began handing out the tests. At first he didn't notice little Maya sleeping in her low-profile front pack resting on my chest. When he reached me, though, he looked at both of us with an unpleasant, this-is-the-last-straw look and said, "You can't have a baby in here." I think he expected me to leave. What he didn't realize was that my whole plan for the survival of the species depended on my taking this exam, and that my years as a Weatherman had completely obliterated any intimidating posture a graying community college professor might have been able to adopt. "No, I need to take this test, and look, she is sound asleep. Thanks," I said, taking a copy of the test out of his hands. He harrumphed and passed on to become a vanishing speed bump on my road to employment.

In Louisa's day, survival was more like a high-wire act than a road. Safety nets were uncommon and there were so many ways to fall – lack of money, lack of health, lack of social acceptability. Louisa and her family faced all three, knowing they had no one but each other to rely on.* Or really, knowing that they had no one but Louisa to rely on. Louisa, the tall, dark, second of four daughters, somehow came to believe that she alone was, had to be, her entire family's primary and eternal source of strength and income.

Perhaps it was her impatience, as she shouldered her way into adulthood. She sometimes gave the impression of being the kind of person who was easily annoyed in the presence of people slower witted or clumsier than she. Perhaps she deeply, secretly hated her father and this was a way to compete and win, spectacularly, against him. Perhaps being the provider gave her a sense of power over her parents and sisters that she found addictive. Perhaps she was showing off to Emerson. There are hints of these dynamics, as well as others, in her writing. However, as forensic psychoanalysis is a suspect game, sometimes couched in disagreeable unkindness, I will abstain and instead let Louisa speak for herself. In her twenty-third birthday letter to her father, Louisa described herself in a long, tumbling, ungrammatical, trying-to-say-it-all-in-a-single-breath sentence:

> I was a crass crying brown baby, bawling at the disagreeable old world where on a dismal November day I found myself, & began my long fight first for a proper quantity of water for my ablutions which was unlawfully withheld from me, then for my rightful food which was denied till I nearly

---

* At the time I took the chemistry class, I was semi-legally collecting both food stamps and unemployment; neither of these cushions was available in the 1850s.

went out of the world I disliked so much, but pork & oysters held me back & supported by these spiritual strengtheners I scrambled up to childhood, out of which after often losing my small self & wandering forlornly thro years of infant troubles & cares, I fell with a crash into girlhood & continued falling over fences, out of trees, up hill & down stairs tumbling from one year to another till strengthened by such violent exercise the topsey turvey girl shot up into a topsey turvey woman who now twenty three years after sits big brown & brave, crying, not because she has come into the world but because she must go out of it before she has done half she wants to, & because its such hard work to keep sunshiny & cheerful when life looks gloomy & full of troubles, but as the brown baby fought through its small trials so the brown woman will fight thro her big ones & come out I hope queen of herself tho not of the world.

Louisa's plan was to accomplish something good in the world *and* take care of herself and her family. It would have been a bold plan for a nineteenth-century man and was a definite stretch for a woman. "Though an Alcott, I *can* support myself," she wrote in a slightly competitive letter to her father on their joint birthday in 1856. She wrote to a friend, with equal parts honesty and irony, "As money is the end and aim of my mercenary existence, I scribble away & pocket the cash with a thankful heart."

At the same time, she loved dancing and parties and fun. Her letters from this period are cheerful and full of funny stories about plays, dances, costume parties, visits to museums, and walks on Boston Common. She was being marginally assisted by her wealthier May cousins, who gave her hand-me-downs, play tickets, dinner invitations, and opportunities to meet people in need of governesses or companions. In 1856 she wrote to Anna after attending the opera *Norma*, "I cried and *enjoyed* my soul almost out of my body with the music." *Norma*, by Bellini, is an extravagant tale of faithless men, sisterhood, war, revenge, final admissions of love and then, naturally, death. The story was perfectly attuned to Louisa's romantic and classics-drenched imagination.

Hard worker though she was, Louisa never lost the ability to take a vacation. As an adult, she took many summers off, playing on New England beaches and picnicking in its forests. She spent several summers in Walpole, New Hampshire, at the invitation of a cousin, writing in her journal, "Up at five, and had a lovely run in the ravine, seeing the woods wake. . . . Busy and happy times as we settle in the little house in the lane near by my dear ravine – plays, picnics, pleasant people, and good neighbors. Fanny Kemble* came up, Mrs. Kirkland and others, and Dr. Bellows the gayest of the gay." Back in Boston, she wrote to sister Anna that she planned to go to a play over the weekend: "Let's be merry while we may, for tomorrow is Monday, and the weekly grind begins again." *Plus ça change. . . .*

When Louisa arrived in Boston, she stayed variously with cousins or employers or in attic space in a boarding-house. Some days she wanted nothing more than good, honest work, and some days nothing short of glitzy fame and fortune would do. She continued her country habits of walking and running, boasting in her journal, "Walked from C[oncord] to B[oston] one day, twenty miles, in five hours, and went to a party in the evening. Not very tired. Well done for a vegetable production!" She wrote letters home, sent gifts and money to her mother, father, and sisters, and formed opinions of life and her place in it that kept her in good stead for the rest of her life.

At twenty-four, she wrote, "I love luxury, but freedom and independence better." To her, freedom and independence meant having the ability and the opportunity to do the right thing. She rejected any freedom that came with the price tag of financial

---

* Fanny Kemble, one of the most famous actresses of her day, wrote after the birth of her daughter, "Though a baby is not an 'occupation,' it is an absolute hindrance to everything that can be called so." I imagine Louisa enjoyed the chance to chat with a successful actress who had a sense of humor.

dependence on a man. Neither did she want her independence to be without meaning, focus, and purpose.

Much later, when she was in her early fifties, she noted in her journal "Freedom was always my longing, but I have never had it." She sounds a bit crotchety and sorry for herself here, perhaps because she had recently realized that her health problems were going to prevent her from going back to Europe to live the bohemian artist's life that her youngest sister May was so ecstatically inviting her from Paris to come share.

※ ☞ ※ ☞ ※

Louisa would ardently wish to be nothing more than a kind, quiet, virtuous citizen, but then all of a sudden she just as ardently wanted to be noticed, applauded, and lionized. She wrote to a friend that she had a "strong liking for people who don't think much of themselves." Down-home, straightforward, taciturn New Englanders were just her style. In *Work*, Louisa's barely fictionalized story of her twenties, her heroine Christie Devon is polite, hardworking, always learning. But then the other Louisa would emerge, standing up for her principles at an antislavery rally, or boasting at a party that "I'll be famous yet!" when she was being teased about being an authoress. Fictional Christie, her eyes ablaze, would suddenly do the same, vigorously defending a coworker unjustly fired for being a "fallen woman," or eloquently turning down a marriage proposal from a rich bounder.

The binding of the first edition of *Work* was decorated with a picture of a bumblebee busily harvesting pollen from the open trumpets of a morning-glory vine. The drawing is graced with a quote from Emerson's English friend Thomas Carlyle,* "An endless significance lies in work; in idleness alone is there perpetual

---

* Carlyle, although he became quite anti-democratic and authoritarian in his old age (like Wordsworth), was initially interesting to the transcendentalists for his anti-industrialist and life-enhancing stance. Carlyle once described Bronson as a "Yankee Don Quixote."

despair." Christie Devon, an orphan (in her fiction, Louisa frequently dealt with the difficulties of parents, particularly fathers, by making them dead or absent) expresses this belief over and over, as she tries out one occupation after another, refusing to become just another farm wife. It is a kind of female *Pilgrim's Progress*, a favorite book of both Louisa and her father. Or perhaps a female *Tom Jones*, but without the never-ending sex. *Work* wastes no time in plunging directly to Louisa's central point: women have a right to do meaningful work, and they will live wretched lives and die dreadful deaths if they don't obtain it. Suicide is close to the surface in the early chapters. So is slavery. So are various debilitating and frightening psychiatric disorders. Louisa was closer to Charlotte Brontë's world than Jane Austen's.

Charlotte Brontë, not Jane Austen, was one of Louisa's favorite authors. It is possible that Louisa never read Austen's delicious comedies and insightful social commentary. Emerson, who guided much of Louisa's reading and taste, saw nothing to recommend in Austen's books, writing in his journal in 1861:

> I am at a loss to understand why people hold Miss Austen's novels at so high a rate, which seem to me vulgar in tone, sterile in invention, imprisoned in the wretched conventions of English society, without genius, wit, or knowledge of the world. Never was life so pinched & narrow. The one problem in the mind of the writer in both the stories I have read, "Persuasion" and "Pride and Prejudice," is marriageableness, all that interests any character introduced is still this one, Has he or she money to marry with, & conditions conforming? 'Tis "the nympholesy of a fond despair," say rather, of an English boarding-house. Suicide is more respectable.

Brontë's *Jane Eyre*, on the other hand, was among Louisa's favorite books. In 1855 Charlotte Brontë died at age thirty-nine during a difficult childbirth that was complicated by tuberculosis. Her friend, the novelist Elizabeth Gaskell, wrote a wildly popular, contemporary biography of her. When it came out in 1857, Louisa read it eagerly.

Charlotte Brontë's life must have struck many familiar chords with Louisa: the family of sisters, the illnesses and death, the authorial endeavors, the grinding poverty. She wrote in her journal on a June day in 1857, "Wonder if I shall ever be famous enough for people to care to read my story and struggles. I can't be C[harlotte] B[rontë], but I may do a little something yet." Louisa's spunky American faith in herself shines off the page. In her fiction, she clearly admired Brontë's passionate heart, but in the end, she couldn't share Brontë's ultimately (and understandably) class-ridden pessimism.

Louisa was forever marked by her parents' declination toward reform. Her father fought the incivilities of progress with words of kindness, generosity, equality, and utopia. Her mother fought personal poverty and despair by running an employment and social service agency for working women (in those days called, interestingly enough, an "intelligence office") and by taking in sick and homeless women and children.* This continual background force steered the rudder and filled the sails of Louisa's life.

But Louisa didn't want to be just like her parents. Who does? Bronson's incompetence put a burden on his wife and children. Her mother's choices left her exhausted before her time. In her twenties, Louisa did judge her parents, but rather than communicate that judgment on to them, as I and many of my 1960s comrades rushed to do (the word "pigs" comes to mind, along with our humorous belief that no one over thirty could be trusted), Louisa simply used her opinions to shape a different life for herself – up to a point.

秘霏秘霏秘

---

* It was one of Abba's homeless families that brought scarlet fever into the Alcott household; most Alcott biographers attribute the death of Elizabeth (the third daughter) to this virus.

The liveliest of Louisa's letters and journal entries spring from her two yearlong trips to Europe in 1865–66 and 1870–71 and on a shorter trip to New York City in 1875. It is tempting to draw the conclusion that her life became more enjoyable the further she got from her parents and from Concord, but being such a loyal daughter, she would likely demur.

Arriving in England by ship in 1865, Louisa had many of the same thoughts Americans before and after her have had: English weather was "abominable." It didn't matter, though, as neither fog nor rain could obscure the delights of literary London. "I felt as if I'd got into a novel while going about in the places I'd read so much of." Her guide later wrote to his wife about Louisa's "enthusiasm and appreciation of drollery." He commented favorably on her as "a jolly Yankee girl, full of old Nick [the devil] and thoroughly posted on English literature, so that it is great fun to take her about, as she appreciates all the literary associations." Louisa returned the favor, writing him into a story she published about Dickens's London.

She enjoyed the English countryside too, finding it interestingly different from the Massachusetts landscape. The hurried and harried American lifestyle was apparently well entrenched by the 1860s, as Louisa wrote:

Everything [in England] was so unyankee, so quiet and well kept. Each field seemed to have been newly weeded, each road freshly rolled, each garden just put in order, and each house newly scrubbed from garret to cellar. . . . Grass was never so green, wheat so deeply golden, woods so dark, or rivers bluer than those I saw under an April like sky, grey and misty one hour, serene and sunny the next; or black with a sweeping shower. Nothing was abrupt, nobody in a hurry, and nowhere do you see the desperately go ahead style of life that we have. The very cows in America look fast. . . . This slow going nation are very interesting, and I find things extremely soothing to my nerves, so I've nothing to do but fold my hands and let myself be made comfortable.

Even in London, she loved the open spaces of the parks as much as she loved Hampton Court, the Crystal Palace, and the British Museum. "None were lovelier to me than the old farmhouse with the thatched roof, the common yellow gorse, larks going up in the morning, nightingales at night, hawthorn everywhere and Richmond Park full of deer close by." On her second trip, in Italy, she commented several times that "art tires, Nature never."

Reading the letters and journal entries from these two trips is like watching a rose open to the morning sun. We can feel frost melting, dew evaporating, and see her petals flaring to embrace a cheerful blue sky. Even though she diligently writes home about how much she misses her parents, even though she complains at times about money or her health or her companions, she is clearly enjoying a freer, happier life in Europe than in Concord.*

In November and December 1865, she had an intense romantic interlude with Ladislas Weisneiwsky, a twenty-year-old Polish soldier, who became, three years later, half of her model for charming Laurie in *Little Women*. The two met in Switzerland, where they took long walks and exchanged battlefield stories. He joined her later for two weeks in Paris, where they stayed on the rue de Rivoli. Why her romance with Laddie, as she called him, proceeded no further is not for us to know. It must have been something other than the difference in their ages. Louisa had just turned thirty-three, but she was still five years younger than her sister May was when, in 1878, she married Ernest Nieriker. In his twenties, Nieriker was as much his bride's junior as Laddie was Louisa's.

Her second trip to Europe kicked off in 1870 just after the publication of *An Old-Fashioned Girl*. It was selling well, adding to the revenue still pouring in from *Little Women*, which had

---

* One aspect of European travel she does not comment on is the food. She wasn't raised to appreciate food and that never changed.

been published two years earlier. On the train going down to New York to catch the boat, a boy was selling *An Old-Fashioned Girl* car to car.

> [The] trainboy . . . put it into my lap; and when I said I didn't care for it, exclaimed with surprise, – "Bully book, ma'am! Sell a lot, better have it." . . . [Later] On the steamer little girls had it, and came in a party to call on me, very seasick in my berth, done up like a mummy.

This second trip was her triumphant reward for writing what the public wanted to read. Louisa shared her success with her youngest sister May, and their friend Alice Bartlett. Louisa and May's diaries and letters are full of "charming weeks in Brittany" and "splendid journey over the Alps and Maggiore by moonlight." In Lugano, in southern Switzerland, their hotel room backed onto the opera house. They were able to see the stage from their window and watched the last two acts of *La Traviata* in their nightgowns, feeling remarkably blessed to hear and see great opera in such comfortable attire.

However, all was not peaches and cream. The Franco-Prussian War dogged them at intervals,* and the two months they spent in Rome saw endless rain and flooding. (Margaret Fuller had complained of the same torrential storms during her winter in Rome some twenty years earlier.) However, having the Tiber spill its banks and make lakes of the piazzas was not without its compensations for a people-watcher like Louisa.

> Being a Goth and a Vandal, I enjoy it [watching the flood activity] more than chilly galleries or mouldy pictures. It thrills me more to see one live man work like a Trojan to

---

* Louisa became quite irritated at Napoleon. "I don't wonder his people curse him after he got them into such a war, & then slipt out like a coward. Hope his ills will increase, & every inch of him will suffer for such a shameful act." She had no patience for the French people either, as they vacillated between wanting the Republic and wishing for a return of the monarchy.

save suffering women and babies, than to sit hours before a Dying Gladiator who has been gasping for centuries in immortal marble. It's sad, but I can't help it.

The trip ended on a sorrowful note, with news from home of the death of Anna's husband John. After the condolences were conveyed, Louisa, trying to stay dry in Rome, immediately began writing *Little Men* "for the good of the two dear little men now left to my care, for long ago I promised to try & fill John's place if they were left fatherless." Perhaps, and this is the tricky thing about people like Louisa, it wasn't a uniformly down-note after all, as it gave her new reasons to work, new people to serve, and more burdens to bear, either quietly or not, as the spirit moved.

February 5, 1888

Dear Kit,

I am reluctantly getting accustomed to the idea that the twenty-first century has seemingly unrestricted access to my journal and letters. However, my declining health tells me that this additional loss of worldly privacy is not a trauma I will have to bear for long. I do hope you are correct that this exposure will be of benefit to the inhabitants of your time zone. I am not naïve: I know as well as anyone that risk & discomfort go hand in hand in many worthy collaborations.

Thank you for reminding me of my twenties. They were fun, despite my precarious finances & occupational uncertainty. I learned about the work of writing in that decade – how to deal with publishers, the pitfalls of contracts & copyrights, all the details that are part & parcel of being a professional. I never wanted to be an amateur anything. I was willing to pull whatever strings I could lay my hands on to get my work in front of a publisher. My first book, those little stories I had told to Ellen Emerson & wrote up as Flower Fables, *was published only because of Mr. Emerson's connections & Miss Stevens's being willing to pay for the printing. Now, that was good pay for all the sewing I did for her!*

I must note, though, that Mr. Emerson, god of my life though he has been, never did anything further to encourage my writing career. He never reviewed any of my books or specifically commented on the worth of what I was wrestling onto the page. Perhaps I was always a child to him. In some ways, he treated everyone as a child – at least in the sense that he always held himself aloof & distant from everyone, even Mrs. Emerson. He was friendly & approachable, but you always got a funny sense that the part of him he let you approach was not his main part.

Once he said that people were like round balls, globes that roll around making contact with one another only at one tiny point, leaving all the rest of their surfaces untouchable and private. I know this is bad gossip, but Mrs. Emerson once complained to Mother that Mr. Emerson defended his lack of affectionate gestures to her by saying he was a "photometer" not a stove: he could measure light but not radiate heat. I didn't mind, though. Better that, I think, than never to have known him at all.

I did occasionally fall very low in those first Boston days. But it was nothing compared to my unhappy state these days. At least then I was healthy. How can any healthy person ever be miserable?

From my sickbed today I would tell every healthy twenty-year-old out there to think carefully about their choices, but not so carefully as to never jump out of the gate. If you start out life aiming for a safe middle ground, then where will you be, thirty years later, when a safe middle ground is all you have the energy left for? It is well worth taking a few chances to find your truth. Believe me, any truth worth finding is not just lying there, like an abandoned shell on the beach, winking up at any Sunday afternoon stroller who happens by. Besides, a little hit-&-miss is part of the game. Without acting, I think we are not fully alive.

Ah yes, Europe . . . those trips were such a pleasure! And dear May found her greatest success there, & her heart's true love too. I did so want to make one more trip, but it will never happen. It's almost as nice, though, certainly quieter, to imagine it & write it into Diana & Persis.

I am curious about the name Kit. I have known some Kittys in my day. I presume it is a nickname. Is it Katherine?

I think our next stop is nursing, am I correct? You say you had to go to college to become a nurse? I hope Miss Nightingale's book was first on your reading list. I certainly gained a great deal from it.

With pillows plumped, I am alertly yours,
Louisa

PS: Thank you so much for not speculating or probing into my affairs with dear Laddie. I would not allow it, even for this project. I am pleased to know – I hope this is true – that you people in the future have not unearthed any of my more serious marriage-related adventures. Some secrets I will take to my Sleepy Hollow grave. I'll leave the money to the living, but the feelings come along with me.

Doing Good: Nursing

*One of the best methods of fitting oneself to be a nurse in a hospital,
is to be a patient there. For then only can one wholly realize
what the men suffer and sigh for; how acts of kindness touch
and win; how much or little we are to those about us . . . .*
Louisa May Alcott, from *Hospital Sketches*, 1863

February 7, 2006

Dear Louisa,

I am so glad you enjoyed the European memories. I love Europe
as well, for the same two reasons as you – literary history and
scenery. I wish I could make the kind of leisurely, yearlong trips
that were the style in your day. I'm not sure I would like the risk
and discomfort of the Atlantic steamer crossings though; it sounds
as if you were seasick most of the time. The habit today, for those
who do travel, is to go by airplane, which is what we call a machine
similar to what Emerson once imagined as a balloon with a rudder
(well, not really, but at least they are both objects to carry people
through the air).

I wish you could see what our wonderful Earth looks like from
forty thousand feet above the surface, which is where our airplanes
travel. The unbelievably beautiful views would take your breath
away. The clouds pile spectacularly all around, the horizon hints
at infinity, and the ground below looks like stiff, folded Renaissance
drapery all strewn with twinkling gemstones. Airplanes go very
fast and get us across the Atlantic in less than a day. That's the

good part. The bad part is that most of us have jobs that allow only one or two weeks of vacation at a time.

I visited our elder daughter Maya when she was teaching in Russia. It was not like Europe – the serfdom of the nineteenth century may be gone but terrible poverty and corruption remain. You would have admired her fellow teachers who were such wonderful women, bravely raising their families under difficult conditions of food shortages, crumbling buildings, corrupt politicians, and uncertain water and fuel sources. Their cheerfulness, generosity, and persistence humbled me. It was a privilege to meet them.

One night, the head teacher hosted a dinner party in her tiny apartment. Immediately upon arriving, we sat down at the dining table. The dining room and living room were the same room, and all the furniture had to be cleared out to expand the table large enough to fit eight of us. We sat on simple backless wooden stools crammed so close to the walls that no one could get up without unseating an adjacent companion.

We were treated to many, many homemade-vodka toasts and a table crowded with their very best rabbit, carrots, potatoes, fish, cucumbers, and cabbage. The Russian custom is that one's entire glass must be drained after each toast. There were songs, jokes, and much laughter, Maya translating for me as simultaneously as possible. They wanted to talk about Pushkin and were taken aback at how little Maya or I knew of his rebellious, romantic life. He was their Keats, Shelley, and Byron all rolled into one.

The meal was served family style more or less all at once, with each of us having a small saucer-sized plate to fill and refill from serving bowls lining the center of the table. We ended with a delicious and celebratory honey torte, made by Ludmilla, a small, blond woman, the quietest of the teachers. She gave me the recipe:

Mix 3 tablespoons honey and 1 cup granulated sugar together and warm in stove. Add 4 whole eggs, $1^1/_2$ teaspoons baking soda and 2 cups flour. Mix all into a rectangular baking pan and cook for a while in a medium oven. When cooked, slice two or three layers horizontally, and pile back on top of each other, alternating with sour cream and sugar. Decorate with candied fruits or fresh flowers or berries.

When I tried this at home, it was not as good as I remembered. It wasn't until I ate it that I realized it contained no oil or butter or milk. A frugal confection; your father might even have approved.

But yes, it is time for nursing, and I am glad to get there as well. It has become an interestingly anomalous profession these days. On the one hand, it is unionized; nurses are workers represented by collective contracts just as if they were factory workers. On the other hand, it is the same indispensable, professional, and honorable work as Miss Nightingale always knew it would someday become. Nurses today have gradually taken on many tasks only physicians used to perform. There was a big fight some decades ago about whether or not nurses could use stethoscopes. (As you may know, stethoscopes were invented by a French doctor in Brittany in 1816.) Today they can.

I became a nurse because I refused to make my living in a business that profited from imperialism or racism (thereby eliminating working for any large American corporation). Health care in some guise seemed a reasonable option and nursing an easy entry point. I had thoughts of working in Vietnam, not to nurse American soldiers, but to take care of the poor Vietnamese who had suffered so much from American guns and bombs.

Today, nursing is sometimes a respected profession and sometimes it is not. It is reasonably well paid, but it won't make you rich. Nursing will always entail a lot of stand-up physical work. Sadly, it doesn't often attract intelligent people anymore. Or, if people start out as nurses, they get tired after ten or fifteen years and change occupations just when they've become reliably good at it. That's what happened to me.

It got too expensive in the United States about thirty years ago to keep people in hospitals for long periods of time. There are only three reasons why a person stays in a hospital nowadays: to have a baby (which is a bogus reason for most deliveries), for major surgery that requires special machines and life-sustaining nursing care, or for non-surgery-related, life-sustaining nursing care. Hospital business managers know that their beds are filled primarily because of the quality of their surgeons and the quality of their nurses. So you would think they would be equally generous to both. But no, they treat the surgeons far better than the nurses because of the way bills are paid for health services.

Surgeons bring in patients and bill directly for their work, but nursing care is not billed directly. It is treated like maid service in a hotel. Hospital managers are always trying to figure out ways to reduce nurse staffing; they see nursing care as a cost, not as a chargeable service or a revenue producer. Do you think the fact that most surgeons and hospital administrators are men and most nurses are women might weigh in here? And doesn't it seem a little backward to have the billing methodology determine our health care priorities and systems? But enough ranting. No reason to ask you to borrow troubles from the future.

I guess there's always something, isn't there?

Trying to keep the lamp lit,
Kit

PS: You are right not to tell me anything you don't want everyone to know. Secrets are never safe with me.

NIGHTINGALE'S NOTES
NAKED YOUNG MEN · HOSPITAL HUMOR
THE PRIVILEGE OF NURSING

Miss Florence Nightingale published her *Notes on Nursing: What It Is and What It Is Not* in 1859. She was then thirty-nine years old, twelve years older than Louisa and a veteran of the nightmare of the Crimea, one of Queen Victoria's more wretched wars. When Nightingale reached the army hospital at Scutari, Turkey, in February 1855, the death rate in the hospital was 42.7 percent. Six months later, she had slashed that to 2.2 percent, thanks to her theories about fresh air, clean linens, sensible sanitation, and decent food; her administrative genius; her own army of thirty-seven handpicked, motivated, and personally trained nurses; and a portion of the Nightingale family fortune. The soldiers, she figured out, had not been dying from their war wounds, but from malnutrition, exposure, dysentery, cholera, typhus, and scurvy. Those were all problems that organization, supplies, and nursing care – not surgical care – could remedy. She came back to London in July 1856, ill in body but vibrating with reforming ideas and powerful intentions.

Nursing, like doctoring, thrives in wartime. Horrific challenges brought on by innovative weaponry, new tactics, and sheer volume create opportunities to invent new ways to take care of damaged bodies. Some ideas work out well, like ether and clean sheets, and others – like treating typhoid fever with mercury – not so well. Nightingale was so appalled at the stupidity and ignorance that passed for military medicine that she spent the rest of her long life (she died in 1910) browbeating the medical establishment into accepting sweeping administrative, technical, and staffing reforms. "She would think of nothing but how to satisfy that singular craving of hers to be *doing* something," wrote Lytton Strachey, who included her with three men in his influential *Eminent Victorians*. Like many men, Strachey found it a bit disturbing that a woman would want to *do* something.

Nightingale established basic standards for sanitation, staff training, and hospital architecture that have since been accepted worldwide. It took endless months of argument, even reaching into Parliament, to convince the military that it was a good idea to wash sheets in hot water and vent the privies away from the patient wards. Nightingale, who took to mathematics with the ease of a genius, invented new ways to analyze epidemiological data and designed new types of pictorial graphs (which are in use today by epidemiologists and statisticians) to get her points across to the political dunderheads.

Louisa devoured *Notes on Nursing*. She also had practical experience of her own, nursing her sister Lizzie through her heartbreaking illness. Nursing, thought Louisa, could be a way to contribute her bit to the war to end slavery. She was as qualified as the best, so why not? But nursing was not the only door she was trying to open. She was also in preliminary negotiations to go to Port Royal in South Carolina to teach at a school for escaped slaves.

The teaching deal fell through. She was rejected because of a strict rule requiring that applicants be married women over forty. Later, when she returned from nursing, too ill to ever take up such physically demanding work again, she tried once more, reopening her discussions with Port Royal, petitioning, "I should like of all things to go South & help the blacks as I am no longer allowed to nurse the whites. The former seems the greater work, & would be most interesting to me. I offered to go as a teacher on one of the Islands but Mr. Philbrey objected because I had no natural protector to go with me, so I was obliged to give that up."

It wasn't Louisa's style to warm the abolitionist bench. She wanted to be out in the field. In September 1859, from Boston, she wrote in her journal, "I can't fight, but I can nurse." If the righteous were going to battle, she wanted to be there. In October 1862 she reported, "War news bad. Anxious faces, beating hearts & busy minds. I like the stir in the air, & long for battle like a warhorse when he smells powder. The blood of the Mays is up!"

The Revolutionary War lineage on her mother's side was always strong and warm in her body. In November 1862, she wrote, "30 years old. Decided to go to Washington as a nurse if I could find a place. Help needed, and I love nursing, and *must* let out my pent-up energy in some new way. . . . A solemn time, but I'm glad to live in it, & am sure it will do me good whether I come out alive or dead."

Leaving home to go to Boston by herself had been a huge step, but it was territory known to the family and a life not all that alien from Concord. It wasn't enough for Louisa. Soon she was tired, not of the poverty and the struggle but of the routine and the lack of adventure. In December 1856 she went to a lecture on courage and commented, "Thought I needed it, being rather tired of living like a spider – spinning out my brains for money." She wanted something more physical, more visibly productive, and more connected to the bigger sweep of human activity – all of which were unusual aspirations for a nineteenth-century girl to articulate.

Margaret Fuller, who boarded with the Emersons for a while, taking part in Louisa's childhood Concord neighborhood, had expressed similar yearnings and nontraditional urges. Like Louisa, she wanted to do things and be somebody. "'Tis an evil lot," Margaret wrote, "to have a man's ambition and a woman's heart," adding, "I feel within myself an immense power, but I cannot bring it out." It wasn't until Margaret found herself in the Italian struggle for independence and unity that she discovered her power away from the printed page.

❋ ❦ ❋ ❦ ❋

Louisa set her own adventurous ball rolling by inquiring into the process for becoming a nurse at a Union army hospital. Established by Dorothea Dix, the requirements for Civil War nursing covered age (not too young), gender (had to be female), marital status (had to be married) and moral character (had to be high). Fighting the bureaucracy every step of the way, Louisa managed to finesse the marital status problem by being of the right age and highly moral. After all, the Union needed nurses.

Her mother's May relatives gave her some sundry and treat money for herself and her patients. After several days' journey by rail and boat, she arrived in wartime Washington in early winter 1862. The town was awash in mud, construction, soldiers, dysentery, and confusion. "Began my new life by seeing a poor man die at dawn, and sitting all day between a boy with pneumonia & a man shot through the lungs. A strange day, but I did my best. . . ."

Some cultural challenges to nursing haven't changed since Nightingale, such as how to prepare young women to take care of naked, prone young men. Louisa had no preparation at all. Poor Louisa couldn't even find the words to describe her first such experience. As the Fredericksburg wounded began to pour into the hospital, her head nurse firmly told her to take off their clothes and begin washing them. "If she had requested me to . . . dance a hornpipe on the stove funnel, I should have been less staggered; but to scrub some dozen lords of creation at a moment's notice was really – really –" It may have been the only time her pen failed her.

Writing to a nurse friend she explains, "Having no brothers and a womanly man for a father I find myself rather staggered by some of the performances around me. . . ." Gradually, she developed a mental approach that turned all her patients into "boys," so she could treat them without getting all muddled up in sexual confusion. For nurses of my generation, our training included such helpful tips as "Don't make eye contact" or "If things seem awkward, use a cold washcloth."

Hospital humor is a defense mechanism that hasn't changed much over the years. All experienced nurses and physicians recognize the value of dark humor as a defense against stress and depression. Neophytes are usually indignant and highly unamused when they first hear it, but that's only because they are still unaware of the enormous doses of pain and death that are out there waiting for them on a daily basis. It doesn't take long to appreciate the value of a chuckle or two to counter the unrelenting awfulness of concentrated human suffering. Louisa was a quick learner. Her short stint as a war nurse – only two months – gave her enough insight to comfortably include hospital humor in her story called "My Contraband." In this scene the physician is asking the nurse to go upstairs to help with a dying Confederate soldier. "When can you go up?" he asks her.

"As soon as Tom is laid out, Skinner moved, Haywood washed, Marble dressed, Charley rubbed, Downs taken up, Upham laid down, and the whole forty fed."

We both laughed, though the Doctor was on his way to the deadhouse and I held a shroud in my lap. But in a hospital one learns that cheerfulness is one's salvation; for, in an atmosphere of suffering and death, heaviness of heart would soon paralyze usefulness of hand, if the blessed gift of smiles had been denied us.

Within hours of Louisa's arrival, her hospital, a wreck of a building, was hit with casualties from Fredericksburg, the Union's worst battlefield loss so far. Inundated with dying men, Louisa felt like "an energetic fly in a very large cobweb." Daily life at the hospital started early and cold, went long and hard, and ended exhausted and dirty. There was so little she could do, and it was endlessly frustrating to see that there was so much to be done.

Owing to the stupidity of that mysterious 'somebody' who does all the damage in the world, the windows had been carefully nailed down above. . . . I had suggested a summary smashing of a few panes here and there. . . .

Bandages had to be washed and reused; many were made from old shirts and pants. Coal fires had to be fed. There were medication rounds. The food – dreadful mealy bread, horrible rotting meat, and weak coffee – was passed around. In addition to the nurses, patients were comforted and helped by ambulatory patients, who, as soon as they were able to get out of bed, were pressed into service as attendants to their prone comrades. Louisa had a strong opinion about this system:

Constant complaints were being made of incompetent attendants, and some dozen women did double duty, that then were blamed for breaking down. If any hospital director fancies this is a good and economical arrangement, allow one used up nurse to tell him it isn't. . . .

Because nurses have the broadest view of how a patient is being cared for and how the hospital is being managed, they are more likely than anyone to see systemic glitches and failures. Louisa quickly became irate at the shoddy state of affairs she observed around her. She visited another, better-run facility across town:

> As I watched the proceedings, I recalled my own tribulations, and contrasted the two hospitals in a way that would have caused my summary dismissal, could it have been reported at headquarters. Here, order, method, common sense and liberality seemed to rule in a style that did one's heart good to see; at the Hurly burly Hotel [as she called her hospital], disorder, discomfort, bad management, and no visible head, reduced things to a condition which I despair of describing. The circumlocution fashion prevailed, forms and fusses tormented our souls, and unnecessary strictness in one place was counterbalanced by unpardonable laxity in another.

She went on to describe a string of frustrating human and organizational snafus as she tried to get supplies from the pharmacy to her patients. In the Crimea, Florence Nightingale had to break open locked cabinets against military orders to find blankets for her patients. Any nurse today would have the same kind of story to tell. Bending, or sometimes breaking, the bureaucracy to benefit one's patients is one of the most valuable of nursing skills.

⁂

The battle of Fredericksburg raged over the day of December 13, 1862,* as Union General Burnside attacked the well-entrenched Confederate forces of Generals Lee and Jackson. Union and Con-

---

* Fredericksburg came just three months after Antietam, where twenty-three thousand other Americans had been killed in just one day, totalling over half of all American deaths in Vietnam. Margaret Fuller's brother Arthur was killed at Fredericksburg.

federate soldiers killed or wounded numbered eighteen thousand between them, with Union losses more than double the Confederacy's. A Confederate officer who directed artillery fire wrote in his diary about riding across the Fredericksburg battlefield after the fighting ended. "Enjoyed the sight of hundreds of dead Yankees. Saw much of the work I had done in the way of severed limbs, decapitated bodies, and mutilated remains of all kinds. Doing my soul good. Would that the whole Northern Army were as such & I had my hand in it."

Some of the 9,600 soldiers whose mutilations were deemed not fatal were sent to Louisa's Hurly burly Hotel. The physical plant was reminiscent of what Nightingale had faced at Scutari: foul air, dreadful plumbing, rats and bugs, damp everywhere – a bacterial paradise. The doctors focused on the war injuries with their primitive surgical interventions. Meanwhile, comforted by nurses, the patients died from blood loss, infection, and other medical causes. Not all the nurses were ministering angels, however. Louisa's sharp eye for detail, which would shortly improve her authorial income, quickly indentified the less than moral specimens. She saw some pilfer the soldiers' belongings and heard others convince dying men to make out quickie wills to their own benefit.*

Dorothea Dix and Clara Barton are the names we remember as the founders of nursing in America. Both were instrumental in developing and managing the corps of nurses who worked on the Union side during the Civil War. (Clara Barton went on to found the American Red Cross.) Louisa met Dorothea Dix and found her, as many did, a dragon-lady of the first degree. Dix had the same singleness of purpose, unbending will, and unshakable confidence in her own opinions as did Nightingale. Louisa wrote, and later crossed out, in her journal "No one likes her [Dix] & I don't wonder." Miss Dix was evidently one of those people who aren't necessarily fun to be around, but who do get things done. She

---

* Beer was a plentiful ration among all hospital staff, but likely not to blame for the nurses' sloppy ethics.

spent some time at Louisa's hospital and visited her as she lay
feverish with typhoid, bringing tea, wine, and a Bible for her
delirious journey home.

Dorothea Dix had already spent twenty years reforming America's treatment of prisoners and the mentally ill when the Civil War
broke out. At age fifty-nine, she talked the Union army into giving
her an unpaid position managing all women nurses working in
army hospitals. She invented the job as she went along, handling
recruiting and on-the-job-training as well as all management and
administration, including (like Nightingale) drumming up supplies from private sources when the government failed to provide
them. After the war, she returned to her work with the mentally ill.

Louisa dived right into the work and rhythm of her hospital.
She relished being present and active in such a heightened environment. By not pretending to know things, she learned a great
deal. She quickly made herself useful to the physicians, the
patients, and her fellow nurses. One of the physicians was a shy,
hardworking Quaker doctor named John Winslow. Winslow
made tentative romantic advances toward her, which she quickly
rejected. "He comes often to our room with books, asks me to his
(where I don't go,) & takes me to walk now & then. Quotes Browning copiously, is given to confidences in the twilight. . . ." That
wasn't what she was there for.

When Louisa graduated to night duty* she spent her days
sightseeing in wartime Washington.

Another of my few rambles took me to the Senate Chamber, hoping to hear and see if this large machine was run
any better than some small ones I knew of. I was too late,
and found the Speaker's chair occupied by a colored gentleman of ten; while two others were on their legs, having a
hot debate on the cornball question, as they gathered the

---

* In my nursing days, it worked the opposite: the least experienced nurses were
given the night shift.

waste paper strewed about the floor into bags; and several white members played leap-frog over the desks. . . . Finding the coast clear, I likewise gamboled up and down; . . . sat in Sumner's chair, and cudgeled an imaginary Brooks within an inch of his life. . . ."

She wrote a cheerful letter to Henry James's brother Wilkie, who was serving as an officer in the Union Army's first and most famous black regiment, the Massachusetts 54th. She invited him to be sure to come to her hospital if he ever needed care and said she would take care of him like nobody's business. Several months later, half of the 54th was wiped out in a brave but unsuccessful attack on Fort Wagner in the Charleston harbor. Wilkie went home with multiple gunshot wounds; Louisa, convalescing herself, knitted him a blanket.

Louisa liked her night shifts, as they left her "time for a morning run which is what I need to keep well, for bad air, food, water, work & watching are getting to be too much for me. I trot up & down the streets in all directions, some times to the Heights, then half way to Washington, again to the hill over which the long trains of army wagons are constantly vanishing & ambulances appearing. That way the fighting lies, & I long to follow."

※ ※ ※ ※ ※

Nursing in the nineteenth century, reflecting contemporary belief, had a very different approach to death than we have today. I was taught that it was kinder to patients, and to families, to pretend that death was not in the cards. We were supposed to hide, at all costs, our inability to vanquish death. When I was in nursing school, a few progressives like Elisabeth Kübler-Ross* were just beginning, to say that it wasn't all bad to admit to patients that they were dying.

---

* Her groundbreaking *On Death and Dying* was published in 1969. I visited Cicely Saunders's pioneering St. Christopher's Hospice in London during my mid-1970s nursing training and was greatly inspired by the humanity and hon-

In Louisa's day, death was so inevitable and so public that only certifiably crazy people could ignore it. Besides, most people believed in an afterlife. Since death was not seen as a full stop, dying was potentially less terrifying. There was useful consolation yet to be provided, there was a comforting conversation to be had, and there was a shared set of assumptions that softened the fact of death. Dying was not oblivion, but a universal transition.

Louisa described one patient's death in particular, a Union soldier from Virginia, her age, dying in great pain from chest and back wounds. He doesn't at first realize that he will not recover, and the physician asks Louisa to tell him so.

> "You don't mean he must die, Doctor?"
>
> ". . . there's not the slightest hope for him; and you'd better tell him before long; women have a way of doing such things comfortably, so I leave it to you. He won't last more than a day or two, at furthest."
>
> I could have sat down on the spot and cried heartily, if I had not learned the wisdom of bottling up one's tears for leisure moments.

The next day, she was talking with the dying man. Proving that most people have an inkling anyway, he said,

> "This is my first battle; do they think it's going to be my last?"
>
> "I'm afraid they do, John."
>
> It was the hardest question I had ever been called upon to answer; doubly hard with those clear eyes fixed on mine, forcing a truthful answer by their own truth.

By the time I did my graduate work in nursing, in the 1980s, the attitude of doctors and nurses toward death had reversed itself

---

esty with which dying patients were being treated. The careful titration of powerful painkillers was key to keeping the patients alert and engaged. What I saw there was not, however, included in my curriculum back home.

from my 1970s training. Our thinking about caring for dying patients was closer to that of the 1860s. We were taught to talk to our patients and families about an impending death, and we were given ways, conversational and pharmacological, to help ease the process. Since I worked in oncology, taking care of children and teenagers with cancer, many of my patients were as close to death as Louisa's. I kept a notebook of stories about each of my patients who had died, trying in my own way to plug up the holes their deaths left in the universe.

Tim was one ten-year-old boy I cared for – a small, pale kid with watery blue eyes squinting uneasily over medication-induced chubby cheeks. Tim's parents wouldn't let us talk with him about his disease. Leukemia and our imperfect treatments had left him weak, anemic, and intermittently whiney. He was what we called a "frequent flyer," a patient who was admitted, discharged, and then readmitted several times a month, as our attempts to stabilize him kept crashing. His parents were terrified and shell-shocked. They couldn't believe that they could neither buy nor pray his way back to health. We all watched as Tim became depressed, and more and more silent and withdrawn.

Nurses and doctors could talk about anything else, but his parents were adamant that we not talk to him about how he felt. On his last admission, Tim was practically transparent; all he had left in his bloodstream were malignant white cells. The slightest bruise, blowing his nose too hard, and he could bleed to death. We expected him to die any day. His parents continued to talk and act as if death were not an option. They restated their orders not to say anything in his presence that would suggest his disease was getting the better of him. It was painfully clear that Tim was being forced to face his increasingly obvious mortality all alone.

One evening, when his parents were at dinner, I asked him, trying to sound casually conversational, busying myself with his IV tubing and not looking at his face, "How would it be if you didn't get home again?" The subtext, conveyed I hoped, by sheer tone of voice, was, "Nothing you can say will surprise or scare me, and anything you say will make you feel better," and also, "It is not cowardly to be ready to die." I glanced at him, saying nothing, to see if he understood. He looked at me for a long frozen time, pale and shadowy. Suddenly, his eyes smiled with relief that he wasn't the only one who knew. He whispered that not going home would be alright with him. That's all it took. Tim and I both felt better. He died calmly a few days later. It was around Christmastime, and before they left the hospital, his mother crocheted me a little pin in the shape of a holly wreath that I take out of its ancient tissue paper and wear every year.

Being a nurse changes your life. Seriously ill people are engaged in a battle, not just for their lives, but for meaning in their lives. It doesn't matter whether they have been attacked by a bullet or a virus or a genetic time bomb. The beauty of caring for seriously ill people, if Louisa's and my experience can be generalized (for indeed they were similar in this respect), is that most people meet their difficulties with unexpected nobility. Patients and their families continually teach anyone who pays attention that people can be generous and brave, that they can leave pettiness and selfishness behind. On the whole, patients give humanity a good name. Much later, Louisa recalled those days:

> I narrowly escaped with my life after a fever which left me an invalid for the rest of my days. But I have never regretted that brief yet costly experience . . . for all that is best & bravest in the hearts of man & women comes out in times like those, & the courage, loyalty, fortitude & self-sacrifice I saw & learned to love & admire in both Northern & Southern soldiers can never be forgotten.

Louisa wrote about her "boys," one by one, as they passed through her hands. Being who she was, she caught their humor, bravery, and conversational quirks perfectly. There was the young man from Michigan who had lost his right arm and was learning to write to his sweetheart with his left. They joked about his awkwardness, and sometimes Louisa stepped in to pen the words more legibly for the girl worried sick at home. John, the dying black-smith from Virginia, obviously struck her more deeply than all the others, if we judge by the number of words she devoted to him. He was dying, not a different fate from most of his ward mates, but he moved her profoundly in the way he did it. His manliness must have been a shade more manly. His stoicism, his Victorian romanticism, his concern for his poor mother on the farm at home – all touched her imaginative heart.

> Mrs. Ropes* & myself love him & feel indignant that such a man should be so early lost, for though he might never distinguish himself before the world, his influence & example cannot be without effect, for real goodness is never wasted.

Louisa's morning runs weren't enough to keep her going, and typhoid caught up with her after only two months of work. Fever-ish and chilled, still she resisted attempts to get her home. Finally, Miss Dix sent a message to the Alcotts, and Bronson came down to Washington to take his fallen child back to Concord.

Some months later, she collected her thoughts and letters into a series of articles for Frank Sanborn's *Commonwealth* and then into a small book called *Hospital Sketches*, which became her first publishing success.† In it, she included a little Q-and-A post-script, answering questions that came up frequently in conversation after she returned. She used the space both to continue her diatribe against thoughtless hospital management and careless care while describing some of her daily experiences in more detail.

She wrote that she "witnessed several [surgical] operations, for the height of my ambition was to go to the front after a battle, and feeling that the sooner I inured myself to trying sights, the more useful I should be. One surgeon confided to me that he

---

* Mrs. Ropes, Louisa's head nurse, was to die of typhoid two weeks later.

† She told her publishers to give most of her share of the profits to various Civil War orphans' funds.

feared his profession blunted his sensibilities, and, perhaps, rendered him indifferent to the sight of pain. I am inclined to think that in some cases it does; for, though a capital surgeon and a kindly man, Dr. P. . . . has acquired a somewhat trying habit of regarding a man and his wound as separate institutions, and seemed rather annoyed that the former should express any opinion on the latter, or claim any right to it, while under his care."

Although she was quick to say that she personally was treated with "utmost courtesy and kindness," she was not shy about concluding, "It's my private opinion, [nurses do] the hardest work of any part of the army, except the mules." A fierce abolitionist to the end, she finished *Hospital Sketches* with the wish that her next assignment would be to a hospital that took care of "colored regiments, as they seem to be proving their right to the admiration and kind offices of their white relations, who owe them so large a debt, a little part of which I shall be proud to pay."

Several years later, she received a visit from an army surgeon, who said *Hospital Sketches* would "do no end of good both in & out of the army &c." She wrote about it to her publisher, adding, "I didn't quite see how but haven't the least objection to its revolutionizing the globe if it can."

February 9, 1888

Dear Kit,

Before we go further, I must protest that I do not approve of using sentences from a person's journal that have been crossed out. Should I have burnt everything? Poor Miss Dix is barely cold in her grave, & I have no wish to malign the departed. I do hope we can continue this project without further incident.

That said, I am awash in tearful thoughts. I so loved all my boys, & still suffer regrets that I wasn't able to get closer to the front. I'm such a sad old donkey, so much of my life has been hobbled in one way or another. But I suppose those are the ties we live to break.

Did your researches tell you that Margaret Fuller actually met Florence Nightingale in Rome? That must have been wonderful – two feisty ladies. I do hope they were in circumstances that allowed them to have a true conversation. I expect they would have traded many a tale of frustrated ambition & difficult families preventing them from serving & living as their spirited natures commanded. Their meeting would have been before the Crimean War. Did you know that Margaret also did her bit as a nurse when the French were attacking Rome? Her hospital, the Fatebenefratelli on Tiber Island, was still there when I visited. I walked around it & mourned once again for her loss at sea.

I am curious that special schooling, even college, is part of becoming a nurse in your century. That surely means we have learned a great deal about the care of the sick & dying. In Jo's Boys, I made dear Nan a productive & happy physician. I wish she were real & here to help me today with my own frustrating maladies. Are we going to talk later about the treatments I am receiving for my calomel poisoning? I certainly believe in progress, but some of the ideas people have talked me into, like that mind cure that has been so popular, have been a terrible waste of my time.

How sad for you to have taken care of dying children. My boys were tough enough, but little children! I could hardly handle fictional child deaths, let alone real ones. I am, however, much heartened that you observed the human tendency to rise to the challenge. If our public institutions could only encourage that aspect of humanity a little more, & reward our ignoble traits a bit less, society would be much the better.

My Washington, D.C., days were my first & last hurrah. I've never been truly physically well since then, but that winter marked the true beginning of my writerly success. I learned that I had won a $100 prize while I was there, you know, for that delectable Pauline – A. M. Barnard's first outing! It had all my favorite ingredients: murder, suicide, revenge & a dark handsome lover from the Caribbean.

But it was in Washington, too, that I learned of dear Henry

Thoreau's passing. I wrote a poem about it, mostly about his flute, &
it helped me remember all the good times we had. He was an amaz-
ing and wonderful man. Once, when we were all having dinner at
the Emersons', Lidian asked him which dish he would like, & he
answered "the nearest." It seemed as if the more he knew, the less he
needed. He knew our woods so well that he could tell the month and
the day simply by looking at what flowers or seedheads were bloom-
ing. He was never wrong by more than two days. The world was
lucky to know him.

I may ask my sister Anna to mix up your Russian cake. I was
given some very fragrant and delicious lavender honey for Christmas.
Father may enjoy it too. I will tell him it is from Russia via the twenty-
first century. That will keep his wandering mind happy for a good
long while.

A bilberry wine toast to you,
Louisa

PS: Nickname for what?

Writing It Down

Women aren't literary in any substantial sense of the term.
Henry James

*[Louisa] infuses her morals so skillfully and her ethical machinery is
so gracefully concealed by the clinging drapery of love, or the thick
foliage of events, that her characters blossom out upon you with
a new grace and beauty as well as being truthful to the Life.*
Abba Alcott

February 10, 2006

Dear Louisa,

"To and fro, like a wild creature in its cage, paced that handsome woman, with bent head, locked hands, and restless steps. Some mental storm, swift and sudden as a tempest of the tropics, had swept over her and left its marks behind." What a great opening for *Pauline*! A. M. Barnard definitely deserved that prize.

By now my friends have learned that you were far more than a writer. But you have more surprises in store for them because they think they know what you wrote. In this project, though, we are going far beyond *Little Women*. We're going to spend our time leafing through some pages they are less likely to have seen.

This part is mostly about what you wrote for grown-ups and the grown-up ideas you sneaked into your girls' books. The adult books are the ones you worked the hardest on, aren't they? They are the ones you care the most about. Especially your stories of women trying to find a way to live with men without letting the men become the molten center of their lives. Sometimes your heroines made it work, and sometimes they didn't.

I remain, admiringly yours,
Kit

PS: Oh, yes, you wanted to know if Kit is a nickname. Yes it is, and yes I think it does have something to do with my father's fantasies about his children's specialness. My real name doesn't begin with a K though. Care to take another guess?

Love versus Duty · Henry James's Insult If I'd Been a Boy · Nathaniel Hawthorne's Rant The Lurid Style · Tired of Moral Pap

Louisa had a dark red velvet rectangular bolster she called her mood pillow. She kept it in the living room at Orchard House. When it was laid horizontally on the sofa, it meant stay away, she was in a bad mood; when it was upright and vertical, she was approachable. Her moodiness was a trait her omnipresent father much disapproved of. Moods frightened him, and he didn't think people should have them. Louisa used her pen to defend herself against his insistent attempts to flatten both her highs and her lows. Her first real novel, published four years before *Little Women*, was called, deliberately, *Moods*. It was published in two forms, once in 1864, and again in 1882 with a revised ending. It was always her favorite creation. *Moods* combines the hearthside tableaux of her girls' books with the very adult action, love, deceit, and trauma of her A. M. Barnard persona.

People write books for different reasons, but the most common ones are for money, for revenge, or to further a cause. Some write because they find it entertaining or find that writing clarifies their own thinking, or because they like the power of deciding what will happen next. Louisa had all those reasons.

If a person makes a living at it, writing becomes a job, freighted with those familiar, job-required compromises most people know so well. Louisa did make a living at it, for decades. In order to do so, she agreed to one major trade-off: she spent most of her time writing what her paying public wanted, instead of what she really enjoyed and wanted to write about. At one point, at the end of the 1870s, she was interested in writing a historical novel for children about the American Revolution, but after doing her market research (asking all the kids she knew) she told her publisher "The dears *will* cling to the '*Little Women*' style" and so she abandoned the Revolution for *Jack and Jill*, serialized in 1879–80.

Toward the end of her life, like a software entrepreneur acting on a never-forgotten dream to be a schoolteacher, she went back to the themes that truly interested her. She didn't finish *Diana and Persis*, but in the four completed chapters we have, she returned to her favorite puzzles, those issues that I think continue to puzzle all thinking women today:

1. Can a productive and creative single woman be happy?

2. Can a married woman maintain her personal life and friends?

3. Can women be both personally happy and professionally successful?

4. Can people be happily married and still respect each other's privacy and basic human rights?

These four were the most important personal questions of her life. She believed neither her mother, nor her sister Anna, nor she herself had answered them well. May, the golden-haired, artistic youngest sister was the only one who had possibly come close. May was more than a weekend artist, although you wouldn't think so from looking at her primitive drawings on the walls of her room at Orchard House, or her illustrations for the first edi-

tion of *Little Women*. But she studied seriously, both in Boston
and in Europe, and she improved considerably. Ruskin once told
her she copied Turner better than anyone he'd seen (and Turner
was Ruskin's favorite painter).

May had pictures accepted in the competitions for the great
Paris Salon in both 1877 and 1879.* The first is a lovely but tradi-
tional still life of fruit, a blue vase, and a straw-covered wine bottle.
The second, *La Négresse*, is quite different. It is an arresting portrait
of a young black woman, a red scarf on her head and a white
sleeveless shift pulled down, exposing her right breast. The
woman's face, turned slightly to the left, compellingly expresses
loss and degradation, but equally hints at strength, wisdom, and
the promise of recovery.

Much of *Diana and Persis* is a straight copy of May's eager,
excited letters home about her idyllic artist's life in Paris and her
courtship and marriage there. Diana and Persis are two best
friends, young American women, one a painter and one a sculp-
tor. The action is centered in Paris and Rome. Louisa must have
thought that if happiness was possible anywhere, it would be in
Europe, not New England. But she knew it was too late for her.
Her mercury-poisoned health was too precarious for any late-
blooming trans-Atlantic rebirth.

≈≈≈≈≈

Louisa worked on *Moods* far more that any of her other books† and
for years didn't let any publisher see it for fear of a rejection that
would hurt more than any other. She was accustomed to rejection,
as she was constantly bombarding, and constantly being rejected

---

* The competition for these events was stiff: only two thousand of 8,500 sub-
missions were accepted. In the 1877 competition, she was the only American
woman to have a picture accepted. May was one of several young American expa-
triate artists who were complimented and occasionally fed by Mary Cassatt.

† *Little Women* was practically automatic writing. The first draft was the final
draft.

by, the *Atlantic Monthly*, much as aspiring authors today are by the *New Yorker*. In the summer of 1864 she "went home & wrote a story, 'An Hour,' for the *Atlantic*, & sent it. As I thought it was good was pretty sure they wouldn't take it." They didn't, perhaps, she thought, because it was about slavery.

But she was more cautious with *Moods*, because it mattered more to her. It is the story of Sylvia, a young woman who is a bit of a tomboy, as are all Louisa's true heroines. Sylvia is courted by two men. Adam is a young, strong, silent stranger who rides into town one day to visit his friend Geoffrey, a kind, gentle, slightly older man who lives next door to Sylvia. Adam is modeled after Thoreau. Sylvia immediately falls in love with him. Adam appears to lead her on and then drops her, disappearing, she has reason to believe, to marry a sultry Cuban siren.* Meanwhile, kindly neighbor Geoffrey, modeled after Emerson and complete with a wonderful library, suddenly realizes that he loves Sylvia as well. After much troubled thought, Sylvia acquiesces to Geoffrey's heartfelt proposals of marriage. But her mind drifts continually to Adam. Only intermittently and with great effort to can she convince herself that she loves Geoffrey. This is a big problem, because Sylvia is ahead of her time in believing that love is a prerequisite to marriage.

Moods is only marginally readable today. Louisa, always in a hurry, and unwilling to let the lessons unfold within the story, created a didactic tale in a two-dimensional world that is overly stiff for today's reader. Lest today's reader feel overly sophisticated, however, *Moods* also leaves us floundering because we are classical illiterates. Louisa's contemporary *Moods* audience would have caught all her literary allusions because in her day, readers dreamed in Greek and Roman mythology and played parlor games based on Milton, Dickens, and Shakespeare.

Henry James could catch all her allusions, but he still hated

---

* When Louisa needed characters to be gorgeous, unpredictable, and emotional, she made them hail from Caribbean or Mediterranean countries.

the book. His scathing review of *Moods* came out in the *North American Review* in July 1865. At that time, James was still living in the United States, writing a few articles and hiding his Civil War draft-dodger status with bombastic talk, but his complex and powerful novels were yet to come. Although his future stories would be populated by some feisty and brave young women, James himself didn't much like *real* women who were getting published when he was not. James excoriated both Louisa and her *Moods*. He slathered on his dislike and jealousy with a masculine superciliousness. "We are utterly weary of stories about precocious little girls," he wrote with a tired and superior sigh. He went on to proclaim, "The two most striking facts with regards to 'Moods' are the author's ignorance of human nature and her self-confidence in spite of this ignorance."

Louisa, exasperated, vented in her journal, that, all right, if the world didn't want ideas, she'd stop including them, and "the people shall be as ordinary as possible" as it would make her own life easier too. Then, she guessed, "the critics will say it's all right." Bronson, on the other hand, liked *Moods*. He told her "Emerson must see this. Where did you get your metaphysics?"

Most contemporary readers thought *Moods* was a story about good or bad choices in marriage. Louisa felt compelled to respond vigorously in the negative. After all, she said disingenuously, she didn't know anything about marriage. The book revolved on two other themes about which she knew a great deal: the pickles a girl falls into when she can't control her emotions and how the sins of the fathers cause harm to the children. It turns out that Sylvia and her brother and sister are all marked by character flaws that were caused by the fact that their father never loved their dead mother and, in trying to atone for this, had made matters worse.

Sylvia's moods are the result of living a lie: she doesn't love her kind, patient husband Geoffrey. She loves protean Adam. *Moods* has two endings, one written in the flush of Louisa's twenties and the second, revised, published eighteen years later. In both versions there is a wise woman, Faith Dane (whose advanced thinking is reminiscent of Margaret Fuller and who shows up later as the nurse in the Louisa's Civil War story "My Contraband"*), who counsels Sylvia to stay away from Adam – telling her that Adam is "too powerful" for her. In the first ending, there is no solution other than death: Sylvia wastes away with a conveniently tidy, unidentified Victorian illness, and for good measure, Adam is shipwrecked and dies as well, after first saving his friend Geoffrey's life.

In the second ending, Sylvia doesn't die, but Adam still does. Sylvia uses her extra time on Earth to wrestle her moods to the ground. She finally attains an adult love for Geoffrey and presumably goes on to live a long and productive life. The last sentence in the revised version reads in part, "for now she had learned to live by principle, not impulse, and this made it both sweet and possible for love and duty to go hand in hand."

The battles between love and duty cause great personal and interpersonal unhappiness for many of Louisa's characters. Surprise, surprise! This was her own life. Louisa grew up on the battlefield of this very personal civil war, as her father solidified his eccentricities into bloodless duty and her mother continued to love and fight for a rich emotional life. As a child cannot choose between parents without paying a huge emotional price, Louisa never gave up trying to join the two. The struggle to love what she understood as her duty but also to indulge and enjoy duty-free emotions were the twin goals toward which she accelerated her fictional characters and drove her own life. When this fusion succeeded, happiness was assured. When it failed, all was lost. The particular failure Louisa repeatedly described was the one in which duty dictated the continuation of a loveless marriage, contracted because the wife chose with her head, usually full of concerns about her empty pocketbook, and not with her heart.

One male reader wrote to Louisa to criticize *Moods* because

---

* Escaped slaves were called "contrabands," an awkward legal term used in those days to tenuously bridge the abyss between being property and being a free person.

she allowed her heroine to have feelings and preferences about her marriage partner. Louisa responded hotly, probably more lengthily and with poorer punctuation than she had intended:

> I honor marriage so highly that I long to see it what it should be life's best lesson and not its heaviest cross. . . .
>
> Half the misery of our time arises from unmated pairs trying to live their legal lie decorously to the end at any cost. Better a few cases of open infidelity that warn & shock than many hidden tragedies that doom the innocent children as well as the guilty parents.

Did Louisa think her parents' marriage was loveless and is that what put her off marriage for herself? Probably not; nothing is ever that simple. By all accounts, Bronson and Abba Alcott were devoted to each other and didn't like being apart. But they also irritated each other and showed it in their different ways – Abba with her quick temper and Bronson with his manipulative intellectualisms. Their persistent poverty likely exacerbated the opportunity for flare-ups. The children, like children everywhere, saw it all.

When *Moods* was accepted for publication, Louisa continued to worry. She cared so much about the story. "Proof began to come, & the chapters seemed small, stupid & no more my own in print. I felt very much afraid that I'd ventured too much & should be sorry for it. But Emerson says 'that what is true for your own private heart is true for others,' so I wrote from my own life & experience and hope it may suit some & at least do no harm."

Although always for public sale, Louisa's transparent writing was never trivial and always stayed close to her most important personal struggle.

※ ⫷ ※ ⫷ ※

Another of Louisa's adult novels, *Work*, centers on the problems of the working girl in the 1850s and '60s. The Wesleyan Chapel at Seneca Falls, New York, hosted a "convention to discuss the social, civil and religious condition and rights of women" in July

1848. The idea was born over tea in Auburn, New York, as several abolitionist friends found themselves unable to ignore any longer the "present condition of women . . . the reality of her degradation."

The group passed a "Declaration of Sentiments," asserting that women had rights equal to those of men with respect to work, marriage, suffrage, property, church, education, and all legal contracts. It was fashioned after the Declaration of Independence and began, clearly enough, with "We hold these truths to be self-evident, that all men and women are created equal." Frederick Douglass, the passionate antislavery leader, was a driving force in getting the mixed gender convention to accept one of the most controversial clauses: the right of women to vote.*

Louisa was well aware of these doings, and *Work*'s heroine Christie Devon fires an appropriate salvo in the very first sentence of chapter 1, "Aunt Betsey, there's going to be a new Declaration of Independence." Christie, a late-adolescent orphan, and her guardian aunt are kneading bread and rolling out piecrusts in their farmhouse kitchen. Christie bursts out, "I'm not going to sit and wait for any man to give me independence, if I can earn it for myself." In fact, she's already decided that independence of the sort she craves is not available in rural America, and she must go to the city. "I'm old enough to take care of myself; and if I'd been a boy, I should have been told to do it long ago."

There is a string of comments like "if I'd been a boy" throughout Louisa's fiction, journals, and letters, all implying that she either wished she were a boy, or that, often as not, she liked doing the things that boys did. I do not propose any interpretation other than the obvious: she took a clear-eyed look around her and saw that, truly, men had most of the power and got most of the goodies.

---

* Douglass withdrew his support later, when the Fourteenth and Fifteenth Amendments to the Constitution were up for a vote and the political winds were saying that the white men in Washington, D.C., were willing to grant either women or blacks the right to vote, but not both.

Like any intelligent woman, I think she was simply trying to muscle a little more fairness out of an unfair world.

Fairness was on my mind too, as I began raising my daughter Maya in the 1970s. I was especially attracted to a story in *Ms. Magazine* about a child brought up in a completely gender-neutral environment. I've forgotten how this was accomplished, but the result was a child who was utterly ignorant of the cultural implications of being either male or female. So, of course it (readers never learned the child's sex) grew up strong and sensitive, the best of both worlds. I was quite taken by this fantasy. Adapting it to one small aspect of Maya's life, I deliberately chose female pediatricians for her, thinking she wouldn't then get stuck believing that only males could be doctors (as they mostly were in those days, at least in the U.S.). So I was startled one day to hear her, at five years old, tell me that girls couldn't be doctors. Clearly, I had not reckoned with the strength of the prevailing culture. My feeble attempt to create an egalitarian reality was no match for the assumptions Maya assimilated every day in neighborhood conversations and normal social intercourse.

But we learn, and we don't give up. In Louisa's *Work*, Christie goes off to do what any man would do – figure out not just how to make a living, but to find a life. At one point a rich man proposes to her, but she refuses him with a speech not unlike Elizabeth Bennet's famous first refusal of Mr. Darcy. She questions his motives and says she doesn't love him.* Living on her own is difficult, though, and eventually, after several scrapes and occupational failures, Christie hits bottom. As she contemplates suicide on a bridge in Boston, she is rescued by a factory mate from a clothing sweatshop where she once worked. Christie is sent to recover in the country, at a sort of halfway house run by a kind Quaker woman and her son, the quiet, hardworking David. Mother and son own a nursery. Amid the flowers and fresh air, Christie

---

* Louisa places this conversation in a room where the prominent feature is the painting of *The Fates* she knew from Emerson's study.

regains her strength and spirits, and inevitably she and David (another Thoreau stand-in) fall in love.

The story does not end here, though, with love and marriage assured. Marriage is only one event in Christie's journey. She and David marry just hours before his Union army regiment is shipped off to the Civil War killing fields. Christie joins up as a nurse. In short order, she is pregnant and David is dead. She and her daughter Pansy return to Boston to live a long life supporting themselves and doing community service from the warm, loving base of a women's commune.

Louisa uses Christie's postwar community work to show how hard it is for the rich and the poor to communicate with each other, despite everyone's best intentions. In one meeting that Christie is chairing,

> the workers poured out their wrongs and hardships passionately or plaintively, demanding or imploring justice, sympathy, and help; displaying the ignorance, incapacity, and prejudice, which make their need all the more pitiful, their relief all the more imperative.
>
> The ladies did their part with kindliness, patience, and often unconscious condescension, showing in their turn how little they knew of the real trials of the women whom they longed to serve, how very narrow a sphere of usefulness they were fitted for in spite of culture and intelligence, and how rich they were in generous theories, how poor in practical methods of relief.

Moods and *Work* were Louisa's two most personal books. Everything else she published was written primarily for financial gain. *Little Women* wasn't even her idea. Her publisher suggested she write a book for girls, and she agreed, reluctantly, to give it a try. She records in her journal in May 1868, "Mr. N. wants a *girls' story*, and I begin 'Little Women.' Marmee, Anna, and May all approve my plan. So I plod away, though I don't enjoy this sort of thing. Never liked girls, or knew many, except my sisters; but our queer plays and experiences may prove interesting, though I doubt it." Some fifteen years later, still raking in the profits, she reread her journal and added the note, "Good joke."

She spent the next twenty years, the remainder of her life, both enjoying and fighting off the rewards of *Little Women*'s success. There were sequels galore – sometimes with the same characters, sometimes not.* She told her readers about the problems and dreams of poor girls and rich girls, orphans and cousins, happy families and miserable ones. By having her archetype Jo run a school, she was able to keep the flow of adolescent trials, tribulations, punishments, rewards, failures, and successes coming.

In the early 1870s, Louisa had a conversation with a society woman in Boston. The woman told Louisa something to the effect that *Little Women* "shows [Louisa's] true style of writing – the pure and gentle type, with innocent young lives. . . ." Louisa interrupted to disagree, "Not exactly that. I think my natural ambition is for the lurid style. I indulge in gorgeous fancies and wish that I dared inscribe them upon my pages and set them before the public." When asked why she did not follow her wish, Louisa responded,

> How should I dare to interfere with the proper grayness of old Concord? The dear old town has never known a startling hue since the redcoats were there. Far be it from me to inject an inharmonious color into the neutral tint. And my favorite characters! Suppose they went to cavorting at their own sweet will, to the infinite horror of dear Mr. Emerson . . . to have had Mr. Emerson for an intellectual god all one's life is to be invested in a chain armor of propriety. . . . And what would my own good father think of me, if I set folks to doing the things I have a longing to see my people do?

---

* After her mother and Anna's husband John died, Louisa apologized to her readership and said she could no longer continue their characters in her books, as their real life counterparts were gone. Amy (May) however continues on as Laurie's wife in *Jo's Boys* even after her real death in Paris.

No, my dear, I shall always be a wretched victim to the respectable traditions of Concord.

In her journal, Louisa's first mention of preferring the "lurid style" is in reference to her neighbor Nathaniel Hawthorne's *Scarlet Letter*, which she liked very much, "I like 'lurid' things, if true and strong also." Hawthorne, like Henry James, was greatly irritated by women authors, writing to his publisher:

> America is now wholly given over to a d****d mob of scribbling women, and I should have no chance of success while the public taste is occupied with their trash – and should be ashamed of myself if I did succeed. What is the mystery of these innumerable editions of *The Lamplighter* [by Maria Susanna Cummins], and other books neither better nor worse? Worse they could not be, and better they need not be, when they sell by the hundred thousand.

In early 1877, Louisa took advantage of an opportunity to sneak some of A. M. Barnard's lurid style into a respectable package. Her publisher asked her to contribute to the "No Name Series," anonymous novels penned by popular, known authors. Reviewers and the reading public enjoyed guessing who had written each one. No one suspected Louisa was the author of *A Modern Mephistopheles*. The *Atlantic Monthly* reviewed it (sharing the same column with a review of Henry James's *The American*) in July 1877.

The staff reviewer hazarded the guess that *Modern Mephistopheles* was by Julian Hawthorne, Nathaniel and Sophia's son, and complimented it roundly: "The language is vigorous and clear, having a sculpturesque effect, and the succession of periods and paragraphs is often so admirable that many pages together seem to be set in solemn rhythm." The lesson of the work, wrote the reviewer, was that, "wanton exercise of the intellect and a suppression of the better forces in the heart are very dangerous and devilish." Hmmm, I wonder if Bronson picked up on that.

Exactly as the title denotes, *Modern Mephistopheles* is a Faustian bargain brought up to Victorian date and yet another opportunity for Louisa to pay her compliments to Goethe. The devil is an older man named Jasper Helwyze, who ghostwrites poetry for Felix Canaris, a young and failing poet who wants fame more than anything. Felix, a heart-stoppingly attractive man with long dark curls who is half English and half Greek (there's that tropical excitement again), moves in with his devilish patron and promises to obey him in all things. Helwyze soon tires of pulling Felix's strings and moves on to two women. Olivia is his age; she had turned him down many years ago, leaving him bitter and angry. Now she's changed her mind and wants him back, but he's decided it is more fun to punish her forever by inviting her into his house so he can refuse her on a daily, personal basis. Olivia has brought a beautiful and artless young girl, Gladys, to live with her.

Helwyze decides to tinker with his houseguests' hearts. He demands that Felix marry Gladys. Felix protests that he does not love her. No matter, says Helwyze, do it anyway. He creates jealousy and competition in Felix's oh-so-manipulable heart. This, along with simple blackmail over the authorship of his poetry, brings Felix to his knees. They marry – Gladys, a romantic, trying hard, and Felix, not in love. Helwyze, after forcing the marriage, taunts Felix by telling him that marrying "without love betrays as surely as to love without marriage."

In the end, Gladys dies in childbirth, along with her and Felix's newborn son. Felix exits the story, heartbroken, saying he wants to live an honest life in whatever short time he has left before he joins his dead wife and son. Olivia remains to nurse Helwyze, who has had a stroke and dies shortly after Gladys. Louisa makes several pointed comments throughout the story about the poisonous environment that created such havoc. Olivia describes Helwyze as having built a world "where intellect is God, conscience ignored, and love despised." Louisa cannot stop herself from ensuring that she has made her authorial point, thinking, perhaps, of Fruitlands:

"Lawless here, as elsewhere, he [Helwyze] let his mind wander at will, as once he had let his heart, learning too late that both are sacred gifts, and cannot be safely tampered with."

You are what you think, and you are what you care about. Shades of Thoreau, conversing happily with Aunt Mary Moody Emerson and writing, "I believe the mind can be permanently profaned by the habit of attending to trivial things. . . . Read not the *Times*. Read the Eternities."

In *Modern Mephistopheles*, we see Louisa once again battling with Bronson's ever intrusive intellect. "Enjoyed doing it," she told her journal, "being tired of providing moral pap for the young." Ten years later, in 1887, word had leaked out that she was the author, and she agreed to reprint it under her name. Ever the professional, she suggested to her publisher that he time the release to match a much-anticipated summer touring production of *Faust*.

Louisa liked writing about people who colored outside the lines and made fun of some who didn't, but she usually chose to live with the neatniks. In 1864, still pre-*Little Women* but post-*Hospital Sketches* and the year *Moods* was released, she refused a publisher's offer of extra money if she would put her own name to one of her more sensational thrillers. No, she said, A. M. Barnard would have to continue to take the credit for those outside-the-lines stories. As (Mr.? Mrs.?) Barnard, she was free to live in Concord but still write stories in which women did scandalous, revenge-filled things to men. Not that she got much writing done in Concord. Much later she told a friend "Very few stories written in Concord; no inspiration in that dull place. Go to Boston, hire a quiet room and shut myself up in it."

❧✦❧✦❧

As she became the best-known children's writer of her day, she inevitably received requests for advice from aspiring young writers. Incredibly, she answered many of them. She always cut to the chase and never romanticized the work. "Mind grammar, spelling, and punctuation, use short words, and express as briefly as you can your meaning. . . . Read the best books . . . see and hear good speakers and wise people. . . . Work for twenty years, and then you may some day find that you have a style and place of your own, and can command good pay for the same things no one would take when you were unknown." Reading this over before sealing it, she must have found it a little bleak, because she added this minimally encouraging postscript: "The lines you sent me are better than many I see; but boys of nineteen cannot know much about hearts, and had better write of things they understand. Sentiment is apt to become sentimentality; and sense is always safer. . . ."

She wrote another book worth looking at for the light it sheds on her and to add to the light she can shed back to us. When she was a teenager, she completed her first novel, called *The Inheritance*. There is no evidence she ever tried to publish it, and she never mentioned it in her known letters or journal. It rested ignored among Anna's sons' papers for years before making its way to Harvard's Houghton Library in 1974, where it continued to slumber until 1988 when it was found by excited scholars Joel Myerson and Daniel Shealy, who were preparing a collection of Louisa's letters for publication. As a teenage author, Louisa was already delving into secret sacrifices, already turning down marriage proposals, already dispensing with fathers, and already, she was drawing on her own and her sisters' lives for material.

"My lord," said the heroine of *The Inheritance* (for indeed the tale is set in England and is replete with lords and ladies of all description), "poor and humble as I am, your wealth can never buy my love." When the lord presses his suit, she rebukes him fearlessly, "I have borne enough, Lord Arlington. Do not turn my indifference into contempt by this ungenerous resentment. I have given you my refusal frankly and with kindness. You have no right to question further. . . ."

For women of Louisa's day, there was nothing more courageous a woman could do than to turn down a marriage proposal.

Remaining unmarried can still take courage, but the financial and social risks are not as heavy as they were in Louisa's day. Today, women have hundreds of other ways to demonstrate courage. It's instructive to note that one way men have tried to discourage women from taking brave stands is by labeling them as crazy. A physician in the early 1900s recalled being pressured to diagnose jailed hunger-striking suffragettes as insane. He refused, saying that he didn't want to contribute to the tendency of mislabeling courageous women as psychiatrically ill.

Louisa also used *The Inheritance* to begin exploring the experience of being lonely even when surrounded by people. For men, loneliness is usually wrapped in major angst and grand philosophical overtones; women are often allowed only a discounted version, as if their loneliness is no more than a weak and childish ennui. Louisa thought otherwise; it was that fairness issue again.

In 1870, Louisa made more money than any other living American author. Her girls' stories were a winning combination of truth and humor, pain and good cheer. She provided the world with a sanitized version of her own childhood, making a self-filling purse out of a sow's ear. She was justly proud that she had found a way to commercial success without sacrificing either of her parents' extremely elaborate, comprehensive, and often conflicting values.

If she occasionally felt trapped in her nicely feathered nest, she also had the pleasure of succeeding where powerful people had told her she would fail. James Fields, the publisher of the *Atlantic*, gave her $40 in 1862 and told her to use it to set up a school so she could be a teacher, because she would never make it as a writer. In 1871, she delighted in paying him back and saying, in a very ladylike way, of course, "I told you so." She recorded that he "laughed and owned that he made a mistake."

She wrote stories the way she did housework or took in sewing: quickly, precisely, and thoroughly, smoothly blending both her mother's energy and her father's scrupulousness. She may initially have thought of writing as an art and an act of rebellion. She hoped she might be improving the world. Eventually, as it does to all sentient wage earners, reality intruded to take the shine down a watt or two. She honed her skills to meet the publishing requirements of the day, turning out just over two hundred stories, often serialized for weekly or monthly publications. She was talking about herself when she wrote that Mrs. Jo was an ugly duckling who turned not into a swan, but a golden goose.

Still, she never gave up writing about the problems she cared about most, and although she liked her lurid style, she never wrote in service of pure distraction, but always with the human purpose of improving her readers' lives with cheerfulness, humor, and usually, a lesson or two.

February 14, 1888

Dear Not-even-K,

Publishers did drive me to distraction. You'd think the worst part would have been at the beginning when they wouldn't deign to pay any attention to me. But no, it got worse when they started bidding against each other – for instance that terrible time I had over Eight Cousins *& the European rights & all. We will continue in mayhem until we get some agreements on international copyrights.*

Illustrators have also been an affliction, having no idea what children are wearing at different ages, making the older ones into babies & putting whiskers on the younger ones. Sometimes I didn't know whether to laugh or to cry, & did both, & it still didn't help much.

The very worst problem, by far, is the autograph seekers, the photo hunters & the silly people mooning around my house with no sense at all that they are being the least bit intrusive. I tried to state my case for being left alone in Jo's Boys, *my last March family story. Poor Mrs. Jo suffered nothing that hadn't happened to me first. I don't have the energy to make up those people! One woman came asking me for a piece of clothing; she was making a "celebrity rug" & said she already had a vest from Mr. Emerson, a dress from Mrs. Stowe, & a pair of pants from Mr. Holmes. I must admit that I capitulated. How could I refuse to be walked on in the company of such esteemed scribblers?*

I have been reading Henry James's recent work, The Bostonians. *As a writer myself, I cannot fail to credit his clever style, but his ignorant & persistent cruelty toward women's suffrage is unexpectedly harsh. The pen is powerful & I fear he has wielded it for the benefit of his personal & warped prejudices. I have amused myself for several days imagining a feminine Hell for both the author & his leading man, Basil Ransom.*

I am also struck with how Mr. James has created an odd & reactionary echo of my Moods. *His Bostonian Verena is much like my Sylvia in her childlike qualities and her confused responses to being pursued by a strong, passionate, essentially alien man. His Mississippian Mr. Ransom resembles my Adam Warwick at his very worst. Ransom is Warwick without a shred of conscience. Ransom doesn't love Verena at all; he just wants to possess her in the most evil sort of A. M. Barnard way. It is the South striking back . . . & winning! Why would Mr. James promote such a plot?*

Poor Verena had no Faith Dane to help her through her agitations & moods, so the ending is far from satisfactory for the characters or the reader. It is no use for Mr. James to say that art is its own justification. It isn't, & won't be until liberty & freedom have spread much farther afield than they are today. He even wastes a paragraph complaining about competition from women writers!

Why is it that male writers must continue to lob these nasty notes about women writers? E. A. Poe, I believe, went out of his way to be rude to Miss Fuller after she left him out of her article about contemporary American authors. Then James Russell Lowell attacked her far more viciously than anyone else in his 1848 Fable for Critics. *At least he tried to be a little funny with most of his other targets, my sainted father and Mr. Emerson included.*

You mention Mr. Hawthorne's dislike of women authors. Perhaps you saw his scurrilous journal entries on Miss Fuller that his son Julian published a few years ago. (This journal publishing is definitely a bad idea). Not content with simply criticizing her writing, Mr. Hawthorne describes her "strong, heavy, unpliable, and in many respects, defective and evil nature . . . a strong and coarse nature . . . a great humbug." He even said it was fortunate that she & her husband & child perished as their ship broke apart in that storm off Fire Island! I feel as if I must dust some shelves or sweep down the staircase to calm myself.

Despite the fact that I took to dodging into the woods, just like Mr. Hawthorne, to avoid reporters & sightseers, I must come clean & admit that being a "famous authoress" has opened a few pleasant & useful doors for my family & me. I did have a wonderful time being wined & dined in New York in 1875, meeting & talking with important & interesting people whom I would not have met without my publishing successes. Similarly, I think my assistance to the women's suffrage movement has been made greater by my so-called celebrity. I think that is our next topic, is it not?

Before we move on, I must say your comment about Diana & Persis *being unfinished caught me off guard. When I am well, I try to complete thirty pages a day. I realize that my health is not improving, but I did hope to get beyond four chapters. Is this something you perhaps should not be telling me? I wish I knew better about how these "time zones" work.*

"Constance"?

Wonderingly yours,
Lu

Reforms of All Kinds

To put a woman on the committee [The Anti-Slavery Society]
with men is contrary to the usages of civilized society.
Lewis Tappan, a founder of the Anti-Slavery Society in 1831,
objecting to the election of Lydia Maria Child and
two other women to its executive committee

If the misery of our poor can be caused not by the laws of nature,
but by our institutions, great is our sin.
Charles Darwin

February 16, 2006

Dear Louisa,

Yes, we have made it to the women's suffrage and other reforms
essay. You have never pulled your punches much, have you? You
have always waded right in, wherever you are, whenever you can.

Do you remember when you had your head examined without
telling the phrenologist who you were? His office was in New York,
near Union Square. You went in 1875 when you were staying on
West 26th Street. You copied out his diagnosis and put the piece
of paper into a book you gave to Anna. Her sons saved it, and now
we can read it too. The phrenologist said you had an unusual
number of large bumps, making you "a person who can row
against the tide & like it." Some of it sounds remarkably accurate
– although of course we don't take phrenology seriously nowadays.
Do you? He also said you were idealistic, but practical; a good

nurse; that you had more friends than you wanted; that you loved praise but could go without it; that you had a gift for drama, language, observation, and mimicry; and that you were a devoted wife and mother. You must have enjoyed the subterfuge.

All sorts of reforms were happening in the 1870s and '80s. Women's suffrage was only one of many that you have cared about, and rightly so. I understand that temperance has always been a concern of yours, because drunken men routinely wreck the lives of their dependent wives and children. You don't like any kind of self-destruction, condemning your overweight character Stuffy to death by apoplexy after dinner in *Jo's Boys*.

I see you also have campaigned to get rid of those awful corsets. Even though I know you have always appreciated stylish clothing, you clearly have taken up Margaret Fuller's sword against the corset. "Yes! let us give up all artificial means of distortion," she said, and I agree too. I think the nineteenth-century reforming term for more comfortable clothing was "physiological dress." That is a war still not won. In the 1960s and '70s, women rebelled against ill-fitting and constricting brassieres. Supposedly a kinder corset, bras began to appear in the 1880s. Maybe you have seen one? Many of us who stopped wearing them in the 1960s and '70s were reviled by men as "bra burners" (to go along with the draft-card burners, I guess), as if not having pointy breasts was some sort of crime against civilization. It's funny, isn't it, how the powers-that-be rail so fiercely about the most random things?

To get back to more serious reforms, you always argued for better education for women and were an early and frequent proponent of the radical notion of coeducation. Your Plumfield College was coed, and you wrote about Harvard student visitors who talked about why they would have preferred coed classes. Other issues, like better care for prisoners, orphans, and the sick have also been constantly high on your list. And over and over – you want choices, choices, and more choices for women. "Women have been called queens for a long time, but the kingdom given them isn't worth ruling," you have one of your enlightened characters say. You have given your own time, money, and good name to all of these causes, and others besides.

It's not just "moral pap" to have a character speak up for the needs of the poor and oppressed. It's really very clever and subversive of you to sugarcoat your radical notions so they come out of the oven tasting like good ol' fashioned values.

I like your persistent mixing of simple and immediate charity with deep social restructuring. That combination needs just as much advocacy today as it did in your time. I've heard people say things just as thoughtlessly inexcusable as you had that spoiled rich girl Trix say in *Old-Fashioned Girl*,

> Well, I'm sick of hearing about beggars. I believe half of them are humbugs, and if we let them alone they'd go to work and take care of themselves. There's altogether too much fuss made about charity. I do wish we could be left in peace.

As if rich people never get any help!

So I'd like you to sit back and appreciate your contributions. I hope you can hear a round of applause from my time zone.

Yours for Reforms of All Kinds,
Kit (not Constance, although I like the name. Try again.)

Liberty Is a Better Husband Than Love
Like Chinese Feet · First to Register
Same Pay for the Same Good Work

In February 1868, a cheerful, mid-thirties Louisa had hyacinths in bloom on her Boston windowsill and a $100 advance payment for "one column of Advice to Young Women" in her pocket. This was pre-*Little Women*. She sat down, ate a squash pie for dinner, and wrote a story called "Happy Women." "It was about old maids," she wrote in her journal. "I put in my list all the busy, useful independent spinsters I know, for liberty is a better husband than love to many of us." She ended the column urging women not to become bitter and useless if love never comes their way.

> No, the world is full of work, needing all the heads, hearts and hands we can bring to it. Never was there so splendid an opportunity for women to enjoy their liberty and prove that they deserve it, by using it wisely. If love comes as it should come, accept it in God's name and be worthy of His best blessing. If it never comes, then in God's name reject the shadow of it, for that can never satisfy a hungry heart.

In marriage, she said, she wants "to look up, not down." She gave her rich, eighteen-year-old heroine Rose a couple of good lines early in *Rose in Bloom*. Rose is replying to advice from male family members, "Would you be contented to be told to enjoy yourself for a little while, then marry and do nothing more till you die?" and again, "I won't have anything to do with love till I prove that I am something besides a housekeeper and baby-tender!" Reform, for Louisa, started at home.

¾⋌¾⋌¾

Although there are hints that Louisa had several admirers, we do not know of any actual marriage proposals she may have rejected. She was evidently adept at scotching ardor before it got to that stage, as we saw in her treatment of the Browning-quoting Dr. Winslow in Washington, D.C. Earlier, in 1860, when she was twenty-seven years old, she told her journal:

> Had a funny lover who met me in the [train] cars, and said he lost his heart at once. Handsome man of forty. A

Southerner, and very demonstrative and gushing, called
and wished to pay his addresses; and being told I didn't
wish to see him, retired, to write letters and haunt the road
with his hat off, while the girls laughed and had great
fun. . . . He went at last and peace reigned. My adorers are
all queer.

In her adult novels, Louisa appears to know what love felt like,
both when it was very, very good and also when it turned hurtful
and twisted. In the end, it seems as if she judged herself accurately
and truly did value independence more highly than the alternatives.
The autonomy of spinsterhood was Louisa's personal version of the
liberty she sought for the slaves, the equality she sought for women,
and the freedom she loved so deeply in her American bones.

We are always curious about women who choose not to marry.
In almost all cases it is a choice, an active turning away from a
particular opportunity. Jane Austen, another famous literary
spinster, accepted an offer of marriage from a local gentleman
farmer, but thought it over during the night and in the morning
told him she had made a terrible mistake. It was very awkward,
because she and her sister Cassandra were staying at the home of
the gentleman's parents at the time. They were so embarrassed
and uncomfortable at delivering the reneging message that they
called for a carriage and left before breakfast. Jane had a raging
headache for days afterwards.

Florence Nightingale also actively chose not to marry. In
deciding to turn down an eligible suitor, she wrote out a private
pro and con list: "I have an intellectual nature which requires
satisfaction, and that would find it in him. I have a passional
nature which requires satisfaction, and that would find it in him.
I have a moral, an active nature which requires satisfaction, and
that would not find it in his life. To be nailed to a continuation and
exaggeration of my present life . . . to put it out of my power ever
to be able to seize the chance of forming for myself a true and rich
life. . . ." That, she decided, was not a life she wanted to live.

In 1852, Nightingale wrote an essay, "Cassandra,"* in which she said that English women's brains had been bound in useless and attractive confinement like Chinese women's feet. She laid out a few other choice observations:

> Women are never supposed to have any occupation of sufficient importance not to be interrupted . . . and women themselves have accepted this. . . . They have accustomed themselves to consider intellectual occupation as a merely selfish amusement, which it is their 'duty' to give up for every trifler more selfish than themselves.
>
> Women never have half an hour in all their lives (except before or after anybody is up in the house) that they can call their own, without fear of offending or of hurting some one. . . . A married woman was heard to wish that she could break a limb that she might have a little time to herself.
>
> The family? It is too narrow a field for the development of an immortal spirit, be that spirit male or female. . . . This system dooms some minds to incurable infancy, others to silent misery.

Florence Nightingale's bitterness frightened the few people she allowed to read her essay, so directly did she attack the prevailing foundations of her class and society. But Abba and Lidian would undoubtedly have sympathized with many of Nightingale's pithy comments, such as, "The great reformers of the world turn into the great misanthropists, if circumstances or organization do not permit them to act. Christ, if he had been a woman, might have been nothing but a great complainer."

---

* In Greek mythology Cassandra was a beautiful princess (daughter of King Priam of Troy) who rejected Apollo's amorous advances. In retribution, Apollo put a curse on her: she could see terrible events in the future, but she couldn't prevent them from happening because no one would ever believe her.

The mystery writer Dorothy L. Sayers (she got irritated if anyone left out the L.) invented Harriet Vane as her ideal of a delightfully complete and total human being. Harriet had her scrapes, even worse than Louisa's Jo, as when she was jailed and tried for the murder of her lover. Sayer's *Have His Carcase*, a witty and agreeably complex murder mystery in which Harriet finds a body on the beach, opens with the sentence, "The best remedy for a bruised heart is not, as so many people seem to think, repose upon a manly bosom. Much more efficacious are honest work, physical activity, and the sudden acquisition of wealth." Severely pressed by her public, Sayers eventually married Harriet off to Lord Peter Wimsey, just as Louisa finally capitulated and married her Jo to Professor Bhaer. Louisa won at least the pyrrhic victory of not letting it be Laurie.

Interestingly, in *Jo's Boys*, the Plumfield neighborhood reunites Jo and Laurie in middle age, as the three sisters Jo, Meg, and Amy live semi-communally with their families. Jo has as many happy scenes with Amy's husband Laurie as she does with her own husband, Professor Bhaer.

⚘⚘⚘⚘⚘

As late as 1913,* the *New York Times* published a speech by Everett Wheeler to the New York State Association Opposed to Woman Suffrage. Mr. Wheeler had a "give them an inch and they'll take a mile" perception of what women wanted.

> Nothing shows more clearly the failure of the suffragists, to realize the facts of the case than their favorite argument, that it is no burden to spend a few minutes putting a piece of paper in a box. If that is all they want let them set up boxes of their own and have a play election once a year.

* Lest we forget, American women's right to vote was not ensured by Congress until 1920. That is well within living memory and only two years before my own mother was born.

But, in fact, the agitation they promote, if it means anything at all, means they want *a full share in civil government.*
If this object was attained it needs no prophet to predict
that it would destroy the peace of families and that in the
end it would destroy the country and the race.

After the slaves had been freed and granted full citizenship rights,
Louisa and many abolitionist women turned to fight for the same
federal protections for women. They quickly fell into sectarian
arguments over scope and sequencing. There were two main
camps. The first, represented by the National Woman Suffrage
Association (NWSA), not only supported suffrage but also confronted other legal problems faced by women, such as unequal
pay, employment discrimination, and unfair divorce laws. They
focused on national, rather than local actions and results. This
group was led by Elizabeth Cady Stanton and Susan B. Anthony.

A second, Boston-based group, led by Lucy Stone, Julia Ward
Howe, and Josephine Ruffin, included many of Louisa's old anti-
slavery set. They believed that by sticking to the suffrage issue
alone and working locally, they could get the vote more quickly.
Then, with the vote, they argued that they could more efficiently
fix the other problems. Mrs. Stone's group broke away from the
NWSA in 1870 and formed the American Woman Suffrage Association (AWSA). Both groups had marches and actions, and both
published newsletters. After twenty years of confusion and lack
of success, the groups merged again in 1890.

Louisa sided with the Boston AWSA. She was wooed by both
newsletter editors, but turned down the NWSA's "gushing letter"
in favor of Lucy Stone's *Woman's Journal.* From her position as
chairwoman of Concord's AWSA chapter, Louisa wrote numer-
ous articles and letters for *Woman's Journal* describing the successes and failures of women's suffrage activities in Concord.

In 1879, the hundred or so women who paid property taxes in
Concord were granted the right to vote for positions on the school
committee (but not for any other positions). Louisa properly saw

this as a tiny but significant step and wanted as many women as possible to exercise their newly won suffrage. To this end, she held sessions in her home to prepare women to jump through the municipal hoops required to register, and then to vote. Louisa, being the first woman in Concord to register, described for *Woman's Journal* readers what the process was like. She carefully noted that she was "kindly received" at the assessor's office, and that she did not have to pay any money at the time. She did admit that there was some official confusion, as it was such a new process, but denied rumors (probably spread by the antisuffrage crowd) that she was humiliated or unfairly treated.

She concluded her report with "I am ashamed to say that out of a hundred women who pay taxes on property in Concord, only seven have yet registered, while fourteen have paid a poll tax and put their names down in time. A very poor record for a town which ought to lead if it really possesses all the intelligence claimed for it." She was even more discouraged in her journal, "Drove about & drummed up women to my Suffrage meeting. So hard to move people out of old ruts. I haven't patience enough. If they wont see & work I let em alone & steam along my own way."

She was particularly disappointed that Ralph Waldo and Lidian Emerson's daughter Ellen chose not to register to vote. Writing to a friend, "I don't know why, but am very sorry for she has much influence in Concord & some already back out because she does. Isn't it a pity? Yours disgustedly, L. M. A." Emerson himself never managed to stretch his revolutionary idealism far enough to cover women's rights. He made a few weak statements of potential support when backed into a corner or pushed onto a lecture stage, but diluted it to nothing or took it all back the next day.

In March 1880 the vote for the Concord School Committee was held at a town meeting, so women had to be invited. Town meetings had been off-limits to women since the founding of Concord two centuries earlier. "Our town meetings, I am told," Louisa wrote for *Woman's Journal*, "are always orderly and decent, this one certainly was; and we found it very like a lyceum lecture only rather more tedious than most, except when gentlemen disagreed and enlivened the scene with occasional lapses into bad temper or manners, which amused but did not dismay the women-folk, while it initiated them into the forms and courtesies of parliamentary debate."

The women, being unfamiliar with agendas, did not realize when the school committee vote was to appear, and some did not arrive in time to cast their ballots. When the item came up, there was discussion about whether the women should vote at the same time as the men, or after them. Bronson, who was an early and strong supporter of women's right to vote, proposed that the women be allowed to vote first. This was accepted, and the women filed forward to drop their ballots in the box. Louisa reported the scene:

> No bolt fell on our audacious heads, no earthquake shook the town, but a pleasing surprise created a general outbreak of laughter and applause, for, scarcely were we seated when Judge Hoar rose and proposed that the polls be closed. The motion was carried before the laugh subsided, and the polls were closed without a man's voting; a perfectly fair proceeding we thought since we were allowed no voice on any other question.
>
> The superintendent of schools expressed a hope that the whole town would vote, but was gracefully informed that it made no difference as the women had all voted as the men would.

Louisa then noted that voting continued for other municipal positions (without the women) "by the few who appeared to run the town pretty much as they pleased."

The regular Concord newspaper reported the same events with the patronizing lies and propaganda that suffragettes had come to expect: the school committee vote "caused many a feminine heart to palpitate with excitement and many a hand to unconsciously glide to a bow or bonnet string, or some like feminine fancy, in preparation for the trying ordeal of passing up in front of . . . nearly 200 great horrid men & boys to deposit their maiden vote. The look of eager expectancy . . . [was] not unlike that seen upon the face of a person who is about to have a tooth extracted."

❧ ⚛ ❧ ⚛ ❧

For four years, repeated motions to expand women's suffrage beyond the school committee were tabled at every town meeting. Louisa found this discouraging in general, and humiliating in particular, as Concord, of all places, should be leading this revolutionary and democratic fight. In the school committee elections of 1884, she reported in *Woman's Journal* that some of the registered women voters arrived too late to vote, owing to household duties. Her frustration showed, but she took the opportunity to counter a common argument against suffrage for women:

> Their delay shows, however, that home affairs are not neglected, for the good ladies remained doubtless to give the men a comfortable dinner and set their houses in order before going to vote.
>
> Next time I hope they will leave the dishes till they get home, as they do when in a hurry to go to the sewing-society, Bible-class, or picnic. A hasty meal once a year will not harm the digestion of the lords of creation, and the women need all the drill they can get in their new duties that are surely coming to widen their sphere. . . .

Toward the end of 1885, Mrs. Stone must have given Louisa some of her own medicine, urging her to do more by accusing her of doing too little. Stung, Louisa wrote her a return letter:

> I should think it was hardly necessary for me to write to say that it is impossible for me ever to "go back" on Woman's Suffrage. I earnestly desire to go forward on that line as far & as fast as the prejudices, selfishness & blindness of the world will let us, & it is a great cross to me that ill health &

home duties prevent my devoting heart, pen & time to this most vital question of the age.

After a fifty years acquaintance with the noble men & women of the Anti slavery cause, & the sight of the glorious end to their faithful work, I should be a traitor to all I most love, honor & desire to imitate, if I did not covet a place among those who are giving their lives to the emancipation of the white slaves of America.

If I can do no more let my name stand among those who are willing to bear ridicule & reproach for the truth's sake, & so earn some right to rejoice when the victory is won.

Most *heartily* yours for *Woman's Suffrage*
    & all other reforms,
Louisa May Alcott

While her active political life focused on winning the vote, in her fiction and her personal charities Louisa felt free to campaign for all the other social, economic, and political reforms she saw as so urgently needed. She was always more comfortable in these private efforts, as she was quite shy in public. She was unable to give a speech to a crowd of any size, even friendly fans. It was only when she was acting in a benefit theater performance for one of her favorite causes that she shed her stage fright. She enjoyed these moments in the spotlight and would grow hoarse from her long and vigorously performed lines.

Poverty always drew Louisa's attention, perhaps because her personal experience with it had been so painful. She believed that ending poverty would reduce the need for those social institutions that she saw as disasters in themselves: prisons, workhouses, and orphanages. During her 1875 trip to New York City, where she was fêted at parties and intellectual soirees (at one literary reception she found herself sharing honors with Oscar Wilde, as they had the same publisher), she took time out to visit orphanages, the infamous Tombs prison, and workhouses for newsboys. She spent Christmas Day at an orphanage hospital handing out presents and candy. She wrote home to her family about the sadness and courage she saw and, characteristically, turned it into a story for publication.

She sent "A New Way to Spend Christmas" to the editor of *Youth's Companion* along with this cover note, "Expecting to have much more time I have been obliged to hurry terribly to finish the story. Now in return for my obliging scramble please send me a nice little check for $100, so that I can make my Xmas story pay for my Xmas shopping."

Abba Alcott had early on concluded that equal pay for women would set right many of the tragedies she saw among the women to whom she ministered in her Boston social-work days. Louisa agreed with her mother, and both were echoing Margaret Fuller. Louisa gave the following advice to her friend Maria Porter, who had been elected to the school committee in neighboring village of Melrose:

> I . . . hope that the first thing that you and Mrs. Sewall propose in your first meeting will be to reduce the salary of the head master of the High School, and increase the salary of the first woman assistant, whose work is quite as good as his, and even harder; to make the pay equal. I believe in the same pay for the same good work. Don't you? In future let woman do whatever she can do; let men place no more impediments in the way; above all things let's have fair play, – let *simple justice* be done, say I. Let us hear no more of "woman's sphere" either from our wise(?) legislators beneath the State House dome, or from our clergymen in their pulpits. I am tired, year after year, of hearing such twaddle about sturdy oaks and clinging vines and man's chivalric protection of woman. Let woman find her own limitations, and if, as is so confidently asserted, nature has defined her sphere, she will be guided accordingly; but in heavens name give her a chance! Let the professions be open to her; let fifty years of college education be hers, and

then we shall see what we shall see. Then, and not until then, shall we be able to say what woman can and what she cannot do, and coming generations will know and be able to define more clearly what is a "woman's sphere" than these benighted men who now try to do it.

In her girls' books, Louisa campaigned relentlessly for the right of women to have both an occupation and a husband. But she also realized many of her readers would find that proposal too radical to swallow. Her intermediate step was to showcase young girls being friends with each other in good times and hard, with some of them getting married and some not, but never letting a husband stand in the way of supportive female ties. She also created beguiling pictures of unmarried women who were attractive, happy, and busy – hoping her female Victorian audience would realize that such lives were not only possible, but always preferable to a loveless marriage.

At the same time, she didn't gloss over how difficult it was for a single woman to support herself and she railed against the economic endgame that drove women to prostitution or suicide. Bottom line, she wanted to show her young female readers that women's lives were worth something. Girls *can* make a difference is what Louisa shouts on the pages of *An Old-Fashioned Girl*, the first book off the post-*Little Women* assembly line in 1870.

With *Little Women*'s immediate success, Louisa knew she had an audience, and she struck while the iron was hot. Polly, her heroine in *An Old-Fashioned Girl*, wants to help Jane, a homeless orphan whom Polly learns is recovering from a suicide attempted because she just cannot earn enough money to survive. Polly's landlady is giving Jane a room in her boarding-house. Polly asks her landlady what she can do to help Jane. The landlady suggests that Polly go to some of her rich friends and ask for some sewing Jane could do.

Polly is afraid to ask, "To tell the truth, I'm afraid of being laughed at if I try to talk seriously about such things to the girls."

The landlady replies, "Can't you bear a little ridicule for the sake of a good cause? You said yesterday that you were going to make it a principle of your life to help up your sex as far and as fast as you could. . . . But, Polly, a principle that can't bear being laughed at, frowned on, and cold-shouldered isn't worthy of the name." Polly, behaving like a good Alcott heroine, stiffens her spine and does the right thing.

Jo's Boys is Louisa's last book in the March family series, published in 1886 and dedicated to her trusted physician, Dr. Rhoda Lawrence. All Louisa's values and themes are present and accounted for: Women need an occupation; children need physical as well as mental activity; good people never forget a kindness; happiness requires meaning, love, and community, and the simple life is the best. In between sorting out her young students' lives and loves, Mrs. Jo writes books that prove that truth and simplicity have not entirely lost their charm or power in this jaded world.

But Louisa was never just about sermonizing. The story is where the life is, and she knew it, putting all her heroines and their young friends through every sort of knee-scraping, hair-ribbon-losing misunderstanding and misadventure. In a letter home from sunny Brittany just after *Old-Fashioned Girl*'s publication, she recalls the "hurry and pain and woe" of writing it; nevertheless reading it today gives the impression that Louisa is having a little fun in her new groove as a successful author. In the last chapter, she speaks directly to her readers, alluding to the message she got from her *Little Women* fans, "I now yield to the amiable desire of giving satisfaction, and, at the risk of outraging all the unities, intend to pair off everybody I can lay my hands on."

February 22, 1888

Dear Cit,

I do hope it's not something silly like Canary or Constantinople. Do people in your day know that Florence Nightingale was named after the Italian city because her parents were visiting there when she was born? I've heard that she has the honor to be the first person named Florence – I think many small Flo's have followed. I do love the eccentricities of the English. Perhaps that tendency is what attracted them to my father's teaching methods those many years ago. He had a crew of followers, you know, who founded & named a school after him, the Alcott School outside London.

I do not like it that you felt the need to speculate about my personal marital history, like some penny novel, although I feel honored to be included in the company of Miss Nightingale. Even so, gossip never dies, I take it. There's a reform worth taking on. I don't think I've whacked this whole marriage thicket any better than I did in Work *where Mrs. Wilkins is advising Christie on what to do with her proposal from Mr. Fletcher. Christie is wavering; she presents the question to Mrs. Wilkins as if it's from a friend. Mrs. Wilkins is one of my favorites, & I never put better words into any character's mouth:*

> *"Ef she loves the man, take him: ef she don't, give him the mittin and done with it. Money and friends and family ain't much to do with the matter accordin' to my view. It's jest a plain question betwixt them two. Ef it takes much settlin' they'd better let it alone."*
>
> *"She doesn't love him as much as she might, I fancy* [Christie replies], *but she is tired of grubbing along alone. He is very fond of her, and very rich; and it would be a fine thing for her in a worldly way, I'm sure."*
>
> *"Oh, she's goin' to marry for a livin' is she?"*
>
> *"But she might do a great deal of good, and make others happy. . . ."*

"She might, but I doubt it, for money got that way wouldn't prosper wal. Mis'able folks ain't half so charitable as happy ones. . . ."

End of story, I say.

I am thankful for the women's suffrage movement because it has kept my mind & body active. Concord irritates my very bones, being so willing to rest on its laurels. Now is not the time for either rest or retreat!

It all comes down to living with purpose & principle, as I have said in a thousand different ways. Without them, "half the women of America . . . are restless, aimless, frivolous and sick," as I took the narrator's privilege to say in Old-Fashioned Girl. *Harsh, but true, at least in my experience.*

But, as I have told Mrs. Lucy Stone, I have high hopes for the next generation. We beginners always look like madmen. Have you read much Elizabeth Barrett Browning? Her Aurora Leigh *is lovely & daring. Now there was a woman who kicked over a few buckets. The poem talks of "Earth's fanatics" being "Heaven's saints."*

Have things improved? You haven't said much about your own reform work beyond trying to end that dreadful war in Vietnam.

I hope we are close to the end. As you can see, I am increasingly tired & irritable these days.

Cranky & sorry,
Lu

ABOVE: *Here I am, a clean-cut nine- or ten-year-old, reading Nancy Drew on our living room floor. Very 1950s.*

BELOW: *My Dad's best friend took this picture of my family in the late 1950s. Dad is in his favorite bow-tie; Mom has heels but no pearls. My brothers and I loved our dog, Angie, whom my Dad brought home as a puppy from a research lab where she had been a blood donor.*

LEFT: *My senior picture from the 1968 Bryn Mawr College yearbook. I am in the bottom corner with my college boyfriend at an anti-war demonstration in New York. My accompanying quote is from Mao: "As long as there are people, every kind of miracle is possible." I have to give Bryn Mawr credit for allowing this in amongst all the other portraits of serious young women leaning against tree trunks or sitting on ivy-draped stone benches.*

BELOW: *I did a lot of cross-country hitchhiking in the late 1960s and early 1970s. This picture was taken in 1967.*

ABOVE: *In Cuba in 1969, I met with a remarkable group of Vietnamese representing the South Vietnamese National Liberation Front and the North Vietnamese Army. Our Weather leader, Bernardine Dohrn is sitting center stage.*

BELOW: *During our Weather trip to Cuba, we met not only with Vietnamese, but with Cubans as well. Here is Ted Gold talking with a group of Cuban construction workers. Adequate housing was a major goal of the Castro government. Ted was killed in the townhouse explosion in New York on March 6, 1970.*

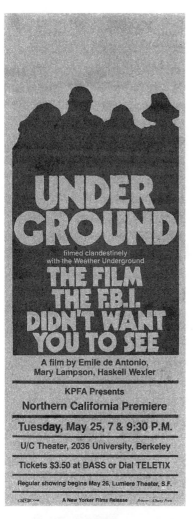

LEFT: *A flyer for the 1970s movie about the Weather Underground. We attracted media people who were interested partly in our politics, but mostly in the drama.*

BELOW: *In Berkeley I spent several years publishing the Berkeley Tribe. One of the actions we supported was a fight against a reduction in food stamp benefits. Here is one of the materials from that campaign.*

UNITED STATES GOVERNMENT

Memorandum

TO :   DIRECTOR, FBI (100-452170)   DATE: 11/6/69

FROM :   SAC, NEW YORK (100-167055) (RUC)

          Classified by 6049
          Exempt from
          Date of Declass
          P C/a

SUBJECT: CHRISTOPHER LYNN BAKKE
             IS-MISCELLANEOUS
             (OO: Seattle)
             CHICAGO

         ReNYlet to Bureau dated 7/25/69 and 9/10/69,
captioned "TRAVEL OF UNITED STATES CITIZENS TO CUBA, 7/7/69;
IS-M", Bufile 100-454734; NYfile 100-166939; NYlet to
Bureau dated 9/17/69; WFOlet to Bureau dated 10/29/69.

         For the information of the Seattle Division, the
following information is set out:

         On 7/22/69,
JFK International Airport advised that the subject
was one of 2 individuals who departed NYC on 7/7/69, via
Eastern Airlines Flight 90/non-stop. All these individuals
obtained one-way tickets through the Harrison Travel Agency,
281 Halstead Avenue, Harrison, New York.

         On 7/22/69,
New York (protect) furnished a rough draft
announcement which he secured from CRV headquarters on
7/21/69, in NYC. The announcement was entitled "CRV members
meet with representatives of the NLF." It is quoted in part
as follows:

         "Three CRV members now in Havanna for a three-week
meeting with representatives of the NLF of Vietnam. They
are part of a group of 40 people from across the country
invited by the NLF to discuss the anti-war movements and
the opposition movements in this country. Most of the delegates
are members of SDS."

2-Bureau (RM)   RFC-19
2-Seattle (RM) (Encl 2)   EX 104
1-New York

WBJ:amw
(5)
NOV 14 1969

---

*Here is a page of my four-hundred-plus-page FBI file, which I obtained after
many years of persistence, thanks to the Freedom of Information Act. The
document is rife with governmental paranoia and illegal wiretapping.*

ABOVE: *Here's Maya in 1973, drooling happily and eating grass in San Francisco's Golden Gate Park. She's the reason I withdrew from violent actions against the U.S. Government.*

LEFT: *I worked as a nurse at Children's Regional Hospital and Medical Center in Seattle for thirteen years, mostly in oncology. We didn't wear uniforms because we didn't want to scare the kids. During that time I went back to school for two masters' degrees, trying to learn better ways to help my patients and their families.*

Getting On

*Of myself there is nothing of public interest to tell,
as the life of an invalid is best left to silence.*
Louisa May Alcott in a letter to Edward Bok,
June 16, 1887, age fifty-four

*"That's another queer thing. Tea is your panacea for
all human ills – yet there isn't any nourishment in it.
I'd rather have a glass of milk, thank you."*
Louisa May Alcott writing as Mac talking to Rose
in *Rose in Bloom*, 1876

February 24, 2006

Dear Lu,

Yes, we are almost to the end. I am so sorry you are feeling poorly, especially because I am not sure this part will cheer you up much. But let's see what we can do. Also, I am trying a little experiment. In addition to words on a page, I am sending you a little bouquet of forget-me-nots and rosemary from my backyard. We have had a good week of early sunshine, as we often tend to do in late February. I hope their message will do you good.

You will be pleased to know it's not a silly C name. At least I don't think it's silly. Knowing my parents, I don't think they would joke about their firstborn's name, even though I was only a girl. They named my brothers with short, one-syllable names and told them it was because when they wrote a book, their name could be printed horizontally on the spine and so be easier to read on the shelf. My name is long, three syllables. Maybe they hadn't thought of the book idea yet. I'd hate to think they had lower expectations of me than of my brothers. I'm sad that my mother will never see this project. But back to my name. It's not generally used as a female name; most people assume my parents wished I were a boy, but I've never believed it.

There has been a trend in the last twenty years or so to name girls by names that are more male sounding, or that sound like surnames. Madison, for instance, and Taylor are popular girls' names these days. Maybe people think that sounding more serious will be an occupational advantage for girls today. Myself, I think that's a superficial approach. The proof is in the pudding, as we've said before.

You obviously had fun with names in your books – changing May to Amy and Mr. Niles to Mr. Tiber. *Diana and Persis* is a clear reference to the Damon and Pythias story of friendship in the face of death. I'm afraid that may be lost on many people today because of our shocking lack of classical knowledge.

You ask about how your reforms have gone. Of all the changes in the one-hundred-twenty-year gap between us, besides freeing the slaves, I think the greatest progress has been in improving people's health. In our political and economic life, much of our so-called progress is negligible. Changes have either created new problems or haven't fixed the old ones. We have outlawed slavery in the U.S., but slaves still suffer in parts of Africa, and discrimination in housing and employment based on skin color has not disappeared here at home. Women work, but typically don't make as much money for the same work as men. But most people today are clearly experiencing better health, less physical pain and longer life than in your century. Childbirth is far safer and children are much healthier. We know how to control seizures and infections far better than we used to. People still die, of course, but at older ages as I mentioned earlier, and for mostly different reasons than in 1888.

The improvements in health will likely continue. Probably fifty years from today my grandchildren will look back and be rightly horrified at how primitively we treated diseases like cancer and diabetes. I can just hear their incredulous tones: "You did what for cancer? You destroyed the patient's immune system in ways that deliberately wiped out masses of healthy cells, making the poor person a sitting duck for any common, garden-variety germ that happened to be floating by? Then you gave them a transplant of cells that you could only hope would rebuild their immune system? And it was touch and go to keep them alive until – and if – that happened? And then the cancer often still came back, or a new cancer would appear because the person was so weak? A little barbaric, wouldn't you say? And weird, Gramma, very weird."

Of course we'll be dying of who knows what by then. Some horrible new version of the black plague could wipe us all out in a minute. Or we'll eat ourselves to death, as seems to be happening right now. Some people, you won't believe this, are having a surgery to make their stomachs smaller as a way of forcing them to eat less.

I guess I should stop. I'll do my best to make this one short and I wish I could say sweet, but maybe "to the point" is more accurate.

Tastefully yours,
Kit

PS: Oh, I forgot to tell you anything about my reform activities. To be honest, I guess I'm just not much of a reformer. I must have run out of steam in the 1970s. As you know with your Lulu, having small children does diminish your civic availability. In California, when I was about four months pregnant with Maya, I was taking part in yet another antiwar street demonstration. It turned a little ugly, as they often did, especially when the police brought in horses. All of a sudden I realized that I had more to protect than my own arms and legs. Running down the street, being chased by police clubs, tear gas, and the occasional drawn handgun, I thought of my expanding belly and said to myself,

"I can't do this anymore; I've got more important things to do."
I veered off into a side alley. The long arm of the law didn't follow,
and that was the end of that.

I'm afraid I have always been fairly cynical about more peaceful change. Greed and self-serving corruption in high places is
rampant – not just in government and business, but in churches
and universities too. Don't even get me started on professional
sports (that probably sounds like an oxymoron to you; I'll explain
it later if you want). The rich and powerful have rigged so much,
and too many of the rest of us are satisfied with the bread and
circuses they throw our way. I am embarrassed to tell you that
half the American electorate, men and women alike, do not even
bother to vote. I think even my determinedly optimistic mother
would have moments of discouragement these days.

So now, it seems you're the one who's caught me in a down
mood. When I get like this, I try to shrink my sights and make a
nice dinner for friends, do a little weeding in my backyard, or sign
up for volunteer work like Christie and the rich ladies talk about
at the end of *Work*.

Realistically(?),
Kit

MERCURY TOXICITY · THE PROLONGED GUESS
OF MEDICINE · MIND-CURE NOT A SUCCESS
A RELIGION OF THEIR OWN

Louisa didn't enjoy getting old, and became occasionally and
understandably vocal about it. Her Civil War mercury poisoning
plagued her for the rest of her life. She complained mainly about
gastric upset, leg pains and tremors, overall weakness and fatigue,
headaches, and difficulty sleeping. To get a sense of how serious
her problems were, here is the Centers for Disease Control
description of a 1996 outbreak of mercury poisoning:

Chronic exposure to mercury salts can result in a variety of manifestations of central nervous system toxicity, including personality changes; nervousness; irritability; tremors; weakness; fatigue; loss of memory; peripheral neuropathy; mental illness, including psychosis; and changes in or loss of hearing, vision or taste. Other classic signs of toxicity associated with exposure to mercury salts include gingivitis, stomatitis, and excessive salivation.

Louisa experienced most of these symptoms. She felt her leg pains all the more deeply because they kept her from the running and walking she so loved and depended on for her mental health. Her headaches, dizziness, and stomach problems increased over time. These various ailments were not accurately diagnosed until they were recognized by a British army doctor she met in France in 1870. She was so excited at having a clear diagnosis that she threw away all her medicines; just having a name for her ills made them disappear for weeks. It's an oddly human trait to feel such relief at learning that there is a name for what was previously a mystery.

The Alcott family leaned toward homeopathy, which was smart in those days, as it tended to protect them from the heroic measures of medical discipline that Abba accurately described as nothing better than a "prolonged guess." Homeopathic physicians were far more likely to do no harm than their nineteenth-century mainstream allopathic colleagues. Louisa fired a few of her doctors and finally settled on Dr. Rhoda Lawrence, who provided her with room and board in a small nursing home she owned in Roxbury. Milbrey Green, who specialized in botanical treatments, was her other trusted doctor.

In January 1888, Louisa describes her days at Roxbury in a letter to a friend.

I still live on my milk, as it gives me all I need & all I can manage with entire ease as yet. Dr. G. says I can eat bread & meat & oysters, but they won't nourish like milk, & that is what I need, & they may upset my cranky stomach if I begin yet. So I hold off & take my milk gruel & cups of warm milk every 3 hours & entire peace reigns. I'm up early & trot round my nice rooms, sew, read & write a little, make things & amuse myself in all sorts of quiet ways. Dr. L. sends me to sleep after dinner for an hour or so of rest, & then I go till 8, bath rub & bed, sleep well & feel all right except a fit of blues now & then, which is naughty as I ought to be good & grateful all the time.

You must perk up, old dear. I wish you had my Milbrey G. I take homeopathic medicine in homeopathic doses, & here I am doing well. Pepsin & Co. forever! Love to all, L.

The medicines she took mostly did no good, and despite her trusted physicians some probably exacerbated her suffering. Joel Myerson and Daniel Shealy, who edited and published Louisa's journal, made a heroic effort to track down all the medicines and treatments she made reference to taking. The list is long and sad: cayenne pepper (said to aid digestion), enemas of all sorts, lobelia, tincture of clomonilla, inhaled oxygen, inhaled natron (a sodium carbonate), the root of the yellow jessamine, various cathartics and emetics, belladonna, morphine, and a mixture of potassium chloride, sodium chloride, magnesium sulfate, and sodium bicarbonate known as Kissinger's Salt.

On the brighter, and perhaps more efficacious side, her physicians also read to her. In February 1888, after visiting her failing father, Louisa recorded in her journal, "A sad p.m. Lay still & Dr read Coleridge, Wordsworth to me so I should not think of sad things. Slept well. Made a poem."

Daringly, or perhaps desperately, she also tried electricity and hypnotism.

My mind-cure not a success. First I am told to be "passive." So I do, say & think nothing. No effect. Then I am not "positive" enough, must exert my mind. Do so & try to grasp the mystery. Then I am "too positive" & must not try to understand anything. Inconsistency and too much

hurry. God & Nature cant be hustled about every ten min-
utes to cure a dozen different ails. Too much money made
& too much delusion all around.

Mrs. Burnett* is trying it. Says it quiets her mind but
doesn't help her body. Too much is claimed for it.

Then a few months later, "Mrs. Newman says 'you've got it!' but
she deceives herself for I have lost my faith & never feel any better after a séance. Try Miss Adams as Mrs. N. says she herself is
'too powerful' for me. Mrs. N. made no more impression on me
than a moonbeam. After 30 trials I gave it up. No miracle for me.
My ills are not imaginary, so are hard to cure." But she isn't sure
that it is not really her fault after all, as she writes to a friend,

> A very sweet doctrine if one can only do it. I cant yet, but
> try it out of interest in the new application of the old true &
> religion which we all believe, that soul is greater than body,
> & being so should rule. This will give you something to
> think of & as delicate, gentle people often grasp these
> things more quickly than the positive ones, you may get
> ahead of me in the new science. Just believe that you will
> be better & you will, they say. Try it.

In the end, though, her natural skepticism and pragmatism won
out. How could a treatment claim to cure cancer, she asked, when
it failed to wipe out a simple headache?

Lulu was perhaps the best medicine, providing pleasure and
meaning to an ailing Louisa. Louisa's sister May had died in Paris
a few weeks after giving birth to a daughter she named Louisa May.
Her last wish was that the baby be taken from Paris to Boston to
be raised by Louisa. The grieving Swiss husband complied, and
sent his sister to accompany little Lulu on the ship to her new
home. Louisa became a first time mother two months shy of her

---

* Mrs. Frances Hodgson Burnett, author of *The Secret Garden* and other novels,
was a friend of Louisa's from the late 1870s on. They met at various celebrity
author events and enjoyed lunches, dinners, and carriage rides together.

forty-eighth birthday. "Happy days . . . getting acquainted. Lulu is rosy & fair now, & grows pretty in her native air. A merry little lass who seems to feel at home & blooms in an atmosphere of adoration." Two months later, "Too busy to keep much of a journal. My life is absorbed in my baby. On the 23rd she got up and walked alone. . . . A new world for me."

⧉⧉⧉⧉⧉

Louisa was writing and thinking more about religion at this time too. Her family's transcendental-universalist inclinations took some explaining. She described her beliefs in a letter to a young friend in 1884:

> My parents never bound us to any church but taught us that the love of goodness was the love of God, the cheerful doing of duty made life happy, & that the love of one's neighbor in its widest sense was the best help for oneself. . . .
>
> One can shape life best by trying to build up a strong & noble character through good books, wise people's society, an interest in all reforms that help the world, & a cheerful acceptance of whatever is inevitable. . . . Have you read Emerson? He is called a Pantheist or believer in Nature instead of God. He was truly Christian & saw God in Nature, finding strength & comfort in the sane, sweet influences of the great Mother as well as the Father of all. I too believe this, & when tired, sad or tempted find my best comfort in the woods, the sky, the healing solitude. . . .

As a postscript she added, "The simple Buddha religion* is very attractive to me, & I believe in it. God is enough for me, & all the prophets are only stepping stones to him. Christ is a great reformer to me not God." She went on in a subsequent letter to say that she liked the idea of reincarnation, as it increased the

---

* The Concord neighbors' magazine, the *Dial* was the first publication in America to print English translations of Buddhist scripture.

chances for people to learn to be better and happier. She believed that people who truly love each other in one life will meet again in a next:

> This is my idea of immortality. An endless life of helpful change, with the instinct, the longing to rise, to learn, to love, to get nearer the source of all good, & go on from the lowest plane to the highest, rejoicing more & more as we climb into the clearer light, the purer air, the happier life which must exist, for, as Plato said 'The soul cannot imagine what does not exist because it is the shadow of God who knows & creates all things.'

Women, she thought, might need a religion of their own, because of their special problems, particularly as their "hearts are usually more alive than [their] heads, & [their] hands are tied in many ways."

Leap Day, February 29, 1888

Dear Cassandra? (No, that's too female; not Charles,
    not enough syllables – Coverdale?)

I've always enjoyed Leap Days; the name gives me a chance to remember when I could indeed leap & prance about. Long gone now, but I've tried to keep the good days alive on paper at least.

    Yes, getting old & infirm has been a bigger challenge than any poverty, punishment, or lost love has ever been. And you say folks in your time zone may have decades left to live, likely charging into your nineties? You do have some work to do, then, to make that extra time as useful & as pleasant as possible. I am glad not to be facing that one. I remember now. That's why you wrote to me in the first place, isn't it? So, have you gotten what you wanted? I have never been short on advice, but I have always given it on a "take it or leave it" basis.

    You might notice that I did not often put old people in my stories.

Was never sure what to do with them. I've always thought – despite my undying dislike of autograph seekers – that a private life is never enough. A good & useful life should include some time on a public stage. Since old people do not have the energy for stage-strutting, they are not nearly so interesting as the young folks, so I've usually left 'em out. I have always been more interested in what's to come than in what's been.

By the way, I am glad to see that my instincts about those silly mind treatments have turned out to be correct. Sorry, though, to see that some of the ones I had hopes for also have been sent to the trash barrel. Never mind, though, we can but try.

I think if this project is to have a final word – do I have the last word? – we couldn't do better than what I said about my charmingly imperfect Rose in Rose in Bloom*:*

> *"Her projects were excellent, but did not prosper as rapidly as she hoped, for having to deal with people, not things, unexpected obstacles were constantly arising. . . ."*

Isn't that always the way of it?

Onward, even so,
Lu

PS: Thank you for the rosemary & forget-me-nots. Blue and green, the colors of the world, have always been my favorites. They came through quite nicely & grace my windowsill still, catching what little sunshine there is – very little I must say, as Boston is still quite cold & gloomy. I take it that the weather in your corner of the country is far friendlier than ours at this time of year. Perhaps I should revise my views of the West.

Finding a Way

The highest that we can attain to is not Knowledge,
but Sympathy with Intelligence.
Henry David Thoreau

I feel considerable regret by turns that I have lived
so many years and have in reality done so little
to increase the amount of human happiness.
John Brown in a letter to his wife, Mary, 1844

March 2, 2006

Dear Lu,

I know your war wounds are getting the better of you. I wish I could stroll into your room with an armload of fragrant blue and white hyacinths and sunny yellow daffodils. I would read a funny play to you and ply you with warm blankets and a milky vanilla-and-honey custard.

It would be ironic and awful if our project has worsened your symptoms in any way. I trust you would have told me if you thought that was happening. Wouldn't you?

This letter has no enclosed project essay. This one is just me, telling you how much you mean to me. A last love letter from a grateful fan. What you have made of your life has brought a great deal of good fun and thought to generations of women, including mine, including me. I feel a little like a junior Miss Sears, the woman who bought Fruitlands and turned it into a museum (what would your father think of that?) The *New York Sun* said that Miss Sears "regards the past as having been lived chiefly for the benefit of the future. The present she regards as a convenient work season arranged for her by Father Time in which she can make the future still more aware of he past." I think I can fairly say, without fear of contradiction, that you have lived most heartily for the benefit of the future.

A couple of years ago, I heard a speech by the president of huge charitable foundation. Besides a description of how her foundation is giving away billions of dollars (yes, billions) to improve health and education all over the planet, she told us about Mahatma Gandhi's list of seven public sins. You haven't heard about Gandhi yet, but he will become like the George Washington of India in the early twentieth century.

His list of sins will be very recognizable to you; they are nothing new, but seeing them all together displays a powerful indictment. You will be heartened to know, I think, that people today are being actively reminded to avoid them – although I guess that also means we haven't beaten them, which isn't so heartening. You have made your heroines face down every one of these. As you have yourself. Here they are:

> *Politics without principle*
> *Wealth without work*
> *Pleasure without conscience*
> *Commerce without morality*
> *Science without humanity*
> *Worship without sacrifice*
> *Knowledge without character*

I cannot imagine sorting them in any priority order, can you? Each is embedded in the others: an endless circle of selfish indifference, stupidity, and pain. To fight these is to make a life worth living.

By now, you know enough about my time zone to know that we are *very* far from keeping Gandhi's words in mind all the time. Sometimes, reading the news from the world, a person might think we go out of our way to endorse and pursue these sins. I used to think I could make a difference – set things on a better track. I'm not so sure anymore. I have this growing tendency to feel small and useless. So I flounder. Sometimes I just care about myself and want to forget everything else. Sometimes I get so frustrated and angry that I want to join some violent revolution and throw myself on a barricade somewhere. Sometimes I just want to get through the next hour without doing anything stupid. With my switchback tracks, I must look like a bug wandering blindly around on the wrong side of the tapestry.

So, as you remember, we've been looking at your life partly for the companionship and memories, but partly to see if the good parts of how you lived your life might rub off on us wandering bugs here in the twenty-first century. So hang on now, because I am going to say some shamelessly nice things about you, and I know you are not used to it. This is the best way to remind myself of what I need to go forward. If you need to stop to fan yourself, go right ahead. Have a little sip of milk. Anchors aweigh, now, ready?

The shortest way to say the first one is: *ideas count*. It matters what *you* think, what *I* think, what *each* of us thinks. You are always telling your young readers to care about themselves – to pay attention to what they do with their bodies and their brains because that's where the real wealth and value always lie. Following fads is lazy; assuming that the people in charge have the best ideas is folly. That's what kept slavery around for so long, and what kept women from owning property, from voting, and from going to school. Make up your own mind, you said, and you multiplied your voice into a whole army of heroines led by Jo, Polly, Rose, Christie, and so many more.

Number two: *persistence*. I was looking at a pen-and-ink drawing of bamboo in a windstorm when I first thought of writing to you. The bamboo is being blown hard and is flapping and curving over a few straight but broken stumps of dead pine. Flexible persistence wins the game, the Chinese artist told my husband and me as we bought his work.

Your life is a wonderfully persuasive example of bamboo-like persistence. You inserted yourself in *An Old-Fashioned Girl* as a walk-on caricature of an author who just happened to write a successful book through no effort of her own. Not accurate. You always pretend that *Little Women* fell into your lap. Not true. In fact, you have always worked a demon, for hours, wearing out bushels of pens, and you never gave up, even when publishers were turning down your stories right and left. You studied your market, you refined your product, and you kept at your other jobs until you could safely afford to quit them. You were a professional and a realist. There was no magic wand or fairy godmother. There was just you, slogging along with paper and ink and very sore hands. You even had to teach yourself to write left-handed when your right thumb gave out.

I'm embarrassed to tell you how easy the mechanics of writing have become. We have personal printing machines that can erase and move text and churn out perfectly legible pages with the lightest touch of our fingers. The machines even correct our spelling, which I know you would especially appreciate (makes it hard to do dialect, though).

Even so, magic machines do not produce persistence. The only way a person can be as persistent as you is by truly following her heart. There is no other place for the energy to come from, especially when everything is going against you. Forgive my saying it, but if your mother hadn't known, deep in her heart, that she truly loved your father, I am sure she would have left him. She suffered so much visible aggravation, with so little visible recompense. She must have had a hot, spinning dynamo in her heart that kept her going. You have written over and over that if you don't feel that dynamo, you shouldn't get married – or make any other big commitment – because you will need every watt to face all the difficulties life is certain to throw at you.

The third good quality about you is your *courageous independence*. You must have had this bred into you from your transcendental childhood. It may well be the only transcendental message

worth remembering. Trust your own thinking. Of course, to be
useful, one must know how to think, and one must take the *time*
to think. You rightly worry that many women are not very good at
thinking, because of their lack of education and because nobody
seriously expects them to do so. You also see women being ridiculed, punished, or just ignored when they do venture to think.
I believe the situation has improved in the hundred-and-twenty
years between us, although the problem has definitely not vanished
– and is still oppressively apparent in many parts of the world.

I wish we could see your smile. "Surely joy is the condition of
life," said your friend Henry Thoreau, and I think you have done
your best to make it so. You have found your joy everywhere and
anywhere. You skilled in navigating all the tangles and snarls in
the world. I think you have sometimes just played at being a
responsible adult, as if the role were a character in one of your
beloved Dickens stories. You have been very convincing in the
role, I might add, but I detect a wise and laughing trickster inside,
reveling in humanity's uncertain footing between the solemn and
the merry.

I wish you could get back to Europe, where you enjoyed yourself
so much. Remember those sunny afternoons in Dinan, in Brittany,
lounging among red geraniums and warm stone walls, laughing
and eating chocolate and berries? And those pleasant days in
Geneva, Bex, and Vevey, where you met old friends? Everyone
either knew you or wanted to know you. As you wrote yourself,

> The other eve, as we sat in our wrappers, the maid came
> up with H. J. Pratt's card. We asked him up and he appeared
> as brown and jolly and handsome as ever. He had been to
> Bex for us and hunted all day along the Lake to find us. At
> Montraux he met Charlie Howe who told him the Alcotts
> were here and on he came. . . . We have had lively times
> since he came, for he has traveled far and wide and can
> tell his adventures well. . . . He dances wild dances for us,
> sings songs in many languages. We had a moonlight ball

in the road the other night coming from the Warrens – fine affair. He is much improved and quite appalls us by talking Arabic, French, German, Italian, and Armenian in one grand burst.

Your sister May spread her wings in Europe, and found work, love, and happiness there. We all know that it never would have happened without your hard work and your generosity in funding her first months there.

Nature, you have said, is a more reliable source of pleasure than art. Either running across the fields, or just looking out from a carriage window has always cheered you up. After your mother died, you found comfort there, writing, "Nature is always good to me." It was true for me, too; after my mother died, I spent several afternoons in a small Japanese garden near our house. The calm water, round rocks, and rooted trees told me what I needed to know.

You said once that you thought you must have been a horse in a prior life because you love to run so much. I can imagine you prancing across a grassy field, yellowed a little from a long summer, with your dark hair flapping and flowing like a mane behind you. It's a picture that makes me smile.

I'm almost done, as I'm sure you are glad to learn. What I *really* like about you – and I hope I have learned from you – is that it *is* worth the trouble to work hard to make your life into something. You have always believed you were worth bothering about, and that the world was worth bothering about. You care about your character. You have acted in the world as if you matter, as if you can make a difference. In your case, it turned out to be true – you have made a difference.

But a person never knows for sure. Your trick, your lesson, is just to start – to make your work worth the effort just by doing it, no matter if anyone is noticing or not. That is what I will take with me into whatever future I have.

Now I am done, and I send this last note to you with much

love and sorrow because I know we have reached the end of our work together. May you feel a friendly fresh breath of spring on the cold March day when you read this.

Gratefully yours,
Kit

P S: I think I'll keep the last laugh: no, not Cassandra, and not Charles or Coverdale, either.

Endnote

Put away papers & tried to dawdle & go about as other people do.
Louisa May Alcott, 1884, age fifty-two

*Sorrow makes us all children again, – destroys all differences
of intellect. The wisest knows nothing.*
Ralph Waldo Emerson,
after the death of his five-year-old son

❧ ☙ ❧ ☙ ❧

Louisa last visited her father on March 2, 1888, just two days before he died. His death was expected, as he had suffered a stroke. She knelt by his bed and said, "Father, here is your Louy, what are you thinking as you lie here so happily?" He answered, "I am going *up. Come with me.*" She replied, "Oh, I wish I could."

She did, four days later on March 6.

❧ ☙ ❧ ☙ ❧

The Concord neighbors today share a dusty little ridge in Sleepy Hollow Cemetery, just over the hill behind Louisa's Orchard House. The summer's day I visited them, there were carnations and snapdragons lying on the stones marking the Thoreau, Emerson, and Hawthorne graves. Louisa's flat small stone, incised "Louisa M. Alcott" was strewn not with flowers, but with pennies, nickels, and dimes.

ACKNOWLEDGMENTS

"Every book is, in an intimate sense, a circular letter to the friends of him who writes it," wrote Robert Lewis Stevenson in the dedication of his delightful 1879 *Travels with a Donkey in the Cévennes*. This book is no less a letter from me, not only to Louisa May Alcott but also to my twenty-first-century friends. I count every reader as a friend; at the very least you are, as Stevenson put it, "a generous patron who defrays the postage." For that, I thank you.

When I naïvely abandoned paying work to see if I could write a book, I had little idea the challenge would be so pleasant. The most fun by far was discovering that writing is not nearly as lonely an undertaking as I had thought. Even during long stretches of solitary writing at home, I had the company of Archie, our extremely sympathetic and attentive cockatoo. But the best part of the process was learning that friends and family were actually interested in what I was doing and were willing to help! Who would have guessed?

Like movies whose credits unroll screen after screen, this book has been no less a collaborative project. My friends had the energy not only to read multiple horrible drafts but to couch their comments kindly enough to enable me to make major course corrections without totally melting down. Among these invaluable friends (apologies to the unnamed because I could have gone on for pages, but the book is on a budget and paper is not free) are Cindy Ayers, Nancy Bourne, Marcia Cantarella, Joan Hockaday, Karen Kapeluck, Darby Langdon, Marcia Ringel, Joy Selak, Jan Schaefer, and Gennie Winkler. Others, including Jane Bogle, Barbara BonJour, Marilyn Goebel, Tina Hetzel, Kate Jackson, Sandi Kurtz, Ann McElroy, and Dianna McLeod endured my lengthy natterings about the nineteenth century during many companionable walks, lunches, and tea breaks. Friends, tried and true.

Early helpers were other writers who were willing to take my word for it that I was a writer – still a daring assertion. Dave Barry, Teri Hein, Clare Meeker, Will Nothdurft, Tom Orton, Marjorie Reynolds, Marcia Ringel, Joy Selak, Jeff and Anni Shelley were all incredibly gracious and patient with my professional baby steps. Most long-suffering and gallantly supportive of all has been Mr. A. L. Hart, a gentleman agent of the old school to whom not even a Mount Everest heap of gold and gratitude would give him the credit he is due.

Louisa May Alcott aficionados became my new best friends. The staff at Orchard House, brilliantly led by Jan Turnquist, was endlessly supportive and hospitable in the midst of their own massive projects to save Louisa's family house and keep the Alcott flame burning. Jan was extremely kind one day as she took me through a back room and allowed me to look more closely at the glowing copy of May Alcott's wonderful painting *La Négresse*. Nancy Gahagan and Maria Powers were extremely patient and helpful with my search for photographs and, always, "just one more question." Leslie Wilson, curator of the Concord Free Public Library's Special Collections, took the time to help me understand that Louisa was likely not involved in the library's banning of *Huckleberry Finn*.

Thanks to Glenn Harrington, whose great-aunt was a family friend of Clara Endicott Sears, and to Michael Volmar, curator and webmaster at Fruitlands, for helping me learn more about the Alcott commune Fruitlands.

David Godine and his talented publishing team have been equally adept at delighting, challenging and teaching me. I am extremely grateful to David, Carl W. Scarbrough, and Sue Berger Ramin as they patiently introduced me to the publishing industry's undeniable oddities. Thanks also to the gracious Toby Lester, deputy managing editor at the *Atlantic Monthly*, who opened the magazine's archives to me as I tracked Louisa's excitement at having some of her early stories accepted by the most prestigious literary magazine in the country.

ACKNOWLEDGMENTS

Most remarkable of all, Madeleine Stern, *grande dame* of Alcottiana, found the time to respond to a question I had about Louisa's funeral arrangements.

The three owners of Point B Solutions Group, who employ me in my business and technology consulting life, blinked not a gentlemanly eye when I told them on very short notice that I intended to take a year off to write a book. Their continuing good wishes (and repeated requests to enlarge on my radical Weather days stories from the 1960s and '70s, in which they are too young to have participated) keep me from feeling overly guilty about abandoning the life of a wage slave.

Even so, I never would have been so bold as to cut the employment lifeline if it weren't for my practically perfect husband, who, being so tired of hearing me complain that I didn't have enough time to write, told me, as a Christmas present, to take the year off.

I can only hope from the depths of my grateful heart that Louisa will now, by the magic of ink and paper, spread her pixie dust of energy, intelligence, humor, and love even wider than ever.

KIT BAKKE
Seattle

PS: The mistakes are mine, all mine.

SELECTED BIBLIOGRAPHY

These books provided me with windows into Louisa's life. I am extremely grateful to the scholars who have directed their professional spotlights and analytical skills on the Alcott family. Their work has helped me to count Louisa as one of my friends.

Alcott, Bronson. *How Like an Angel I Came Down: Conversations with Children on the Gospels*, recorded by Elizabeth Peabody. Boston: Munroe & Co., 1836–7.

Baker, Carlos. *Emerson Among the Eccentrics*. New York: Penguin Group, 1996.

Bedell, Madelon. *The Alcotts: Biography of a Family*. New York: Clarkson Potter, 1980.

Du Bois, W. E. B., *John Brown*, Philadelphia: G. W. Jacobs, 1909

Elbert, Sarah. *A Hunger for Home: Louisa May Alcott and* Little Women. Philadelphia, Pennsylvania: Temple University Press, 1984.

Fuller, Margaret. *Woman in the Nineteenth Century*. New York: Greeley & McElrath, 1845.

Hawthorne, Julian. *Nathaniel Hawthorne and His Wife: A Biography*. 2 vols. Boston: James R. Osgood and Company, 1884.

Hawthorne, Nathaniel. *The Blithedale Romance*. Boston: Ticknor, Reed and Fields, 1852.

James, Henry. *The Bostonians*. New York: Macmillan and Co., 1886.

James, Laurie. *Men, Women, and Margaret Fuller*. New York: Golden Heritage Press, 1990.

Myerson, J., and D. Shealy, eds. *The Journals of Louisa May Alcott*. Athens: The University of Georgia Press, 1997.

Nightingale, Florence. *Notes on Nursing: What It Is and What It Is Not.* New York: D. Appleton and Company, 1860. (First American edition; also published London: Harrison, 1860)

Perry, Bliss. *The Heart of Emerson's Journals.* Boston: Houghton Mifflin, 1926.

Saxton, Martha. *Louisa May Alcott: A Modern Biography.* New York: The Noonday Press, 1995.

Sears, Clara Endicott. *Bronson Alcott's Fruitlands.* Boston: Houghton Mifflin, 1915.

Shealy, D., and M. B. Stern, J. Myerson, eds. *Louisa May Alcott: Selected Fiction.* Athens: The University of Georgia Press, 2001.

Showalter, Elaine, ed. *Alternative Alcott.* New Brunswick, New Jersey: Rutgers University Press, 1988.

Stern, Madeleine B., ed. *L. M. Alcott Signature of Reform.* Boston: Northeastern University Press, 2002.

Strachey, Lytton. *Eminent Victorians.* New York: Harcourt, Brace & Co., 1918.

Thoreau, Henry David. *Civil Disobedience and Other Essays.* New York: Dover Publications, 1993.

Ticknor, Caroline. *May Alcott: A Memoir.* Boston: Little Brown & Co., 1928.

Yates, Gayle G., ed. *Harriet Martineau on Women.* New Brunswick: Rutgers University Press, 1985.

For complete citations, contact the author through
www.kitbakke.com.

READERS' GUIDE

1. How would you answer the questions listed on page 182 for women's lives today?

    1. Can a productive and creative single woman be happy?

    2. Can a married woman maintain her personal life and friends?

    3. Can women be both personally happy and professionally successful?

    4. Can people be happily married and still respect each other's privacy and basic human rights?

2. Louisa May Alcott lived in a neighborhood of people who, a century later, are still widely remembered and respected. She grew up with them and knew them on a day-to-day basis. Do you think they knew they would be leaving such a powerful intellectual legacy? Discuss any of your close friends or family whom you think will be remembered and respected (outside their families) in a hundred years.

3. *Little Women* was published when Louisa was thirty-six, and its success changed her life. She appreciated the money, but resented the bother of celebrity and the restrictions she felt the book's style put on her future writing. Discuss this trade-off. Were the "golden handcuffs" worth it?

4. Louisa never indicated any interest in seeing the Midwest or the West Coast, although many Americans (and Europeans) in the mid-nineteenth century were caught up in the romantic adventure stories coming out of Chicago, Kansas, California, and

Oregon. Why do you think she showed no inclination to explore the American West?

5. There is no evidence that Louisa ever read Jane Austen, although we know that Emerson read *Pride and Prejudice* and thought it was tedious. We also know that Louisa loved Charlotte Brontë's *Jane Eyre*. If Louisa had read Austen, do you think she would have enjoyed Austen's irony, humor, and exquisite writing style, or would she have seen Austen's stories as Emerson did – unduly focused on marriage as the only proper goal for a woman? What do you think she found so attractive about Charlotte Brontë?

6. There is a French proverb that translates as "the more things change, the more they stay the same." This book makes some comparisons between the middle of the nineteenth century and the middle of the twentieth century – in civil rights, women's rights, social change, and health care. What do you think has changed substantially between those two centuries, if anything, and what do you think is still basically the same? What might you predict in these areas for the middle of the twenty-first century?

7. When discussing the shock of having to wash and care for soldiers in the Union army hospital, Louisa says she was unprepared for the naked male body because she grew up with only sisters and that her father was a "womanly man." What do you think she meant by this?

8. Is there anything in Louisa's life that speaks to how you live your own life today? What does she tell you about what is important?

LOUISA MAY ALCOTT CHRONOLOGY

1832 Louisa May Alcott born in Germantown, Pennsylvania, November 29

1839 Bronson's Boston Temple School closes; end of Bronson's schoolteaching career

1843 The Alcott family lives on Fruitlands commune, June to December

1845– Alcotts live at Hillside in Concord (house later purchased
48   by Nathaniel Hawthorne). The events of *Little Women* mostly occurred at Hillside

1851 Louisa's poem "Sunlight" appears in *Peterson's Magazine* – her first publication. She uses the by-line "Flora Fairfield"

1854 Louisa's stories invented while babysitting the Emerson children are published as *Flower Fables*

1858 Alcotts move to Orchard House (next door to Hillside); Louisa's sister Elizabeth dies; The *Atlantic Monthly* publishes Louisa's first story, "Love and Self-Love," about a young girl cruelly manipulated by an older, cold, heartless man

1862 Louisa volunteers to work as a nurse at a Union army hospital in Washington, D.C.

1863 Louisa's story "Pauline's Passion" wins $100 prize. Set in a tropical landscape, the story includes a betrayed, intelligent, passionate woman, forgery, implacable hatred, murder, gambling, and wife abuse

1864 *Moods* is published

1865 Louisa's first trip to Europe (as a paid companion to an invalid rich girl)

1868–9 *Little Women*, Parts I and II, published to great acclaim

1870   Louisa goes back to Europe, taking sister May and friend Alice with profits of *Little Women* and advance on *An Old-Fashioned Girl*; sister Anna's husband John Pratt dies; Louisa vows to support her two nephews and writes *Little Men* while in Rome

1877   *A Modern Mephistopheles* is published; Louisa's mother dies in Concord at the Thoreau family house, which Louisa had purchased for Anna

1879   Louisa's sister, May, dies in Paris shortly after giving birth; May names the baby (nicknamed Lulu) after Louisa and sends her to Louisa to raise

1880   Lulu arrives in Boston; Louisa sets up housekeeping in Boston at 81 Pinckney Street on Louisburg Square, and devotes last eight years of her life to being a mother

1883   Hillside is purchased from Nathaniel Hawthorne's daughter Rose by Harriet and Daniel Lothrop. Daniel was a children's book publisher, and Harriet wrote *The Five Little Peppers and How They Grew* under the pen name Margaret Sidney. Today, Hillside is now owned by the National Park Service.

1886   Louisa's calomel poisoning from treatment for her Civil War typhoid gets the better of her; she moves to a nursing home run by a physician friend, Rhoda Lawrence; *Jo's Boys*, her last book, and the last in the March family saga, appears

1888   Bronson Alcott dies in Boston house owned by Louisa, March 4; Louisa dies at Dr. Lawrence's, March 6

1900   The Lothrops' daughter Margaret donates Orchard House to a group of ladies to run as a Louisa May Alcott museum. They also had a plan (never carried out) to use part of the house as a "summer vacation place for working girls"

SUGGESTIONS FOR READING
MORE LOUISA MAY ALCOTT

For readers wishing to read more of Louisa May Alcott's words directly, here is my list of Alcott favorites.

Hospital Sketches. There are several editions of Louisa's Civil War nursing stories, originally serialized in the *Commonwealth* and then printed in book form by James Redpath in 1863. My choice is a facsimile version printed by Applewood Books, 2004. In addition, the entire text is available from several online sites.

A Modern Mephistopheles. Originally published anonymously in 1877 as part of Roberts Brothers' "No Name" series, it is now available from several publishers, including Random House and Greenwood Publishing. The latter edition (1987) includes an introduction by Madeleine B. Stern, still the most comprehensive and astute Alcott scholar we have.

An Old-Fashioned Girl. Louisa's first post-*Little Women* book, this excellent story can be found in several paperback editions geared for her teenaged audience, including from Dell and Puffin. The full text is also available from several online sites.

The Selected Letters of Louisa May Alcott edited by Joel Myerson, Daniel Shealy, and Madeleine B. Stern (Athens, GA.: University of Georgia Press, 1995). These Alcott scholars have also edited Louisa's journals. While both are interesting, Louisa's letters are more entertaining and descriptive of herself and her times than her journal entries. I found the introduction, editing, footnotes and indexing of both volumes endlessly helpful.

Transcendental Wild Oats. Louisa published this delightful gloss on her commune days in 1873. Called both "gentle" and "biting" satire, it highlights Louisa's consummate skill at turning hard times into good reads. The full text is available online. I recommend the 1975 Harvard Common Press edition because it includes Louisa's no-frills journal entries, written at Fruitlands in 1843 when she was eleven years old.

Work. Originally published in 1873, this is Louisa's thinly-disguised fiction of the difficulties faced by a woman trying to make a living in urban mid-nineteenth-century America. I recommend Penguin's 1994 edition with its excellent introduction by Jo Kasson.

I have not included *Little Women* in my shortlist of suggestions: Louisa did not think it best represented her life or her work, nor do I. However, if you must read (or re-read) it, please find an edition that follows the 1869 original language and characterization, not the Victorian "clean up" that was done in 1880. Two sources for the original are the Oxford University Press edition (1994) edited and with an introduction and notes by Valerie Alderson, and the Library of America edition, 2005, edited by Elaine Showalter. The latter also includes *Little Men* and *Jo's Boys*.

ILLUSTRATION CREDITS

Pages 69–71 used by permission of Orchard House / The Louisa May Alcott Memorial Association; page 72 (top left and top right) used by permission of Orchard House / The Louisa May Alcott Memorial Association; page 72 (bottom left) courtesy of Concord Free Library; page 73 (top left and top right) used by permission of Orchard House / The Louisa May Alcott Memorial Association; page 73 (bottom right) National Portrait Gallery, London; page 74 used by permission of Orchard House / The Louisa May Alcott Memorial Association; pages 141–143 used by permission of Orchard House / The Louisa May Alcott Memorial Association; page 144 (top) used by permission of Orchard House / The Louisa May Alcott Memorial Association; page 144 (bottom) and pages 217–222 courtesy of the author.

A NOTE ON THE TYPE

Miss Alcott's E-mail has been set in Scala and Scala Sans, a family of types designed by Martin Majoor in the 1990s. A distinctly contemporary face, Scala roman marries the proportions of old-style types, the monoline strokes of geometric sans-serifs, and the slab serifs of the so-called Egyptian faces. The harmony between roman and italic reveals the designer's attention to detail, as does the balance between serif and sans-serif. Although the family's ancestry is traceable to no single family of types, Scala succeeds (much like its distant cousin, W. A. Dwiggins's Caledonia) by virtue of its clean drawing, its vertical emphasis, its regular rhythm, and its somewhat casual letterforms.

DESIGN AND COMPOSITION BY CARL W. SCARBROUGH